I0647002

Southern Discomfort

Southern Discomfort

Ben Witherington, III

WIPF & STOCK · Eugene, Oregon

"Do not be deceived, God cannot be mocked. A man reaps what he sows."
—ST. PAUL, GALATIANS 6.7

"The violent bear it away . . ."
—FLANNERY O'CONNOR

For my Mom, on her 90th birthday. I'll bet you'll recognize that determined and splendidly strong-willed woman in this novel :). Consider this a love offering for all you've done for me and for all our family over the course of your rich and full life.

And for my wife Ann, in love and appreciation for 39 good years of marriage.

Contents

Part Two: Consequences

Part One

Truth Or . . .

Chapter One

Change Will Do You Good

Masey Bumgarner did not like airports. She didn't like all the new TSA procedures, she did not like paying for bags at the counter, she did not like waiting and waiting for planes to show up, and then waiting some more to board by zones, and she really hated it when they lost your luggage, which had just happened!

Muttering to herself that she should never have listened to her sister Sharon when she told her it would be "fun" to go on one of those Carnival Cruises, she waited for the person at the ticket counter to track down what had happened to her bag between Miami and Charlotte. Not only was the coming and going an aggravation, the cruise itself was full of boozers and losers as far as she was concerned, people she had no desire to hang out with, even on a ten day cruise. How had she let her sister talk her into doing this? And then, on top of all that, Sharon had bailed out of going on the cruise at the last minute because her ne'er-do-well son had been thrown in jail for selling marijuana to an undercover cop in Gastonia!

As far as Masey was concerned, he behaved little better than the trailer trash she had to deal with regularly in her part time job at Wal-Mart in Pineville. Yes she knew her preacher told her regularly that everybody was of "sacred worth" to God, but as far as Masey was concerned that didn't excuse their bad behavior, it just made things worse.

"Ms. Bumgarner, it looks like your bag is still in Atlanta, unfortunately," said the elderly black man at the counter, "but when it arrives we can have it delivered right to your house if you like. That would happen tomorrow. Would that suffice?"

"I suppose so. You give me your word that it will get there tomorrow so I can get the laundry done, and go back to life as I used to know it? I have to go back to work on Wednesday in Pineville."

"Not to worry Mam, this delivery service is very reliable."

"As reliable as the baggage handlers in Atlanta?" said Masey, her forehead wrinkling up.

"I take your point Mam, but no. Better than that. I've worked with them right regularly and I've no reason to complain."

"Well I guess not, they weren't hauling your luggage," retorted Masey, "but then what choice do I have? I need to get home, but first I must rescue my cat from the cat hotel, and check my mail."

"Well then fill out this form with your full address and phone number and cell phone if you have one, and they will call you in the morning to tell you the window of hours between which they will deliver your suitcase."

Masey just grunted, got out her best ball-point pen, and commenced to filling out the form. Masey Bumgarner was sixty-three years old, 5' 2", 150 pounds, gray haired, and spry for her age. Her husband Buford had died three years previously from throat cancer, and the three years before that had been something of a nightmare as he went downhill, despite all the chemo treatments.

Now it was just her, and the cat she called Miss Perkins, and a big ole ramshackle ranch house on a mostly rural road just off of Highway 51, the Pineville-Matthews Road. Her proper street address was Buttermilk Lane, which most people supposed was so named because there used to be a dairy farm on this side of Pineville, but actually it was because there had been a pasteurization plant on the road back in the 50s.

Having finished describing her bag, and filling in all the necessary particulars, she remarked to the man at the counter who was obviously bored and staring off down the concourse, "I presume you will be here tomorrow to receive and reroute my bag?"

"Yes Mam, sho will."

"Good, thank you for taking care of it as soon as possible. Now I'm heading out into the sauna bath that is the parking lot where I left my old Rambler. I'll be in touch if the bag doesn't show up on time." She had taken the card with the phone number for the bag service, and put it in her huge Carolina blue pocket book.

When she walked out the front door of the terminal, the heat hit her like a ton of bricks. It was August in Charlotte, and she had managed to come home on the hottest day of the summer and, having already been irritable, only made things worse.

"That car is going to be 200 degrees at least. I'm going to have to turn on the car, roll down the windows, and crank up the AC until it blows all the heat out of the car. When she got in the car, she immediately smelled something funny emanating from the trunk. Having turned on the engine and the air conditioner on high, and leaving the car in park, she popped the trunk of her old car, went around to the back of it, and looked inside, and her mouth fell wide open. "How in the world did I forget to take that chocolate cake to Mrs. Anderson at the nursing home? I meant to go by there on the way to the airport, but then plum forgot it, as I was late leaving home."

The cake, if it could still be called that, had developed a good crop of beautiful green and grey mold all over the icing, which was the major cause of the smell. Picking up the dead dessert she deposited it in the nearby waste can, and exclaimed "Now I'm gonna have to go to the car wash and have them clean out the smell! It's just one thing after another today! Can anything else go wrong? Some days it just doesn't pay to get out of bed."

The air conditioning had now run enough to make it possible to sit down on the front seat of the car without burning one's bottom on the vinyl seat cover, and so Masey got in and started heading to the gate to pay for the parking. In her head she was enumerating the things she did and didn't like about her cruise.

"Did like the music—classic rock all the way! Didn't like most of the desserts. They were the store bought kind. Did like the swim in Jamaica. Didn't like the junk shops in the Bahamas. Did like the visit to the old plantation in Puerto Rico. Didn't like the dance instructor on the boat—just too effeminate." And so it went as she headed for the cat hotel, thinking her days of adventure were over for a while. Little did she know what was waiting for her when she got home.

Chapter Two

A Peck Of Trouble

Masey Bumgarner's home was an old brick ranch from the 50s. Set well back from the road, and with a long driveway and a large front yard to mow, Masey felt like she had reasonable privacy where she lived. There was a long row of pine trees lining the right side of the driveway, some crepe myrtles in various spots in the front yard, boxwoods right in front of the house, and some old oak trees dotting the back yard. The location looked well lived in and well taken care of on the whole, so Masey was more than a little dismayed when she turned the corner into her driveway and found a yard with grass about two feet high! Obviously, her nephew Delbert had completely forgotten his promise to mow her lawn a couple of times while she was gone. On top of that, the old silver mailbox at the end of the driveway was overflowing with junk mail and some other things as well.

"I'm gonna ring that Delbert's neck!" said Masey. "He's got nothing better to do than to play those interminable video games, and yet he can't even bother to get his hide over here and help out his Aunt Masey." Sighing deeply, Masey got out of her car, grabbed the mail in two hands and dumped it in the front passenger's seat in the car and drove down to the house itself. Miss Perkins was sitting in her cage in the back seat meowing as loudly as possible. The vet said she had eaten alright while at the cat hotel, but Masey could tell she looked a bit thinner, not that losing a little weight was gonna hurt that tubby tabby.

Masey was about to go in the kitchen door, which was on the left underneath her carport, when her eye spied something sticking in her front door in a yellow envelope. The envelope, even from a distance, had a sort of official look, and so Masey figured it deserved immediate attention. No telling how long it had been there.

Snatching the envelope, which was firmly wedged into the crack between the door frame and her front door, Masey immediately noticed the official logo on the front of the envelope which read CITY OF PINEVILLE, CITY HALL, FOR IMMEDIATE ATTENTION. It certainly looked important. Opening the envelope from the back, she slid out a three-page stapled document that read on the top of the first page NOTIFICATION OF RE-ZONING HEARING. Glancing quickly down she saw that the hearing had transpired almost a week ago, and so if she was expected to attend, it was too late for that now. At first she felt relieved, but then she read down further. The meeting had been about the city's plan to rezone the whole of Buttermilk Lane in such a way that a new bypass could be built off of Highway 51. It would become a four-lane road with a median and wide shoulders, which would be achieved by claiming "eminent domain" to about ten feet of Masey's front yard. All of a sudden her quiet little lane was going to become a busy four-lane road. But that was not all. The city also wanted to build a sidewalk on her side of the street too, which required another eight feet of her front yard!

Immediately, Masey was scrambling to find the Pineville Courier from her pile of mail in the front seat. She needed the one for August 5th to find out what had happened on the 4th while she was gone. With the cat caterwauling to get out of her cage, and Masey hot, tired, and frazzled, it took a couple of minutes to find the right paper.

There on the front page read the words half way down on the right: CITY APPROVES BYPASS. The vote apparently had been unanimous even though there were lots of protests from irate citizens whom the action would affect drastically. But the ordinance had indeed passed with flying colors. What this meant was the city had a right to set its own price for the land they would claim domain to, and if Masey wasn't satisfied, well that would be just too bad.

Staring at Miss Perkins she muttered "This is not good for you. No night prowling for you before long!" And suddenly the seriousness of this whole deal began to settle in for her. It might even mean she would need to fence in the front yard for the sake of her cat, or worse, have to sell her house at a knock down price and move somewhere. This was just too much for her to take all at once, and she found herself just sitting down suddenly on the pile of mail on her steps and little tears began to run down her cheeks.

How could this happen and she have no say in the matter? Wasn't this America? But then she reasoned, that even if she had been at the hearing she probably would not have been able to affect the matter. Those big contracts for street projects had behind them a whole slew of politicians and contractors. Those councilmen may even have been paid off in advance! Masey was not usually given to conspiracy theories, but she had her suspicions about this whole deal. How had it passed with just *one* public hearing?

"So what do I do now? Do I just take this lying down, or do I call up Benjie?" Nephew Benjie was the lawyer in the family, and he had a big office in downtown Charlotte. He was actually the child of Masey's no good oldest sister Nadine, but she had flown the coup before Benji could even go to kindergarten. Masey had taken the responsibility to raise him ever since then.

Benji hung around with corporate types and Hornets basketball players. He had won some notable cases in his day, but had lost some as well. He was given to drinking a bit too much, but he was a smart boy with a law degree from Carolina. In a split second, she decided she would call him and see what he had to say. "Can't hurt," she said.

Now Masey was a Christian person. She believed in the power of prayer, and that it could change things. So she also resolved to call up her prayer circle, and get them on the line with the Almighty about this matter. Something for sure had to be done or she would have to move. And at sixty-three, and just home from her first real vacation in years, with her hair all curled up and her skin brown, she was in no mood to take this scenario lying down.

Grabbing her mail under her arms, and unlocking the kitchen door, she stepped inside and noticed the musty smell, and so she immediately turned on the window AC in the kitchen. She put all the mail down on the counter, and then went back to get the cat and her luggage. A plan was beginning to form in her head. Slowly, but surely.

Chapter Three

Counselor Moore

Counselor Benji ("don't call me Benjamin, I'm not a paint") Moore was a no nonsense kind of lawyer. He was old school in the sense that he did not chase ambulances, and did not endlessly advertise for business on the basis of class action lawsuits about prescription medicines that proved, on further review, to grow horns on your head, or hair on your feet, or caused breasts to grow on young men. He mainly concentrated on trial law, and stayed away from large corporate and class action lawsuits, preferring to litigate for particular individuals or very small mom and pop businesses. His turf was defending the under-dog and usually he was not involved in murder trials where there was too much momma drama and problems abounded. In short, his work did not cause him a lot of lost sleep at night, but it did provide him with a handsome income. Benji was proud to say he now had his own firm, *Moore and Lessing*, and with three junior partners all kept very busy, he saw himself, at age thirty-eight, as an up and comer on the legal scene in beautiful downtown Charlotte.

The phone range at precisely nine on this Tuesday morning as Benji was staring out the window of the 22nd floor towards Bank of America Stadium where the Panthers played, and was daydreaming about going water-skiing later in the day on Lake Norman, north of town. He could hear the muffled voice of his uber-efficient secretary Mary Lynn dealing with this first caller, and before he could even become curious about who might be calling, Mary Lynn, looking fine in her new business suit from Banana Republic, knocked on the door, stepped in and said, "It's your Step-Mom Masey, Masey Bumgarner, will you take it?"

"Yes, I'll take it," sighed Benji. Masey had in fact mostly raised Benji, having no children of her own, Benji being without a real Mom (his mother had run off with a truck driver when he was just four, and his dad had joined the army and got himself shot and killed in Kuwait during the Gulf War). His father's military pension had at least got him through college at Pfeiffer and law school at Carolina. But Masey had been the constant in his life, his main lifeline and support in all his growing up years and during his education. She had scrimped and saved to help him pay for the living expenses his father's military fund didn't cover. He owed her a lot. But what in the world could she want?

Clearing his throat, he picked up the snazzy red cordless phone on his desk and said, "Hi Mom, what prompted you to call so bright and early on this morning?"

"Son" (for Masey always called him son), "I've got a big problem looming on the horizon, and I need your advice and probably your legal help. While I was away on that once in a lifetime cruise that my sister Sharon and I were supposed to take, only she bailed on me, it seems that the Pineville city council had a rezoning meeting and voted with all due haste to put a four-lane highway right in front of my house, declaring some of my property 'condemned' for use in the public domain. I want this stopped, or at least I want another hearing.

"They only had one quick hearing earlier this month, and apparently there was a lot of opposition to the decision. They had to clear the meeting room at the end of it, so many people were irate, according to the paper. Could you use your legal beagle skills and poke around and see if there was any foul play involved in this, any paying of city council members, any greasing of the wheels, any contractors offering bribes? I hear that Salvo Sand, Gravel, and Cement got the multi-million dollar contract, and that doesn't smell right, because Vernon Lanceford who owns that company is the brother of Mayor Tom Lanceford of Pineville!"

"Hmm, I see as usual Miss Masey that you've done your homework, and this does sound a little hasty pudding to me. So I promise I'll look into it. But don't you go blabber mouthing about the possibility of a legal action. Mum's the word. This could be a sticky one. I'll need to research the zoning ordinances for Pineville, which I'll bet don't match up with the ones here in Charlotte at all. They are probably pretty antiquated. What I do know is Vernon Lanceford is a nasty piece of work, so whatever you do, don't go sticking a stick in that hornet's nest just yet. That boy has sued half of Mecklenburg County to get his way in the past."

"O.K. son, I hear you, and thanks so much for helping me with this, I'm much obliged. You know I don't like to bother you with trivial things, so thanks for seeing that this is very important to me and my future here. I'm too old for this nonsense, but it seems it came calling for me. Love to you and the family. . . . Give me a ring as soon as you know something."

"Will do," said Benji, and slowly hung up the phone. "Whoo-eee. This could be a big mess, but since I am the attorney for the under-dog, or in this case for the little old lady and her under-cat, I'd best gear up."

Yelling out the door, he said, "Mary Lynn, would you get me the zoning ordinance files for the surrounding towns in Mecklenburg County. I need to do some comparisons. So much for water-skiing this afternoon. . . ."

Chapter Four

Miss Perkins In Charge

Miss Perkins was a tad over nineteen pounds, and on that red tabby frame of hers this made her right portly. In fact her girth was such that she no longer found it easy to get out the cat flap in the backdoor into the back-yard and give the birds their comeuppance on a regular basis. She had less and less inclination to do that anyway, as she was a lap cat and preferred to sit in Masey's lap sleeping away while Masey watched her soap operas. Masey would stretch a little shawl she had on her lap and Miss Perkins, after circling and circling would finally jump up on Masey and then Masey would hit the recliner button and they were set for a good portion of the afternoon, and of course later in the evening when the game shows like *Jeopardy* came on. Masey only worked two days a week at Wal-Mart, so she was often home during the weekdays. She had enough Social Security, and insurance money from her husband that all she needed, as she called it, was "walkin around money,"—money for extras and fun things. As for the television shows, Miss Perkins seemed to be partial to *Wheel of Fortune,* as she would actually pay attention to the wheel as it went round and round.

Masey's house-keeping was pretty good, but once every month or two she would call in Molly Maids to make everything spiffy. Because Miss Per-kins was a longhaired cat, the cleaning ladies had to do double duty on the carpets and the furniture to get rid of the excess fur. This was necessary not just for appearances but also because Miss Perkins tended to get fur balls. Masey would comb her out fairly regularly but that fur just kept coming. It was a nuisance, but not as bad as when her husband Buford used to dip snuff. Masey had tolerated this as an alternative to smoking in the house, which she could not "abide," but then even the snuff finally did its work and snuffed out her husband prematurely.

It was a lonely existence at home with only Miss Perkins around, although Miss Perkins was quite the conversationalist when she wanted to be, especially around suppertime. Miss Perkins liked a bit of mischief as well, like the time when she jumped up on the mantle piece, knocking off Masey's prize-winning Waterford crystal vase with flowers in it. Masey had won the prize at Belk's department store by entering her name in the contest there when Belk's opened at the Southpark Mall back in the early 70s. The worst of it was that Miss Perkins wasn't even ashamed of what she did. She spooked for a minute, and then proceeded to sniff all the broken pieces on the hearth below.

Needless to say, Miss Perkins lived a rather sedentary existence, with little excitement from day to day. She did not quite qualify for being an attack cat, but she did fit the old adage about curiosity and cats. She was always exploring something. In her younger days, she had had a couple of litters of kittens which Masey had managed to give away, with a few ending up at the animal shelter from the second batch.

Masey reminisced about the day when Miss Perkins was nursing the second batch underneath the old Rambler in the carport, when an overly familiar German shepherd started sniffing around the car. Before you could say "Jack Robinson," Miss Perkins had rolled out from under the car and jumped right on the back of the stupefied dog and rode him right out of the yard, yelping all the way. He was not seen again in Masey's yard.

Like any self respecting mother cat with good maternal instincts, Miss Perkins knew how and when to protect her young, not to mention her turf. Even Masey couldn't win an argument with Miss Perkins when it came to turf, for example, what quadrant of Masey's bed the cat would sleep on at night. Masey finally had given up moving the cat, and just moved herself to another spot instead. Miss Perkins was like an incorrigible strong-willed child who you had best not say "no" to, too often, unless you wanted trouble.

As for where Miss Perkins got her name, it had come from an old friend of Masey's, now long dead, named Agatha Perkins. The woman was a red-head with lots of hair, indeed her puffy hair had come to mind when Masey picked Miss Perkins from the animal shelter largely because of her beautiful orange puffy tale, and Masey had thought it only right to name her new found friend after her old one. Besides, both Miss Perkins's had personality plus, and were so strong willed they almost always got their way. Masey had plenty of determination and work ethic and "gumption" herself, but nothing like the steamroller determination of the original Miss Perkins.

At the DAR meetings the original Miss Perkins was known behind her back as the velvet sledgehammer, so often did she rule and over-rule the agendas of the meetings. Ironically she had died on the battlefield, that is to say, at the state park in South Carolina that commemorates the Revolutionary War Battle of Cowpens. She claimed to be personally related to the Revolutionary War hero Francis Marion, otherwise known as the Swamp Fox, but all her ancestry research had shown was very tenuous connections. The historical data had outfoxed her.

Masey's Miss Perkins was now in her seventh year, which in cat years is close to fifty. But she was still pretty spry for an old girl, and Masey liked to tell her that she had now become the real old lady in the house. Miss Perkins merely sniffed at this suggestion, knowing that she had lots of tricks still up her sleeve, like catching the occasional mouse that dared to enter the Bumgarner house. She was always sniffing around looking for an occasion when she would be required to prove her mettle.

Chapter Five

Clerical Help

The Reverend Taylor Sampson had just sat down to swill his second cup of morning coffee, complete with Italian Sweet Cream creamer in it, when the phone rang. Seeing as how he was the only one in the office at the moment, it being lunch hour, he picked up the phone and said "Grey's Chapel UMC, this is Reverend Sampson."

"Good mornin' pastor," said Masey, "I'm in a bit of a dilemma" (she pronounced it as if it were two words—"die" then "lemma") "and need some clerical help, and I don't mean secretarial."

Taylor smiled. Masey was one of his stalwarts at Grey's Chapel. She seemed to be there almost as much as God himself, which is to say, whenever the doors were opened. Lately he had not seen her very much since both she and he had taken an August vacation. Reverend Sampson was in his early thirties, newly married, and a Duke Divinity grad with a great penchant for touting the accomplishments of the Duke Blue Devil basketball team. This did not sit well with Masey, who was a dyed in the wool Tar Heel fan, but otherwise she liked Taylor quite well, and trusted his judgment. He had helped the church through some real difficulties in the past three years, and she was prepared to give him a pass on his basketball preferences, putting it down to the foolishness of youth.

"Tell me about it Masey, or if you prefer, since you live not far from here, I'd be happy to meet you for lunch since I was just heading that way with no definite plan in mind."

"Perfect," said Masey. "How's about you meet me at Spoon's Barbecue on South Boulevard as I've got to run an errand over that way anyway at a nursing home after lunch?"

"Spoon's it is," said Taylor. "I'll see you in twenty minutes or so. They should already be busy by now." Looking at his watch as he hung up and put on his coat, he noted it was just now 11:30, and Spoon's was probably doing a land office business already by that hour. That place ran out of barbecue by two in the afternoon it was so popular, serving up that good Eastern North Carolina "cue" as it was called.

Taylor Sampson was a native North Carolinian, from Sampson County no less. He had attended Methodist College in Fayetteville before going on to Duke for his divinity degree. He was an Evangelical Methodist with lots of good Biblical knowledge, which showed in his preaching. He also had High-Church leanings, but he was smart enough to realize that you can't change local churches overnight, so he had just gone with the flow for a while before initiating some little changes he thought enhanced the liturgical and spiritual life of his people. The church had its first Tenebrae service under his tutelage just this past year and it had gone well. He and his wife Sarah really liked living on the edge of Charlotte, and he had no inclination to ask for a different appointment from the bishop any time soon. As far as he was concerned, he was just settling in for a good tenure at Grey's Chapel.

The trip for Masey to Spoon's involved a slight detour over to the Grove Park nursing home on Sharon Road, where she finally delivered a chocolate cake for her old friend Marcie Anderson, who had been at the nursing home with a slowly mending broken hip for some time now. Her family had simply parked her there after her latest surgery with the excuse that they did not have the expertise to give her the proper care, what with her brittle bones.

It irked Masey to see her there, but she had made a point of "doing the Christian thing" and visiting her regularly, and taking her to the K+W cafeteria after church from time to time. Marcie had been sleeping when she arrived, so she just left the cake with the head nurse at the desk with instructions to surprise Marcie when she awoke. She had recently had her 90th birthday.

The line at Spoons was out the door, and that was not comfortable on an August day when it was 95 in the shade! Fortunately the good Reverend had gotten there before her and was in the little breezeway in line waiting for his turn for the table.

"Hello Reverend," said Masey taking off her sun bonnet which she wore to fend off possible skin cancer. "It's a tad warm out there" she added, mopping her brow.

"More than a tad Masey. How was your trip to the islands? Did you pick up any Bob Marley reggae CDs for me whilst in Jamaica?"

"Darn, I forgot that. It was on the 'to do' list, but my mind is sometimes like a sieve these days. When you start having a cluster of senior moments, it's not a good thing. One senior moment once and while just reminds you your memory's almost full. At least I didn't have to remember to call the airport this morning 'cause my suitcase was delivered first thing and I was able to do the laundry before I headed this way."

Just then Bill Spoon's grandson came out and said, "We have your table for two Reverend Sampson, if you'll follow me."

The restaurant was small, and the décor typically rustic, with little wooden tables and chairs and red-checked plastic table clothes. On the tables themselves there was catsup, a bottle of Tabasco sauce, salt and pepper, and napkins. The divine swine was much in the air in the whole room, and the aroma was wonderful. Spoon's only served eastern N.C. style barbecue, which meant hickory smoked pork shoulder, chopped up fine with a vinegar sauce and little tiny red peppers and crunchy bits in it. It came with hush puppies and orange blossom butter, and sweet tea usually.

"Now Reverend this is my treat, because I'm the one who needed advice, so please don't haggle with me about it, I can afford it, and I appreciate your ministry."

"O.K. Masey, if you insist, as Kenny Rogers once sang 'You gotta know when to hold them, know when to fold them. . . .'"

Masey just smiled. It was nice to have a preacher who knew a little bit of popular music and he had a good singing voice too. She really couldn't much stand those preachers who ranted and raved about rock and roll and country music being all the Devil's music. Her view was—why should the Devil have all the good music?

Gracie, the long time head waitress at Spoon's brought them their tea almost as soon as they sat down and they both ordered the barbecue plate with the potato salad (and banana pudding warmed up later).

"So spill the beans Miss Masey. What's bothering you?" said Taylor with a grin.

"Well, I reckon you've heard about the new bypass off of 51 out Pineville way."

"Yes, I glanced at that headline earlier this week, seems there was quite the kerfuffle at that meeting."

"And rightly so. This is going to mess up a lot of people's yards and lives out that way, putting a four lane highway there, and it involves taking at least eighteen feet worth of my front yard! And I didn't even know about this until I got home and saw the notice on my door. I think this matter was railroaded through to suit the contractors and the city council, and did you know that the contract was awarded to the company that is owned by the Mayor's brother? Something's not right there either. Anyway, here is my question. I've read that bit in 1 Corinthians 6 about Christians not taking other Christians to court, but I would reckon that doesn't apply in this instance since the city council and the zoning commission can hardly be called a Christian group. Am I right about this?"

Taylor scratched his head and said, "Are you really thinking about going to court over this? I mean I understand it is a disruption but, they are not condemning your whole property are they?"

"No, but what they are doing is making it far less valuable, and I would have to sell it at a knock down price and move probably, knowing all of what they are planning to do. That eminent domain rule is just not very fair at all. They just take your land and give you nothing, or next to nothing for it, declaring it condemned! It ain't right, as the old man said."

"Well I agree with you there, it hardly seems fair. And to answer your original question, no I don't think 1 Corinthians 6 applies in this instance, and I'm glad you thought to ask and wanted to do the right thing by God's Word. Maybe if you go to court, you would be like that widow in the parable by Jesus found in Luke's Gospel."

"Maybe, but I hope I don't have to keep going to court and then threaten to punch the judge in the nose and shame him in public if I don't get what I want."

"And what is it Masey, that you really want? You're not a materialistic person, not a possessive person to my knowledge. What do you really want?"

Masey looked Taylor right in the eyes. His blue eyes were sparkling and she could tell he was really concerned. "Well to be honest, I want to be left in peace. I want to live out my days in peace and quiet in my home of long standing where Buford and I made a life together. ANDDD . . . I don't want Miss Perkins to get run over by all that new traffic."

"Ah the formidable Miss Perkins. I have made her acquaintance you'll remember."

"Indeed, so you can see what I'm saying. And besides, there are lots of other people on Buttermilk Lane and the adjoining streets that will be affected that are up in arms about this whole deal. I would like to force another rezoning meeting at the least, and a delay in any action on the construction, and a reconsideration of the whole matter, so I've called my Benji, and asked him to look into things."

"Now I don't like the idea of being litigious, goodness knows we are the most litigious culture on the planet and generally I think that's appalling, but in this case, a widow has little other recourse but prayer, and trust me I've been praying, and my conscience is clear on this matter. Something should be attempted to slow down this freight train before it runs over people and messes up their lives. In addition to what I've just asked about 1 Corinthians, I have one further question—Would you support me in this action, especially if it gets serious? I need some back up, and moral support, so to speak."

Taylor looked up and could see Gracie coming with two large plates of barbecue and hush puppies, and he said, "I think it's just what Jesus would want me to do, supporting widows and the defenseless, so yes—you can count on me!"

Masey put her hand on Taylor's and said "Thank you. You have no idea how much that means to me. Now enough business talk for today, please say a blessing over this good food and let's enjoy lunch now."

Taylor folded his hands and said "Dear Lord, we all have our troubles along life's path, and Masey is facing some upsetting ones just now. We pray for your guidance in this situation, and we ask on this day your blessing on our food and fellowship in Jesus' name, Amen."

And they did indeed enjoy the conversation and the barbecue. But Masey's mind was racing. One of the next steps would be to notify other interested parties, and get their names and addresses to Benji's office. She loved it when a plan began to come together. How to notify the neighbors and organize? Should she go door to door? She wanted to keep it quiet until things were well underway towards the injunction she wanted Benji to get to stop the process. She would have to ponder all this some more.

Chapter Six

The Sand Man

We are all a product of our upbringing to some extent, and the upbringing of the Lanceford boys was certainly not stellar. Vernon Lanceford and the phrase "the milk of human kindness" did not belong together in the same sentence. He was indeed a nasty piece of work. His father had been the same way, a smoker, a heavy drinker, a gambler, and someone descended from the original runners of moonshine from the Blue Ridge Mountains to the middle of the state.

His brother Tom had somehow escaped that whole ethos and had become the "white sheep" of the family and the mayor of Pineville. Mostly he hid under the bed when his father, in a drunken tirade, would beat his older brother Vernon again and again. This toughened Vernon up, he had to survive somehow, but it also made him mean as a snake. Nevertheless, the two brothers got along fine with each other, and stood up for each other, but at the same time held each other at arms length, and did not move in the same circles. Tom's view was "give Vernon something constructive to do and it will keep him out of trouble" which is what had prompted him to quietly support Vernon's bid for the contract on the bypass.

At this point in his life Vernon, at fifty-five years of age, but with a lot more miles on him than years, was trying hard to make as much money as he could so he could retire early. This recent winning of the contract to build the bypass around Pineville was to be his crowning achievement which "cemented" his legacy, paid off all his bills, and made retirement possible. Vernon was prepared to deal with most any obstacle that might get in his way, and deal with it with dispatch!

Vernon had his finger in a lot of pies, and he had "ears" in high places in Charlotte as well, so he was on red alert to listen for anything that might mess up his multi-million dollar construction deal. So far, there had been nothing to set off his early warning system. Still, he had some "bad dudes" on his speed dial list just in case. His plan was to start the project just as soon as September rolled around, which was barely a week and a half away. He had already notified his surveyors they would be needed soon.

On this day Vernon was just hanging out in his office well out on Highway 51, chewing on a toothpick, and glancing up at the little TV hanging in a box up on the wall which was showing Sportscenter. The sound was on mute as the highlights of the previous evening's games rolled by. Vernon was a person who had had a hard time keeping help, by which was meant secretarial help. He was too abrasive, too rude, too abrupt, and too crude as well, if the secretary was good-looking, and so he had to keep calling the temp services. Likewise, Vernon had had a hard time having intimate relationships with women. He was twice divorced, and had been known in recent years to frequent strip clubs, or as they were euphemistically called in Charlotte, "Gentleman's Clubs." As Masey would say, "trust me, those kind of men are no gentlemen."

Recently Vernon had favored a club way out on South Boulevard called "The Platinum Club" where he had met his current favorite liason— Sheri, whose chief assets apparently began below the neck. Sheri, it turned out, was more than just entertaining for the right kind of money, and she had become Vernon's favorite bad habit rather quickly. Of course, he had to keep it all on the QT as he was still owing alimony to both of his exs, who did not live in Texas, but rather in Charlotte.

Vernon was busily fantasizing about Sheri coming over to his place that evening when the phone rang loud and insistent, and his new secretary "Miss Marsh" (whom Vernon insisted on calling Miss March) picked up.

"Salvo Sand, Gravel, and Cement, no job is too hard for us," she answered.

"I see, let me check and see if Mr. Lanceford is in." Putting her hand over the phone she said softly, "Mr. Lanceford it is your lawyer who would like to speak to you, what shall I tell him?"

"Connect me," said Vernon, spitting out the toothpick while picking at his nose. Usually lawyers only called with bad news, so the habitual frown on Vernon's face only got deeper.

"Hello Mr. Hightower, to what do I owe the pleasure of this phone call?" Jason Hightower was a "high cotton" Charlotte lawyer, who did not come cheaply, but he had managed to keep Vernon's sorry hide out of jail despite drunken driving, slugging someone in a bar, and other unsavory incidents along the way. Vernon was in Jason's file labeled "high maintenance clients" and Jason had a monthly retainer fee coming to him from Vernon, which so far, Vernon had not missed a payment on. He had however missed a payment to one of his ex-wives and so not surprisingly Jason said . . .

"Suzanne Ledbetter called me this morning to say that her client, your first ex-wife Jane, had not received her checks the last two months, and was demanding payment. What do you want to do about that? So far there is no threat of litigation, just a reminder."

"Well, since I just got this major paving contract I suppose I'd better be on my best behavior, so you can tell Counselor Ledbetter that a check will be in the mail tomorrow, and sorry for the delay."

"That's nice and contrite of you, I'll tell Ms. Ledbetter you've seen the error of your ways."

Vernon laughed, "That's a good one counselor. Thanks for the heads up, I guess."

"No problem. Oh, one final thing. I hear from my sources that you've been frequenting some Gentlemen's clubs."

"Yeah, what of it. I'm a grown man."

"Well, it might be wise to avoid that for a while, since you were late on the alimony. It could give one of your exs the idea you were flush with money, which could lead to further trouble. Kapish?"

"Yeah, I catch your drift. O.K., low profile for a while, especially now with this new public contract."

"Especially in light of that, and the fact that your brother is the Mayor out there in Pineville. You could mess up his re-election campaign if all your carousing showed up in the paper."

"Do tell, but I see your point. Thanks for the words of warning. Gotta go."

When he hung up Vernon muttered "Damn it! Am I ever going to shed those ex-wives, and get them off my back?" But he knew perfectly well the answer to that question. The legal system was on their side, and unless he was prepared to hire a real thug to do them in, he had to just live with the consequences of his previous mistakes. Even for Vernon, murder was a solution that didn't bear thinking of. . . . At least until he was a lot more desperate.

Chapter Seven

Randle Radcliffe: Ace Detective

Wherever there is sin and crime, there must always be police and legal processes to help clean up the mess. And one necessary cog in the wheels of justice is of course investigation, because criminal activity is generally done in secret, in the dark, under the table, out of the sight of the cameras and the reporters. In downtown Charlotte, near the corner of Tryon and Trade streets, there are not only a surfeit of banks, but a ton of legal offices, and then also the offices of the support industries, such as bail bondsmen and investigative detectives. Not far from that intersection, down towards Green's Hot Dog Stand, was the office of one Randle Radcliffe, an eager beaver detective if there ever was one, with his reputation on the rise.

Randle, aged thirty-five and unencumbered by marriage or children but rather married to his work, was one slick and smooth operator. After spending ten years on the Charlotte police force as an investigative detective, he had decided to go private which had its virtues, but also its drawbacks. At first, Randle had trouble drumming up business. He had taken most any case, only drawing the line at searching for lost dogs and cats. He had bought himself two really good Nikon cameras for "surveillance," and managed to build a reasonable clientele of aggravated divorcees, scheming businessmen, and cheated on wives and girlfriends of Charlotte professional athletes (whether Panthers or Hornets). So it was somewhat of a pleasant surprise when he got a phone call from Counselor Benji Moore. Maybe, he thought, when he saw the caller ID on his phone, he might at least begin to move beyond digging up dirt on relationships gone wrong.

"Mr. Radcliffe, I've watched your progress as a private detective with interest, and I now have a job for you of a different sort if you are interested," said Benji.

"And what sort might that be?" asked Randle, running his hands through his slicked down and ever thinning black hair.

"No doubt you heard about that big construction job of building a new bypass off of Highway 51 down Pineville way."

"Yes, but what of it?"

"Well the zoning hearings turned out to be a single zoning hearing at which someone too quickly 'called the question' and a vote was taken to approve the construction project down there, over the protest of many of the residents that would be affected, without proper debate or vetting of the project. It looks very much like a railroad job, and all the more so when the construction company that got the contract is owned by the brother of the mayor of Pineville.

"Something is not right in this whole business, and I'd like you to investigate and see if there were any 'golden handshakes' given to the honorable councilmen who voted on this project in such haste. I'd like to know who the person was in the audience that forestalled any lengthy debate and 'called the question'. I'd like to know whether the contract was put out properly for bids or not, or if the law in that city allows city hall to just pick someone they like for the job.

"What I already know is that any eminent domain case, which is what we are dealing with here, should be appealable before the circuit court if there are grievances. I intend to file a grievance in court to stop this project before it starts, but I need more ammunition, which it is your job to supply. Are you game? The pay will be better than average, and it will broaden your profile and portfolio."

Randle had been listening with increased excitement to this proposition, twirling his pen again and again, with his leg starting to jiggle. He replied at once "You've come to the right place Mr. Moore. This is right up my alley, considering I was a cop who had to deal with what goes on in the suburbs in Matthews and Pineville on many occasions, and I've still got good connections with the police out that way. How soon were you wanting this information?"

"Ideally ASAP," replied Benji. "Certainly, as quickly as you can start providing it. You will need to keep a record of your billable hours please, and go to work even today, if possible."

"I'm on it," said Randle with a grin, "and I won't let you down." Life and his work had just gotten a lot more interesting.

Chapter Eight

Politically Correct?

Masey Bumgarner was an old school Southern Democrat, which admittedly was an endangered species in 2014. What this meant is that on personal ethical issues like marriage and abortion and homosexuality, she tended to agree with what had come to be the conservative Republican stance, but on everything else she pretty much agreed with the Democrats. She was sorry the ultra liberals had high-jacked the Democratic party, just as the ultra-conservative and Tea Party folks had tried to do to the Republican party. It was hard to know who to vote for in such a situation. The choices were not clear-cut.

On top of all that, Masey had in recent years become something of an activist when it came to issues like gun control, renewable energy, climate change, fracking, and in general saving the environment. She had protested the Duke Power mess when their sludge polluted the Tar River, going with others to downtown Charlotte to hold the protest. Recently she decided she would trade in her vintage car for a Toyota Hybrid and she had been twice to the local dealership and had narrowed it down to the Camry Hybrid and the Prius V with the hatchback. On this morning she was favoring the latter.

On war issues she was a pacifist and thought we had wasted a ton of money and lives fighting useless wars in Afghanistan and Iraq. You might say she was an activist pacifist, and her old Rambler reflected it, with the bumper stickers it had including "Save the Whales," "Clean Energy—What a Concept!" and "Jesus said Blessed are the Peacemakers, not Blessed are the Warmongers."

While eating her morning bagel with cream cheese and drinking her coffee, she was also reading an article about Christian members of the NRA who wanted no restrictions at all as to what guns a person can buy at a gun show or shop. She had a word for such belligerent or paranoid Christians—"fruitcakes for Jesus" she called them.

She had nothing against people having hunting rifles or, if need be, hand guns for protection, but nobody needed an automatic weapon, a machine gun, to go hunting with or for self-protection. No one. She was pretty sure the Founding Fathers would have laughed at the suggestion that when they said "in order to have a well ordered militia" what they really meant was "private citizens should be able to buy any guns their little hearts' desire." "This would be like George Washington arguing that private citizens in Virginia had a right to have a loaded cannon in their front yard!" she exclaimed.

Masey frequently got worked up about issues like this, especially when Christians were aligning themselves with ideas and practices that seemed to her to be clear violations of the Sermon on the Mount. "Have mercy," she said, as she read on in the article and came to a part where a Christian said that, "I am building up a personal arsenal for when Big Brother (aka the Federal Government) comes for us and tries to take away all our freedoms."

America had been binging on fear-based thinking ever since 9/11 and it wasn't getting any better. And oddly, at the same time, real democracy in America had gotten weaker and weaker with more and more power brokers trying to get their way with the use of money and influence, whether it was PACs, or businesses, or politicians, or just anyone with money to burn trying to circumvent democratic processes and elected officials making good decisions purely on the basis of what would be best for all their electorate. As Masey pondered these things and was about to get up and get dressed for the day, her phone rang.

"Miss Masey, this is Benji, I just wanted to give you an update. I've hired a private detective to check into things regarding the councilmen in Pineville, and I expect to hear back from him before too many days. When that happens, we need to talk before I draw up a petition for an injunction to block that construction. I'm just giving you a heads up for now, but expect to hear from me soon."

"Alright Son, much obliged for the update. I'm heading to the cemetery to visit with Buford, bring some fresh flowers, and I'll pay your respects while I'm there as well."

"Thank you so much. I know you miss him a lot, and we all do. He was a good soul."

"Yes, but more importantly, he was a committed Christian, and that's the one thing that gives me peace about his passing. Talk to you soon."

Having "fixed her face" and put on her sun bonnet and her nice gingham sun dress, she got the fresh flowers she had bought at Harris Teeter the day before, carrying them in a little plastic vase with water in it, to keep them alive. Masey hated the plastic flowers on most of the graves in the cemetery. So fake, and just as dead as the persons buried there. In general Masey despised artificial things of any sort.

The ride to the cemetery took about twenty minutes and ended on Sharon Amity where there was a huge cemetery. This was one of those that no longer allowed headstones, but Masey had been grandfathered in since Buford had bought the plot many years ago, so she had been allowed to have a small headstone. It was another scorcher, so Masey hadn't planned to spend much time there, just change the flowers and say a little prayer, but when she got there, she found herself talking to Buford.

"Honey, I'm in a pickle. The city of Pineville is trying to condemn the front portion of our land for a highway they want to build right in our front yard, and I have concluded there is only one way, humanly speaking, to stop them, namely legal action. Now I know you weren't partial to taking people to court, and I'm not either, truth be told, but it appears I have no alternatives. Benji is helping me, and I'd be obliged if you'd put in a good word with the Lord about this little project, as there could be trouble.

"All I want until the time when I come to be with ya'll is to be left in peace and quiet. Oh yes, I almost forgot, that Benji sends his love. I'm doing o.k., just anxious and frazzled about what's happening. I'll have you know I went to see the parson, and he approved of my dealings in this matter. So, I've done due diligence in consulting on this deal. Miss Perkins and I sure do miss you. I'm going to sign off now, but I brought you some of your favorite irises in your favorite color. Hope you like them. Bye, Bye for now." Then there was silence as Masey said a silent prayer and wept for a few minutes before rising and going back to the car. The sweat had already begun to bead up on her forehead.

"Good thing I came right after breakfast before it gets too darn hot to be here. It does look like the cemetery folks could plant a few shade trees here, but I reckon they don't want anything to get in the way of their mowing."

The Rambler started right up, as usual. Soon would be the day when she purchased her newer car, the first one in decades. She had resolved that she would do her best to haggle well on price, just like Buford would have done, and not let those Toyota salesmen take advantage of her. She was still trying to make Buford proud of her.

Chapter Nine

Randle's Ramblings

The city council of Pineville had exactly seven sitting members, with one alternate who sat in if someone was sick or could not be present at the meetings. Seven was the number because there would not be ties when the council voted on things, unless somebody abstained. In regard to the vote in question, the public had been told that the vote was unanimous. The council consisted of four good ole boys, one elderly black, one young man who was an Iraq vet, and one relatively young woman. Randle stared down at the list of names while sitting on a bench outside the mayor's office.

Jack Rubenstein, Oliver Swafford, Ricky Vaughn, Grace McGhee, Ezekiel Bennett, Brad Street, and finally Andrew Withrow. The names were ordinary, no Muslim names, only one "Christian" first name, which belong to the African American gentleman. Randle had gotten far enough in his snooping to know that Grace McGhee was a ball of fire, no push over. She was what one person had called a moderate feminist, which sounded to Randle like an oxymoron. She might not be a burn your bra feminist, like in the 60s with Gloria Steinem, but she was a pot stirrer. It was hard for Randle to imagine she could be railroaded, but then maybe there was something in this deal she found appealing. Turns out her father had been Highway Commissioner for many years for the great state of North Carolina. She knew something about the value of good roads. Maybe she was just tired of piddling down Highway 51 with bumper-to-bumper traffic stopping at one of the some thirty-three stoplights on that part of the road before you could get out of town. This bypass would solve much of that problem.

Jack Rubenstein was Jewish, but not an observant Jew, indeed, he liked to call himself an atheistic Jew, which again sounded like an oxymoron to Randle. Ezekiel Bennett had been a state legislator at one point, and was a highly respected man in Charlotte. He was now pushing seventy-five years of age, but still active for his constituency in politics. What was in this road deal for him? Maybe it gave jobs to some of those in his district. The others Randle had found rather boring, and with no obvious connections to Vernon the contractor. But it was the early days yet.

Randle had an ace up his sleeve, which meant he didn't even need to bother his police buddies in Pineville. The head secretary in the mayor's office was Ms. Charlotte Tate, whom Randle had gone to junior and senior high with and had even dated at one point. They had remained friends for many years. Randle figured he might be able to wheedle some information out of dear ole Charlotte over lunch, and so he had called her and asked if she was free.

Now Charlotte was a shy gal, not likely to sign up for ChristianMingle. com much less FarmersOnly.com, and in fact she had never married. So far as Randle could see, she wasn't courting anyone either, and so was in the old Southern parlance "available" and "bonafide." Not that Randle was very interested in sparking the girl at this late date. That ship sailed some years before Randle told himself, but Randle had always had the gift of sweet talking girls, so he figured he might be able to get Charlotte to talk, especially after a margarita or two at Applebees.

So it was that at precisely high noon, Charlotte came waltzing out of the mayor's office looking fine in her navy blue business suit. Randle noticed that she had put on a few pounds here and there, but she still looked good, and did not yet qualify for being "pleasingly plump." She came right over to Randle and gave him a brief hug saying, "It's so good to see you Randle. What bush have you been hiding under for the last decade or so?"

"Well Charlotte, I think you know the answer to that. I was in the police department for ten years, but now I'm a private investigator."

Charlotte blushed and said, "Did you come to investigate me Randle?"

"No mam," said Randle, "but I will tell you that I am working on a case which involves the Pineville city council and the Mayor. Coming clean, I need to ask you a few questions, but truth be told, I also wanted to see how you were doing. It's been a long time, hasn't it?"

"It sure has, but enough chit chat, I'm starved," said Charlotte as she hooked her arm in Randle's, "let's find some food." Randle made a mental note—"this is not the same shy girl I used to know in high school. She might even qualify as 'forward' now."

The drive to Applebee's only took about ten minutes, and the place was already packed, but the waiting time was only ten minutes.

"I hope you don't have to be back at the office right at one," said Randle. "We've some catching up to do."

Charlotte smiled and said "since I'm the head secretary I've got some leeway, and besides the Mayor is off on a junket to recruit more business for Pineville, he'll not be calling for me."

Finally the hostess came and seated the two old acquaintances in the very back of the restaurant next to a window where it was quieter, just as Randle had requested.

"So tell me about you," said Randle, "but right after we order drinks, and of course this is all on me. Your money is no good here today." Randle winked at Charlotte, who in turn blushed again. Randle had memories of their first date, a school dance, in which on the first slow dance she had laid her head on his shoulder, which certainly had gotten his attention.

Charlotte had ordered an iced mango margarita with Cuervo Gold, and seemed to know what she was doing, so Randle got his usual martini on the rocks. This could be interesting.

"After high school, I went off to Meredith, being the Baptist girl I am, and I enjoyed Raleigh, though, to be honest, many of the boys from State were just uncouth and too rowdy and redneck for me. So, I didn't do a lot of dating, and instead concentrated on my studies, and got a good business degree and graduated magna cum laude, or as we used to call it 'hey lawdy momma' back then, in honor of that Steppenwolf song they used to sing at Wolfpack games.

"I was hired in Raleigh right after graduation and worked in the Governor's office for three years, but I really missed Charlotte, and so I got a good recommendation from the Governor himself, and came home. Working for the Pineville Mayor's office (this is now the second Mayor I've worked for here), has been just fine. I have a lot of church friends at Grace Baptist, and since my folks live in nearby Shelby, all is well. Now how about you? I bet you have a less boring story to tell."

"Well I could definitely tell you some police stories that would curl your hair in ways you wouldn't like, but I'm not as well educated as you. I went to CPCC (Central Piedmont Community College in Charlotte), and got a degree in law enforcement focusing on investigations. So I did that for ten years, but got a hankering to be my own boss, which I reckon you can understand. I've dated a lot of folks over the years, but, I too am footloose and fancy-free. To be honest, my police work was not conducive to married life, as I kept a lot of odd hours, and was in some dangerous situations. Being a P.I. is a little more mundane most of the time, you know—angry divorcees, equally angry wives who have been cheated on, angry business men who think their accountant has cooked the books, and so on. Did I mention anger? I've gotten used to dealing with ticked off people, and try not to let it bother me. It's just part of the job, is what I tell myself."

By now Charlotte was on her second margarita and didn't appear to be likely to slow down anytime soon. Her face had begun to turn a pleasant cherry red, matching the blouse she had on under her business jacket. Finally she stopped drinking and asked . . . "and how can I help an old friend?"

"Well Charlotte this recent rezoning vote, and the action which will follow it has gotten a lot of folks upset, and it seemed odd that there wasn't more discussion and debate allowed, and equally odd that the vote was taken so quickly, and without a further meeting being called so that people had time to study the plans and proposals and make an informed judgment."

"Yessss . . . That was a bit unconventional, and actually I asked the Mayor about it and he simply told me not to worry my pretty little head about it. But then when I got curious and went to look up the rules, it appears that while what was done was not completely illegal, it was highly irregular, and was a rush job. And then I found out the Salvo Sand, Gravel, and Cement belonged to the Mayor's brother, and that seemed fishy. So I asked the Mayor about that as well, and he got pretty irate with me. He said it was none of my business, and that anyway, he had absented himself from the meeting where they evaluated the bids for the job, and had not made any suggestions about which company to pick, so as far as he was concerned it had to mean his brother's company must have made the low bid and was the best company for the job. And that was that . . . I was not to bring it up again . . . until . . ." At this Charlotte paused, as the waiter was standing there, and so they ordered their meals, and Charlotte ordered yet one more margarita, promising, "This will be the last one for me, as I will be sufficiently surrencified, as my granny used to say, which I suppose means 'satisfied' or 'full.'"

Charlotte, under the influence of Cuervo Gold, was no shy person. In fact she could talk the horns off a billy goat in that condition. Randle patiently let her rattle on about her apartment and her mean old landlord, and how her preacher was so young and handsome, and how she had only just gotten a third week of vacation time having worked for the Mayor's office for some eight years, and on and on. Finally Randle steered the ship back in the right direction.

"So you were saying that, you had had to drop the subject of the zoning meeting and the vote and your suspicions until . . . "

"Until, one day I saw something that raised the hair on the back of my neck. I saw someone in a camo jacket come into the Mayor's office area and put seven envelopes in the mailbox for the seven city councilmen. And these were fat envelopes too. I went over during a quiet moment long after the man left, and though I did not tear them open, I could definitely tell they were jam packed with bills of some denomination, and I'm wagering it didn't involve pictures of Washington or Lincoln on them. This of course was after the votes had been taken, recorded, and it was a done deal, so if there was a bribe involved, it was apparently not paid in advance, but as a kickback, after the fact."

"Now of course I have no idea if it was solicited, or promised in advance. I have no idea if some of the councilmen knew about this deal, or how many. I have no idea if some of the councilmen objected to this deal, or not. I have now told you, all I can tell you, and at this point I'm remembering what my Momma told me when I had said too much namely 'Shut Yo Mouth!'"

"And my response to what you did say is 'Well hush my mouth'", said Randle with a grin. "Charlotte, this is enormously helpful, and I will tell you now I am working on behalf of a grieving widow who does not deserve to lose a good deal of her front yard, and the sale value of her house as well. What you've told me confirms my suspicions, and it will be up to me now to begin asking questions of the councilmen themselves. I will leave you entirely out of the matter, and not mention you are my source. But I do have one further question—What happened to those seven envelopes, and how long before it happened?"

"I did not see it happen directly, but what I know is, those envelopes disappeared later the same day, and were not there by end of working day, AND, I did not see anyone unusual in the offices the rest of the day, which is puzzling. I suppose that means someone in the office actually collected them. But who?"

"Who indeed, who indeed," said Randle. The rest of the lunch went well enough, and Randle decided it would be wise to keep in contact with Charlotte in case something more developed so he suggested, "This has been fun, maybe we could do it again in a week or so, if you are game?"

Charlotte, a little bit tipsy smiled and said, "If your pocketbook's the same, then I am game."

Chapter Ten

Vernon's Adventures

Vernon's house, while large, and sporting a swimming pool in the back, in a fashionable neighborhood near Myers Park Country Club, had been a pig sty inside, that is until Sheri Lavalier (not her real name) came along and would not put up with it. She told Vernon she was not coming to his house at all until Molly Maids totally cleaned up the joint. Sheri saw herself as a no nonsense business woman, whose chief business asset just happened to be her body, and not surprisingly, therefore, she was a neat freak. While maybe her mind was rather like that of Lady MacBeth's trying and trying to get rid of that darn spot that she couldn't quite erase, at least she *could* demand external cleanliness and control her circumstances. While Vernon had a reputation of being a cruel coarse dude, around Sheri he was a whipped puppy, especially if he got what he wanted out of her. Sheri may have looked like a prostitute in her neon clothes with plunging necklines, but she had the mind of a fancy call girl, and she had learned how to use the whole package to her advantage.

Sheri quickly realized that Vernon had money, and not just "walk around" money but presumably access to lots of money, for she had even taken a trip to Vegas with him one time and watched him gamble away several thousand dollars without sweating it. Lately, he had been talking big things, like maybe a new car for Sheri, or a trip to the French Riviera once this new construction project got going. Sheri liked the sound of all this, so she had dropped her "hard to get act" and had made Vernon a happy man . . . at least once a week. She had not quit her night job at the Platinum

Club just yet, but Vernon was making noises about her doing so, talking about "exclusive access to my honey" and things like that.

Being observant, Sheri had watched Vernon's wheelings and dealings of late when it came to getting that construction job. There had been a lot of phone calls, a lot of chats with his right hand man Vinny, and then a bunch of sealed envelopes, which Sheri assumed was hush money, or bribe money, or something along those lines. Still, she was smart enough not to ask questions. Instead she focused on the possibility of the hot car Vernon had hinted about. Truth to tell, she could use some new wheels. Her old Honda Accord was on its last legs. So on this Saturday morning, now that the behemoth called Vernon had arisen (Vernon was 6'3" and weighed at least 250 pounds) she was fixing some breakfast for them both and suggested, "Why don't we run over to Carolina Chevrolet and look at those hot Corvettes we talked about last night? I saw a red one in a magazine at the beauty parlor the other day and it looked perfect."

Vernon was in no mood to argue after the previous night's calisthenics. Sheri had basically worn Vernon out, but then, Vernon told himself that she was twenty years younger than him and it had nothing to do with his fitness level.

"Whatever you say honey bunch. It looks to be a nice morning. Let's have a leisurely breakfast on the patio out back, and then we can go for a ride."

"Great minds think alike, sugar. I've almost got this breakfast cooked, so why don't you put on your initialed robe I got you, so you don't spill anything on that sleek frame of yours, and we'll have a nice morning together."

To the outside observer, the Vernon which was waiting for his victuals and coffee on the back patio would have borne no resemblance to the Vernon one saw at work, or at the gambling table. Here at home, he appeared to be rather like a dog who had successfully passed the course at obedience school and was eager to listen to the voice of his master, or in this case, his mistress. Not just any kind of dog, but an eager dog in heat, and it was clouding his reasoning capacity.

The trip to the Chevrolet dealer did not take more than fifteen minutes, and since Vernon was pretty good at striking a deal, before lunchtime rolled around he had worked out a leasing agreement for a 2014 cherry red Corvette Sting Ray with very low mileage and affordable payments. He kept the car in his own name, but he told Sheri that so long as they were doing well and sticking together, she could look forward to a nice gift on her next birthday, which did not come until the following July.

Sheri was allowed to drive the car off the lot, with Vernon by her side. The old Honda that they traded in had barely paid for the down payment, but who cared? Sheri was happy, and Vernon was happy because Sheri was happy, and we all know that the reverse is a disaster—because when "Momma's not happy, no one is happy." Sheri with her newish cherry red Corvette counted herself a lucky girl on this morning. She had an open mind as to what the future might bring.

Chapter Eleven

Randle Reconnoiters

Sitting at the desk across from Benji, Randle sipped his coffee and waited for Benji to finish his first phone call of the day. It was Monday morning, and there were usually a lot of calls. Randle felt he had enough evidence to help Benji make the next move, but Benji was the legal expert, so he awaited instructions for his own next move.

Hanging up, and telling his secretary Mary Lynn to hold calls until further notice, Benji stared across his big desk and said, "O.K., what have we got, what do we know for certain?"

Clearing his throat, and sitting up straight, Randle said "we know for sure that money showed up in the Mayor's office in sealed envelopes and were deposited in the little pigeonhole mail boxes for the seven city councilmen. Seven envelopes and only seven envelopes. We also know that they magically disappeared the very same day, but no one saw any councilmen come and collect them. Charlotte, my friend who works in the Mayor's office, was clear about that, and she was there the whole day working. She would have seen or heard something. What we do not know is whether this payment was a kick back promised in advance, or a second payment, or what. But it was cash. Straight cash, untraceable cash, and that makes it immediately suspicious.

"What we also know is that the vote of the council on the rezoning was taken quickly and surprisingly, despite the protests, it was unanimous. Not many votes on that city council have ever been by acclamation or unanimous. So something's fishy, but I'm going to have to interview several of those councilmen and see which way they jump, before we can absolutely conclude that funny business was going on. I need to talk with the person who called the question in the audience as well. But it certainly looks like funny business to me on first blush."

"Yes it does," said Benji, tapping his pen on the desk, "And I have discovered something else that suggests funny business. I've been pouring over the zoning laws for greater Mecklenburg County and for Pineville, and I discovered that it was absolutely the normal protocol to have two required hearings before accepting a bid on a highway contract. HOWEVER, last Spring, in April, the city council of Pineville, in their wisdom, amended that rule insofar as it applied within their jurisdiction to say "but in circumstances where immediate attention to a road problem is required, the second hearing may be waved, and the contract bids evaluated, voted on and concluded at the closed meeting of the city council, and then ratified (unless there are 'inordinate' objections from the citizens), by a simple majority vote at the public hearing for rezoning."

"I wonder what counts as inordinate objections, as there were plenty of protests at that zoning meeting from irate citizens? In any case, there seems to be enough here from what you've found and I've found to go to the circuit court judge, present this evidence, and ask for a stay on the execution of the contract. And that is what I intend to do, this very morning. That phone call was confirming I have an urgent appointment with the judge out there in Pineville late this morning. The good news is, that judge is a no nonsense 'hanging judge' and if he even smells a rat, he is likely to take action. His name is Judge Sawyer Martin, but everyone calls him 'the Hammer', and he's been on the bench for some thirty years, riding hard on crime and punishment all that time. I expect a favorable response."

"That's all to the good, but I suspect you want me to continue to snoop around, and to begin talking to these councilmen, discretely of course, and in a non-threatening way."

"Exactly. You carry on, and so will I." The conversation was at an end, but the fun was just about to begin.

Chapter Twelve

Prayer Meeting

Grey's Chapel was a historic old Methodist Church. The story goes that it was founded by one of Francis Asbury's circuit riders in the early nineteenth century. It was a white-framed church with the typical adjoining fellowship hall. In the breezeway between the two buildings, two additional rooms had been added on at some juncture, one of which served as a sort of parlor, or small meeting room. It was filled with second hand furniture that did not match—the castaways, or donations of church members of an earlier generation. Here the saints had been praying for decades, and this week was no different.

Masey Bumgarner was as regular as clockwork when it came to the Wednesday evening prayer meeting at Grey's Chapel. She was actually one of the leaders of the group, and she knew the group well. It was this group of ladies who had brought food into her home the entire week of the funeral when Buford had died. It was this group of ladies to whom Masey had confided her grief and her anxieties after her husband was gone. It was this group of Christian friends that had held her hand and given her Kleenexes whenever she needed them, and had burned up the phone lines whenever she wanted to talk. On this evening, as the sun was setting through the window in the old church parlor where they met, she shared her concerns about what would be happening to Buttermilk Lane.

"Goodness knows, I'm not a trouble maker, but this is too much. To come home from a vacation and discover not only that there had been a rezoning hearing, but that a final vote had been taken and that some eighteen feet (ten for the road, eight for the new sidewalk) of my front yard was about to be taken from me under the eminent domain provisions of the law without me having so much as a say so about it . . . well that's just too much."

"So I went to Pastor Taylor and he agreed that it was o.k. for me to seek legal relief from this problem. So my step-son Benji, whom some of you met last Christmas when he came to the Christmas Eve services with me, is doing some investigating, and is planning to file an injunction halting, at least temporarily, this construction project. Ladies, I've been in a swivet ever since I got back from that cruise, worried about what was going to happen to me and Miss Perkins."

Sally Smithfield, a tall slender lady with blue-tinted hair and a high voice chipped in, "And rightly so. Miss Perkins could get run over if a major highway is built in your front yard, that's for sure. And then of course there is all the traffic to worry about too. Charlotte traffic is terrible, and there are lots and lots of careless drivers. Just the other day some preoccupied teenager bumped my back bumper by accident while I was waiting for the light to go green. Turns out she was texting her boyfriend while driving!"

"That's just appalling," said Madison Smith, the elderly stateswoman of the group. "They need to ban hand held cellphones being used at all in a car, if you ask me. It's already caused all sorts of accidents."

"Too right," said Jane Dozier, "too right. We need some better laws, and better law enforcement. So Masey, how would you have us pray about this matter? What shall we be asking the Lord for this evening?"

Masey paused, contemplating what to say, and then found herself asking: "Perhaps we could first ask the Lord for guidance in this matter. How far should I pursue objecting to what has happened? Just until there is another zoning meeting? Until the original decision is reversed? And then if things don't go well at the hearing, do I file a lawsuit? I feel a little uncomfortable about the latter, but if push comes to shove, what else can I do besides pray for a miracle? Pray somehow that the Lord will derail or de-fund this project by a means I haven't even contemplated? Its hard to know what to ask for." And at this point Masey just put her head in her hands and rubbed her forehead and said in a soft voice, "I am almighty tired of this aggravation already, and contemplating a lot more of a hullabaloo isn't something I relish. I'm not spoiling for a fight, that's for sure. But I guess if that's what it will take . . . it is."

"I say, don't let those men take advantage of you without a say so. Life's too short to just lay down and take an injustice and say nothing," said Madison.

"Amen to that", said Jane. "Besides the Bible is full of evidence that the Lord is on the side of widows and orphans, both in the OT and NT, and Jesus didn't tell that parable about the widow and the unjust judge for no reason. So let's pray with expectation. Let's pray with assurance. Let's pray with a hope that doesn't disappoint, remembering that faith is the assurance of things hoped for, yes it is."

For the next hour and a half, the room was filled with petitions to the Higher Court and the Highest Judge of human conduct. There was something cathartic about it for Masey. It lifted her spirits and did indeed give her hope of a positive outcome. She ended up shedding a few tears of joy, and said "I don't rightly know where I'd be without ya'll, and without your support. It means the world to me that you actually care about what happens to me and Miss Perkins. Sometimes I feel so very alone, though I know the Lord is with me. But when I'm with ya'll I feel stronger again, more confident. So thank you so much for this, and I will keep you apprised at how things go, blow by blow."

The meeting was over, and it was already dark in the parking lot. Time to go home and feed Miss Perkins. "She's probably sitting on top of the fridge by now wondering where in the world I could have gotten to," murmured Masey.

Chapter Thirteen

R And R

It was so good to get away, especially to a place like Cancun. Mayor Lanceford had already done his wheeling and dealing with Mexican officials in
Mexico City, and now he was on the R+R side of the trip. He had to admit
that the job had some good perks, but at the same time, the excitement of
being elected Mayor had long since worn off. Now in his seventh year as
Mayor, but facing an upcoming re-election bid, he found the job increasingly boring and had let things slide, going along with most of the proposals
that came across his desk, including the one from his brother. He reasoned
that since his brother had not asked for any help previously, no one could
say there was a pattern of nepotism, so "just this one time" it felt alright to
help him get the contract he both badly needed and wanted.

Lying on his lounge chair with his Dos Equis beer in a little foam
holder, he smiled at the ingenious way he had handled the matter. In effect, he had told the city council that if they really wanted to do something
about raising the pro-business profile of Pineville, they would first have to
improve the road system, which had been neglected for so many years.

"Developers don't want to come to Pineville unless there are good
roads, sewer systems, curbs, sidewalks and the like, so their businesses
have good 'curb appeal', so to speak" he remembered telling the council last
summer. After a two hour meeting, the group had not only agreed with this
proposition, but agreed they should go with the lowest bidder, whoever that
was (being a bunch of fiscal conservatives, concerned about balancing the
city budget) and this meant going with Salvo Sand, Gravel, and Cement.

So it was that the zoning meeting became a mere formality, rubber-stamping the decision already agreed on in private sessions beforehand. Yes there were protests, but there are always a few sore losers in such matters, and Tom Lanceford was not too worried about a few poor or blue collar folks protesting losing some of their yard. He couldn't imagine that causing any real trouble down the road. What he did not know is that his scheming brother had sent thank you packages to all the councilmen after the fact, with anonymous notes saying it was an early Christmas gift from "the workers who will be improving your roads."

Lance Corporal Lanceford was one tough customer, though she hardly looked it being 5'2, 130 pounds, and not an ounce of fat on her body. She had done two tours of duty in Iraq and two tours in Afghanistan. She had also been on the elite team that went into Libya undercover and extracted some Americans after the fall of the dictator Khaddafi. On the outside she appeared not only normal, but impervious to pain and suffering. But on the inside, the wars had taken their toll. She was having nightmares and flashbacks to incidents where her battalion had been ambushed by the Taliban and they had to fight their way back to safety, leaving many of her fellow soldiers to die at the hands of the enemy. After a while these things take a toll on even the toughest of individuals, and so Liz Lanceford was Stateside for some recovery time, suffering from PTSD.

At first, she thought it wise not to tell her mother Jane about this, but then she concluded she would find out eventually anyway. And Liz had exactly no contact with, or relationship with, her father "Big Vernon" whom she had not seen since the nasty divorce had gone through. Whenever she thought of him, and how he cheated on her Mom, she just got angry, very angry. At the moment, she was at Atlantic Beach, having driven down from Fort Bragg in Fayetteville, with her one true comrade in arms, Nancy Meyer, likewise a corporal in the Army.

"So Nance, how do you cope with the nightmares when they come? Do you get up in the middle of the night, and try and change the subject, so to speak? Or do you just roll over and try to go back to sleep, and pretend like you were not reliving some of the horrors? What works for you?"

"To tell the truth", said Nancy, "I really haven't developed a consistent strategy. Sometimes just getting up and having a beer seems to help, sometimes watching a little TV, and sometimes I'm so groggy, I do just roll over and go back to sleep. Nothing eliminates having such episodes, so I just hope to cope at best. Those meds they give us make me too foggy and I need a clear mind to sort things out, so I've not been taking them."

"Really?" said Liz. "Seriously? I find I need to take something to blot out the instant replays of scenes in my head. I don't know where I'd be without the Darvon, to be honest. And I'll tell you something else. I'm not signing up for another tour of duty. I've had it with that. I may move over to the National Guard, but that's about all. No more hostile foreign countries for me. I may even decide to go back to civilian life. It's bound to be safer and easier. I don't want to spend all my life looking over my shoulder afraid of what's coming after me."

"What? And lose out on your good pension and medical coverage which would kick in in five more years? Not me baby. I'm going to stick it out. By the way, did you get anything out of those mandatory counseling sessions when you got back?"

"Not much. Just a bunch a psychobabble if you ask me. I don't see how bad memories or flashbacks can force you to do something you don't want to do. Come on now! I'm in better control of my actions than that!"

The rest of the conversation was mundane, as they resolved finally to have some good seafood at the Sanitary Seafood market in Morehead City down the road. But the result of the conversation was that Nancy was worried that her friend Liz might be a ticking time bomb, and might not be thinking straight either.

Chapter Fourteen

"Stay . . . Just A Little Bit Longer"

Benji figured he needed to look his very best, so he put on his most expensive Joseph A. Bank black pin-striped suit and headed to the circuit court building in south Charlotte. The traffic was its usual bumper-to-bumper self, and the ride from his condo took about thirty minutes even on a good day. Once he got to the parking garage, he then had to cross over on the footbridge into the third floor of the courthouse building, and then go sit and wait in Judge Martin's office. Petition in hand, he came with his full file in his briefcase to back up his request for a stay, and possibly another rezoning hearing.

Judge Martin was the senior member on the bench of this particular circuit court, having been a judge for close to thirty years in Charlotte. He was an African American, a family man, had an elderly mother in the Myers Park nursing home, loved golf and the Tar Heels (his alma mater), and in general had been the protector of the disadvantaged and vulnerable in the Charlotte area. He also was very efficient and to the point. He didn't like dragging things out, believing justice delayed was justice denied.

Benji was only the second plaintiff to visit with the Judge on this morning, and so Benji reckoned he surely could not be tired out from a long day just yet. When the secretary with the bifocals called out "Counselor Moore" in a high shrill voice, he almost jumped out of his seat. He was ushered into a paneled conference room, with high back leather chairs around a long oval conference table. The diffused light came in from the morning sun through the whole wall of curtained windows facing the backside of Quail Hollow Country Club.

"Some coffee for you Mr. Moore?" asked the secretary, pushing her glasses up her nose.

"Thank you ma'am, but no. I've had mine for this morning and am good to go."

"Alright," said the woman quietly, "the Judge should be with you directly."

It took only five more minutes before the Judge, already robed for his busy day in court, and rubbing his balding head, sat down across the table from Benji and said, "Let's get right to the point, how can I be of service to you counselor."

"Judge, I imagine you are familiar with the recent action taken at the rezoning hearing in Pineville where a vote was taken to create a whole new bypass down Buttermilk Lane to Highway 51."

"Yes, I saw that in the papers. I was surprised that with all the protests from the locals the council went ahead and approved the matter. How does this concern you or me?"

"In several ways Judge. Firstly, the normal protocol was to have more than one hearing so grievances could be aired and discussed. This didn't happen. Not only so, but someone in the audience 'called the question' before many of those who wanted to speak could do so, and then suddenly a vote was taken by the council, which was unanimous. If this was not rigged in advance, it was at least rushed. Furthermore, I have learned that the contract for the job was awarded to the company of the Mayor's brother, and surely that smells foul. The various bids were not even publicly discussed or published."

Benji continued, "Worst of all, the Mayor's secretary, who by the way is sworn to silence, saw packets of money show up in the pigeonholes of the councilmen after the vote was taken, packets which disappeared by the end of the day. Something is rotten in Pineville for sure. What I am here for today is simply to ask for a stay, to put the whole building project on hold until this can be properly investigated. I'd like to ask for another hearing as well, if that's not too much to ask."

The Judge said, "Well, I'm afraid not on the second hearing. I did hear that that council had voted earlier in the year that one rezoning hearing was all that was legally required, and since they have already taken a vote, we can't back track on that. But I am prepared to issue a 'stay' while your client or clients, whoever he or she may be, can have time to prepare a proper lawsuit."

"Thank you, your honor, my client is a widow named Masey Bumgarner, whose front yard is about to be confiscated, at least eighteen feet of it, when they build the road and the new sidewalk. Quite naturally, she doesn't like this plan as it will drastically devalue her property, and she has lived there for a long time and doesn't relish moving, buying even less of a house than she now has because she would get less money for hers, what with a major road in the front yard. I suspect that whole street will be rezoned commercial before long if this goes through anyway, putting a lot of blue-collar families out of their homes."

The Judge frowned, rubbed his chin and said, "Not good. You may have your stay, and I suggest you file your motion for a trial in my court rather quickly, as once the news of the stay gets out, there are going to be some irate people in Pineville."

"On behalf of my client, I can only thank you for this and your wise council. You can expect that I will file suit before the end of the working day either tomorrow or the next day, depending on how fast I can have this typed up. Thank you Judge. "

"Very well, I will look for the paperwork, and see you in court, hopefully soon, depending on what's on the docket in the next few weeks."

All in all Benji was pleased as he mulled over the clock that was now ticking. The publishing of the "stay" would not happen before tomorrow at the earliest, and it would not be in the papers until two days hence at best. It was time to burn the midnight oil and get this lawsuit going, but first he needed to apprise Masey of what was happening.

The Bluetooth technology in his car worked very well, and so Benji was able to call hands free by just the touch of a button on the steering column.

"Masey, I've got some good news for you."

"Son, you sound like you are in a well. Are you in the car?"

"Yes mam, I am, and the good news is the Judge has issued a stay, but we have to file a lawsuit almost immediately, as he had to deny the appeal for a re-hearing since the final vote was already rendered. So I will need to get the paperwork to him in a couple of days, and before that we need to go over what all we want in the document. So, we need to get together in the morning and talk this through. Are you good with that?"

"Lord have mercy, things sure do move fast sometimes, but yes, I'll come to your office in the morning. Is ten o'clock alright?"

"That'd be fine."

"And thank you son, you're a good son, and I sure appreciate this. Maybe we can head the pavers off at the pass, the bypass that is!" And with this, they both hung up. The process was now in motion, and the engines were revving.

Masey showed up bright and early to Benji's office, and they spent a good three hours ironing out the details that would be in the lawsuit. She was not suing for compensatory damages. She was simply suing to stop the construction project dead in its tracks. Named in the lawsuit as potential witnesses were the Mayor, the Mayor's secretary, all the city councilmen, Vernon Lanceford, Vernon's secretary, and the yet to be named person at the zoning hearing who called the question. Randle needed to hurry up and find this person.

By the end of that day Randle had tracked down one Jimmy Grimes, a paver working at Salvo Sand, Gravel, and Cement, and had called Benji to give him the name so he could be listed as a potential witness in the lawsuit. Randle would still need to interview the young man who apparently had "called the question" at the rezoning hearing. The suit was properly filed on Thursday morning of the same week, Benji hand delivering it to Judge Martin's secretary so it could be put on the docket.

Chapter Fifteen

Boom Goes The Dynamite

Looking tanned and relaxed, Mayor Lanceford came to his office on Friday for the first time in over a week with a bounce in his step. The Mexico trip had been successful, two companies down there were looking at investing in projects in Pineville that Lanceford had made presentations on while visiting, and all seemed right with the world. But this illusion of well-being lasted all of about fifteen minutes, because when Lanceford sat down at his desk, Charlotte brought him his messages, the Charlotte Observer, and an oral message "on the QT" from herself.

"Mayor, if you don't mind, I'd like to have a word before your day really gets busy. Is now a good time?" asked Charlotte.

The Mayor was feeling mellow and well rested, not stressed in any way, so he said, "Sure, Charlotte, how can I help?"

"Earlier this week while you were gone, something very peculiar happened. I am not a nosy person, but I could not help noticing that there were unmarked envelopes delivered to the seven little pigeonholes where the city councilors receive their mail, identical envelopes. Because this had never happened before in my tenure as secretary here, going back to before your time, I went over to see what had been delivered. I picked up one of the envelopes, and for sure, there was a considerable sum of money in it. I did not open the package or any of the other packages, but by the end of the day, I noticed that they had all disappeared."

Mayor Lanceford was not a person with a blood pressure problem, but he could feel his temperature rising as Charlotte laid out this scenario to him. Getting a grip on his temper, he managed to ask in a somewhat civil tone of voice,

"And did you see who delivered these packages?"

"Well sir, not exactly. It was a man, but I only saw his back as he was leaving. It was not someone I could immediately recognize from the back. He was wearing a camouflage jacket, but that was all I noticed."

"Thank you Charlotte, for keeping watch on things while I was gone. You can go back to work now." The Mayor suddenly found himself in need of some Tums. But what happened next made him need a whole bottle of Tums.

Looking at the morning's Charlotte Observer, he turned to the section that dealt with land development, easements, and other legal decisions, and saw the headline "Bypass Project put on Hold by Judge Martin." Reading quickly he discovered that a lawyer named Moore had filed a grievance with the Judge, and the Judge had agreed to a temporary "stay" until the matter could be resolved legally. The article simply mentioned in a general way "certain irregularities in the rezoning meeting where the vote was taken on the project" without giving details.

Suddenly, the Mayor felt like the world was beginning to spin out of control. Much of the future planning, indeed both of the projects he had interested the Mexican investors in, depended on the building of the Highway 51 bypass. And as for the money that mysteriously showed up and disappeared, Mayor Lanceford had a sinking feeling he knew exactly where that came from. He called his brother on speed dial . . . waking him up.

"Hullo," said a groggy Vernon Lanceford.

"Good morning brother, sorry to bother your beauty sleep, but I have a question for you . . . and you had better give me a straight answer. Did you by any chance decide to give the various city councilmen a golden handshake, perhaps in thank you for the vote taken on the bypass."

"Ummm . . . well, let me think. Yeah, I reckon I did. Seemed appropriate to say thank you. It wasn't a bribe or anything since the vote was already taken, and nothing was said about this in advance. Maybe you could call it a thank you present."

"Do you have any freaking idea how that is going to look if the press gets hold of this information, never mind if there is a court case? And while I'm on that subject, have you read this morning's Observer yet?"

"No, too early. Why?"

"Because, you idiot, someone has filed an injunction and gotten a stay from Judge Martin on our building project due to 'irregularities', and a 'stay' is of course only temporary . . . until a lawsuit is filed. This means it is highly likely there is going to be a lawsuit involving you, and this project, and me, and it will tie things up for the foreseeable future. . . . And who knows how that will turn out?"

There was silence at the other end of the line for what seemed like an eternity and then Vernon said, "That is soooo not good, but perhaps I can fix it."

"I would advise against trying to *fix it,* Vernon, before the case goes to trial. You might well make it worse."

"Yeah, well, you politicians are always waffling around, but I am a man of action. I'll see what the lay of the land is."

"Do not DO anything, unless I agree to it—you hear me?"

"Yeah, alright, I'm going to find out what the facts are and who's responsible. I'll get back to you." And he hung up.

"I've got a bad feeling about this whole deal," said the Mayor to himself. And of course, the Mayor had enough experience to know when an ill wind had just blown through his office.

Chapter Sixteen

The Trade In and the Run Off

Wal-Mart was an emporium of the rainbow coalition of humanity. You could see every size, shape, and age of humanity in that store, not to mention walking advertisements for how not to dress when going out in public. Masey was simply dumbfounded with what she saw on a daily basis in that store. Down one aisle there was a fat lady in what looked like a small orange tent of a dress, with curlers in her hair, shopping for shampoo and other household items. On the next aisle there was a man in a camo jacket and with a beard looking like an extra from Duck Dynasty. In the pet department there were small children running wild, and thumping the fish tanks and hollering "Nemo." In the grocery section, there was an elderly man with only the following items in his cart: 1) a six pack of prunes; 2) two six packs of Budweiser; 3) eight packages of macaroni and cheese; 4) four packages of cigarettes, not to mention a sealed package of eight Skoll snuff cans. Fortunately for Masey, her shift was over, and she got to escape from Fantasy Island to the relative sanity of the parking lot. She decided she wasn't going straight home.

Masey needed something to take her mind off the impending legal hassles and so she drove her car over to the Toyota dealer to finally do something about getting a newer car. Benji had helped her out by looking at Auto Trader and Car Max online, and had determined she could get a very good used Prius V at Brown's Toyota in Matthews, with low mileage, and even in her preferred color—Carolina Blue. She was wearing what she called her haggling clothes, and her little ole lady hat, to draw as much sympathy as she could from the used car salesman, and had headed off to the car lot, leaving Miss Perkins at home. At least she didn't still have her Wal-Mart apron and button on.

Meanwhile, Vernon Lanceford had gone into action trying to get to the bottom of the impending lawsuit. He had called the circuit court Judge's office, and his secretary had read him the formal injunction, listing the plaintiff as one "Masey Bumgarner" Buttermilk Lane, Pineville. He decided to go and "case the joint," survey the house where Masey lived, and maybe leave a little warning note. Lanceford had decided not to call in the goon squad just yet, but rather thought a little intimidation might work. He crafted a little sign before leaving the house, a sign he was planning to leave taped to the front door or some door at the house. The sign read YOU'D BETTER DROP THAT LAWSUIT IDEA LADY, OR YOU'LL BE SORRY. In fact, the lawsuit had been filed by Benji Moore that very morning so that ship had already sailed.

When he drove in the driveway of Masey Bumgarner, it occurred to him that she might actually be home, being an elderly person. So, at first he left the sign in his car, and thought a little verbal abuse might be sufficient to accomplish his aims. After all, Vernon Lanceford was a big ole boy, and fully capable of intimidating smaller people. He had done it many times. But as it happened, there was no car at the Bumgarner house, and so Lanceford went back to his car and got the sign, placing scotch tape to the four corners of it. He determined that the door that looked used was the carport door, the most logical point of entry to the house once one got out of the car under the carport.

What Lanceford had not noticed is that right next to the carport door there was a kitchen window, and in that window was a window air conditioning unit, which just happened to be one of Miss Perkins favorite places to take a little snooze. On this morning she had just settled into her spot when this strange hulking man came walking up to the house, walked right into the carport, and up the three little stairs to the kitchen door. By now, Miss Perkins was on high alert, because she had never seen this ugly looking person before, and was dubious about his intentions. And then when he began putting up a sign on the kitchen door, Miss Perkins figured it was time to go into action. This man was trespassing on her turf, and not in any friendly way. He had not even bothered to bring any cat crunchies or treats to pacify her.

Just as Lanceford had gotten the first two corners of the sign attached to the door, Miss Perkins leaped onto the mostly bald head of Vernon Lanceford and inserted her claws, preparing to ride him out of the yard the way she had done the German shepherd sometime before. Lanceford screamed "What the hell???" and when he swiped at the cat with his left arm he stumbled over the lower step below him and fell hard to the carport floor, which was a greasy old concrete slab. The Rambler had left regular deposits on the floor.

With Lanceford in the prone position, and waving furiously to get the cat off his head, Miss Perkins decided she would jump onto his midsection and insert the claws once more, nimbly leaping over the flailing arms of her victim. This produced a second yelp of pain, and then Lanceford rolled over and decided he had best minimize his losses and skedaddle. His arm was hurting like the dickens, and he was afraid he might have broken his wrist when he tried to brace himself as he was falling. There was oil residue all over the back of his new leisure suit pants.

When he got back to the car, having dislodged himself from Miss Perkins who was standing sentinel in the middle of the driveway, making sure that the stranger beat a fast retreat, he realized he needed something to sit on so as not to mess up the clean seat of his truck, and so he grabbed the old Krispy Kreme doughnut box which had been languishing awhile in the passenger seat, and he sat on it . . . completely forgetting there was a Boston Cream-filled doughnut still left in the box, which his oil soaked behind squashed like a bug when he sat down in the truck. He revved the engine and backed out of the Bumgarner driveway, leaving the sign hanging cock-eyed on the door underneath the carport.

As he drove off, he could feel the blood from the scratches on his head starting to roll down towards his brow, and he swore a couple of times and cursed the cat. "Never did like those damned creatures" he mumbled to no one in particular. He resolved that was the last visit he would personally pay to that house, but he was by no means done with Masey Bumgarner. This whole misadventure had simply gotten his blood up, or trickling down if one looked at his noggin.

Masey was in deep conversation with Mr. Enoch Silver at the car lot, and was asking at this point to see the Car Fax, so she could make sure this previously owned vehicle had not been in a wreck. Mr. Silver had patiently taken her over to the computer and shown her the particulars, and then said, "And the former owner is local, you could call him and ask him why he traded the vehicle, if you like. He left a phone number. His name is Tom Lanceford, you might recognize that name, he's the mayor out in Pineville. It was his wife's car to run around town, and she wanted something a bit more luxurious, once he got re-elected."

"Well that's an interesting coincidence," said Masey. "I think I'll not bother the Mayor, but give me his wife's number. After a couple of rings, a husky voice picked up and said, "Yes, this is Amber Lanceford, to whom am I speaking?"

"Hello Mrs. Lanceford, my name is Masey, and I'm at the Toyota lot looking at possibly buying your former car, and wonder if you could tell me if you had any trouble with it, and I wanted to ask why you traded it."

"Oh no, it ran just fine. I just wanted a larger vehicle to haul all my interior design stuff around with me. Maybe you've heard of Pining Away Designs?"

"No mam, I can't rightly say I have, but you're saying the car was fine, and not in any accidents, you simply traded up—right?"

"That's exactly right, and I enjoyed the car too, hope maybe it will serve you well. Gotta run now, nice talking with you."

"O.K. Mr. Silver, now we need to talk turkey. I've done my homework, and with a car like this with 20,000 miles on it, I should not have to pay more than 20,000 dollars for it, less, counting my trade in, though I realize there's not much call for a vintage Rambler these days with over 100,000 miles."

Mr. Silver smiled and patiently said, "Well how about we call it $19,500 plus taxes and fees, since your car is worth less than 500 dollars at this point."

"Really? Only $500 you say, well I guess I'm not entirely surprised. How about $19,000 all in taxes and the lot."

"Ms. Bumgarner you drive a hard bargain, but I'm in a generous mood this morning so let's just shake on it and call it a deal, shall we? You won't regret it."

The paperwork took another hour, and when Masey drove into her driveway with her new bright and shiny Carolina Blue Prius V, Miss Perkins was back on the air conditioner, and did not recognize the car. But when Masey got out of the car, she jumped down, came right over and rubbed her legs, and starting purring. As Masey was looking up toward the door, and fumbling for her house key in her purse, she noticed the crooked sign, swaying in the breeze on her door.

"Oh no . . . here comes trouble," she whispered. Little did she know that Miss Perkins had already dealt trouble an initial defeat.

Chapter Seventeen

Stumped

Randle had to admit that this was a head scratcher. So far he had interviewed five of the seven Pineville councilmen and they appeared genuinely shocked to hear that some kickback money had come their way, and they all denied in strong terms that they had taken any such money. Randle still had to interview Ezekiel, the African American member of the council, but he thought him an unlikely candidate for taking money, and then there was Brad Street. Brad Street was one of the less well known, and quieter members of the city council. Randle had a very difficult time digging up any dirt on him at all. In fact, he looked like a model citizen. He had a wife who was a leader of the women's league at Grace Baptist Church, he himself was a decorated veteran of the war in Iraq, and he currently worked a nine to five job at Belk's in the men's clothing department. He paid his taxes on time, and there were no liens on his mortgage.

"So if five of the councilmen received no money, who exactly took all that money out of all those mailboxes, and where the heck did it go?" pondered Randle. He had hoped by now to have something to report to Benji, but he had to admit he was stumped. He had arranged for a meeting during lunchtime at Belk's with Brad Street, but he realized that might not be enough time to get to the bottom of things. Nevertheless, he had to make a good faith effort, as time was moving quickly, now that the lawsuit had actually been filed and a court date would soon be announced. Everyone concerned with this case was now on the clock, and how good a case Benji would have depended in part on how good his "intel" reports had been. Randle knew he needed to come through.

The drive from downtown to South Park, by way of Queens Road, took about twenty minutes, and it was 11:30 when Randle reached the mall, parked his car in the parking area underneath the mall, and took the escalator up to the main floor where the Belk's store occupied a huge area on the east end of the mall. Randle was to meet Brad at just before noon at the main mall entrance to Belk's and they were going to have lunch at Mc-Cormick and Schmick's, which required a walk through the main corridor of the mall, and out the side door to a little strip mall area that adjoined the main buildings.

Sure enough, Brad showed up right on time, wearing a nice navy blue suit, and looking nothing like the commando he had previously been only a few short years ago. He was 6'2", dark haired, and ruggedly handsome. Randle noticed the scar on his right cheek, presumably acquired in Iraq.

"Thanks for taking time to see me," said Randle. "I'm just trying to get to the bottom of a mystery involving the city council office, and I was hoping you could help me."

Brad smiled and said, "I'll do my best." He did not seem ill at ease. The conversation went no further until they had gotten to the restaurant, been seated in a nice enclosed area where no one would trouble them, and had ordered their drinks and appetizers.

"So how has life back stateside been for you? How has the transition gone?" was Randle's opening gambit.

"To be honest, it's been a harder transition than I expected. I was so looking forward to coming home and getting back to normal life with my wife, and starting a family, but I came home just after the crash in 2008, and work was hard to find, even for a vet. For a while, I lived on what pay I still had coming to me from the Army, but then finally, John Belk heard about me and hired me to work here at the store at this mall. That happened about 2010, and I've been here ever since. As you probably know, being a city councilman in Pineville is a very part time job, with little pay or thanks, so you could call it my 'night' job sort of."

"Tell me about this city council group itself. Are they good to work with? How do ya'll get along?"

"Well to say the least it is a diverse group of personalities, but I'd say we work reasonably well together. For example, in that last rezoning issue we had met before hand and had all agreed that the wise thing was to take the lowest bidder on the paving contract, whoever that might be. It was only later I discovered that the owner behind the scenes of that company happened to be the brother of the Mayor, or I would have raised some questions about nepotism. But since nothing like that had happened before, I thought it probably didn't matter much. The Mayor had not tried to force the issue one way or another. He stayed right out of our deliberations, as he should have done. I must admit, I was a little disturbed that more time had not been allowed for discussion at the hearing, but then someone called the question from in the audience, so we had to act.

"Yes, who exactly was that person who called the question?"

"I don't know his name but he was sitting in the third row, and we were up on the platform, but I got a fairly good look at him. He looked like a refugee from Duck Dynasty. I mean he had a bit of a beard, was fairly dark skinned, wore a camo jacket and a ball cap. I'd never seen him before, or since, for that matter. I just assumed he was a citizen tired of debate."

At this juncture the appetizers came, shrimp cocktail for both men, and Blue Moon beers. Randle could tell Brad was enjoying himself, and didn't seem in the least nervous. He figured now was the time to ask the more difficult question.

"Were you aware that money in an envelope was put in your mail box and that of other councilmen in the Mayor's office after that rezoning hearing, money that seems to have disappeared by the end of the work day, according to some of the staff there?"

Brad looked away for a minute, then deliberately brought his focus back on Randle and with a frown said: "Are you suggesting we took a bribe?"

"Honestly, I don't know what to think, but I have to ask these questions."

"Well, I can tell you right now, our votes at that closed door meeting were not bought or coerced. Nobody offered us anything upfront to vote a certain way. That's ridiculous. We would have rejected it anyway, had it been offered."

"O.K.," said Randle carefully, "but this was after the fact. Are you sure you've never seen such an envelope with money in it?" There was a rather obvious pause before Brad responded.

"Even if I had seen such a thing, what business is that of yours? You say you are working a case, what case would that be?"

"The case just filed in circuit court to stop the construction of the bypass off of Highway 51, a case based on some very fishy goings on in the City Council building, including of course some surprising appearances and disappearances of money."

Brad swallowed hard and said, "Well I think at this point, since there is a legal process ongoing, I'd best say no more until I talk with my lawyers."

"That's of course your prerogative," replied Randle, "but if they discover you've been hiding something, your co-operation sooner rather than later will serve you well. The lawsuit doesn't accuse you of anything, so you're not on trial for this matter, though you are likely to be called as a witness, and I tell you that as a former law enforcement officer here in Charlotte."

"I've had enough cross examination for one day, and so I think I'll scoot now. You enjoy the rest of your lunch." And so Randle watched Brad grab his coat and walk slowly away.

"That man looks as guilty as sin to me," said Randle to himself, "but guilty of what? I'm going to have to find out."

All the way back to work, Brad's brain was racing and racing. What nobody knew, not even his wife, is that he had developed a cocaine habit while in Iraq, and when he got home, his addiction level was such that he had to go find himself a dealer in Charlotte, a dealer to whom he owed several thousand dollars last week, that is until he, quite innocently and unexpectedly, had discovered money in his mailbox, and then noticed there was lots more of the same in the other councilmen's boxes. The temptation to suddenly take all the money and pay off his debt had proved to be too severe of one, and he had literally taken the money, stuffed it under his bomber jacket, and walked out of the building, no one the wiser, as no one gave a second thought to seeing him in the building since he was well known as a councilman.

There had been enough money not only to pay off the dealer, but to buy a little supply for his next several fixes. Now he was thinking, there is no end to the trouble this habit is going to cause me. I'd better go over the VA and get help before it is too late. Squirreled away with the extra money and the stash was also one copy of the letter that came with the money. Something had told him he might need that later, so he had saved it. When Brad got back to Belk's he was quite unable to clear his mind of all these thoughts, never mind the conversation at lunch. Finally he told his boss he wasn't feeling well, and headed home to have a talk with his wife. He needed to talk to someone just now, and he loved her enough, and knew she loved him, so he figured it was time to come clean about the drugs. Hopefully she would be supportive of his freely seeking help. She, after all, was a Baptist, and last he checked, they did believe in redemption and forgiveness.

Chapter Eighteen

G.I. Jane

Jane Smithwick Lanceford (reverting to her maiden name of Smithwick after the divorce from Vernon) had been an Army brat, who, herself had been in the Army for some ten years before she ran into rough and tumble Vernon. They had had a tempestuous courtship, followed by a hot and heavy first two years of marriage, producing one Elizabeth Lanceford, the only child of that union.

Liz as she had always been known, was never much enamored with her boozing, stay-out-late father, and when she got to an age when she could figure out what was going on, she realized her father was a world class jerk and an unfaithful one at that. Quite naturally, she bonded with her mother, and indeed modeled herself on her Mom, joining the Army right out of high school. Now, after having been toughened up in the military, she was herself one tough customer.

She had come home to visit her mother, only to discover that once again Jane was getting the shaft from Vernon when it came to the alimony payments, and she resolved, if the opportunity presented itself, to do something about. In other words, she was planning a confrontation with "Big Vernon," though she had not thought far enough ahead to start making plans as to when this clash of the titans would happen, or how.

"Honey, it is so good to have you home," cooed Jane, while they were eating breakfast in the little kitchen nook in Jane's modest condo. Jane worked at Lowe's to make ends meet, especially since the alimony checks only came sporadically, and sometimes it would be months in between the checks.

"Yep, and I wanted you to be the first to know, I'm ditching the military. I've had enough of being yelled at and being told what to do day in and day out."

"Tell me about it. That was what life with Vernon was like after the first year or so. He turned into a real mean so and so. Still is, I hear, but I give him a wide berth. I only talk to his fancy lawyer when I absolutely must."

"So, is the rumor true that he is hanging out with a strip tease artist?"

"That's more than a rumor. It's a fact. Her name is Sheri Lavalier, supposedly but I doubt it, and she works at the Platinum Club way out on South Boulevard. I honestly can't figure out what she sees in Vernon, and I expect she will drop him like a hot potato if he stops being her sugar daddy."

"I suspect so," said Liz, lost in thought.

"Did I tell you about what was just in the Observer?"

"No, do tell."

"Looks like Vernon's company may be blocked from building the new bypass out here off of Highway 51. Seems there was some slight of hand involved in getting him that contract, which I am betting his aloof and arrogant brother helped him get."

"Vernon involved in monkey business? Surely not," said Liz in a sarcastic tone of voice. "Sometimes that fellow strikes me as dumb as a bag of hammers, if you know what I mean. And yet somehow, someway he keeps landing on his feet."

"Yeah, I haven't figured that out, even after all these years. How has he managed to stay out of jail and one foot in front of the Law? It's a mystery. I really could care less at this point, I'm glad to be shed of him."

"Good riddance!" said Liz, "but now he can't pay the alimony if he's in jail, so you must have mixed feelings about the coming trial—right?"

"Yeah. I do. . . . One part of me wants to see him get hung out to dry. The other part of me says 'Naw, it will be bad for my bank account,' not that he pays regularly."

This conversation went on for some time, and during it Liz had begun to formulate a plan that just might set up her mom for the rest of her life. A smile crept across her face as she began to see her way clear to being able to make this happen.

Chapter Nineteen

Charlotte's Web, And Masey's Weeping

Now that the "you know what" had hit the fan in the Mayor's office, Charlotte's radar was on full alert to notice any possible abnormalities going on in her midst. She was attentive to every request of the Mayor, and not bringing up any sore subjects, but at the same time her self-preservation instincts had led her to file away certain kinds of information she overheard. For instance, this morning, Vernon Lanceford had come into the office looking like something the cat dragged in. He had a series of Band-Aids on his balding pate, and an air cast on his arm. While the door was closed in the Mayor's office once Vernon had gone in, the conversation obviously got heated, and Charlotte "could not help" over-hearing (especially since she stood by the closed door and listened) what went down, which was something like,

"You idiot, didn't I tell you not to do anything. Not to try anything without checking with me. And tell me did it dawn on you that someone might be able to discover your finger prints on that sign you left at the Bumgarner house and trace it right back to you! To us! Have you got no brains left in your head?"

There was a muffled response in a low voice, but Charlotte caught the words "I wore gloves." Then the Mayor was shouting again.

"Gloves when you were at the house, or gloves the whole time you handled the sign, and wrote the sign you took with you?"

Vernon must have answered the former, because there was an explosion so big in the office that Charlotte was about to knock on the door and ask if everything was alright. There were a couple of minutes of silence after which the door opened and Vernon slunk out of the office, like a dog with his tail between his legs. A few more minutes passed, and the Mayor said in a loud voice "Charlotte!"

Standing up, then smoothing out her dress, she walked right into the Mayor's office with a smile on her face and said "How can I help?"

"Get me my brother's lawyer on the phone, ASAP."

"Yes sir," she said, and went out into her antechamber to dial the number. She made a mental note, "Randle will sure want to know about this."

To say that Masey was shaken up would be an understatement. She was sitting in a kitchen chair staring at the refrigerator magnets and church reminders there, and mustering up her courage to call Benji. When she picked up the old phone receiver, her normally steady right hand was shaking, and tears were streaming down her face.

"After several rings, Benji's secretary came on the line and said, "Can you hold for a minute, I've got two people on two other lines," and Masey said in a soft contrite voice, "of course." It took what seemed like ages before the secretary got back on the line and said, "Sorry for the wait, now how can I help?"

"Mary Lynn this is Masey, I need to speak to Benji right away. It's important."

"Just give me a second, he's in a meeting, but its not a critical one, so I'll walk in and leave him a note that you're on line three and it's urgent."

It was another three to four minutes and Masey's hand would not stop shaking. Finally Benji came on the line. "What's happening Momma?" he said.

"Son, I've been violated . . . well not exactly, you see there was a threat sign left on my kitchen door this morning. I'd been gone for a bit, and came home and there it was. Funny thing is, it was just dangling there not properly hung, like the villain had been interrupted while he was taping it to my door. And there was a big smudge in the oil slick on my driveway where it looked like someone fell before they left. There are even a few little blood droplets near the smudge."

Benji replied with some urgency in his voice, "Momma I'm so sorry this has happened but whatever you do—DON'T touch the sign or any of that whole area. I'm calling the Pineville police right now, and I'll debrief them as to what's going on, and they will come and talk with you and dust for fingerprints. This could be crucial evidence for our case, so whatever you do, don't 'contaminate' the crime scene, as they say on TV. You just stay in your house, maybe drink some comforting Lemon Lift tea or something to calm you down, and wait for the police to come. I'll be right behind them, as it will take a bit for me to get there from downtown. Don't you worry, this is going to be alright."

"Son, don't you think I'd better just drop this lawsuit, before things really get nasty? I mean the Bible does also say 'why not rather be wronged'? Maybe I should just accept defeat and quietly move somewhere else?" And she began to cry again.

"Don't even think about that! That doesn't even sound like the strong woman who raised me!" said Benji. "If you do that then the bad guys just win and get away with criminal activity, and you don't want to be an unintentional accessory to a crime. No, we've come too far to turn back now."

"O.K.," said Masey, choking back the tears, "I figured you'd say that. Besides, I'm staring at Miss Perkins, and she just vetoed the idea of our moving. She's looking mad at me right now."

"I'll be there in a jiffy," said Benji and hung up.

"What in the world have I got myself into?" whispered Masey, "and do I have enough intestinal fortitude to see it through?"

Chapter Twenty

Randle's "Wrasslin"

Randle was having a conflict of conscience . . . sort of. Not that Randle was any denizen of absolute purity when it came to affairs of the heart, but what he was wrestling with was whether it was right or not to continue to pump Charlotte for information, under false pretenses—namely that he was interested in her. But . . . much to his own surprise, he really had become interested in Charlotte. He liked everything about her, and they certainly seemed compatible. So despite his protests to the contrary at the outset . . . he was prepared now to admit . . . he *was* sparking that girl! Somehow, he was going to have to convey this to Charlotte without sounding stupid, or at least not too stupid. And today was the day to do it, as he and Charlotte had a lunch engagement at Ruby Tuesday's in Pineville.

Getting dressed in his best suit, and remembering to even put on some men's cologne, Randle increasingly began to feel amorous, with an equal quantity of the jitters one got when one was afraid one's moves might be rejected. He had been thinking about Charlotte all morning—her soft hands, her dimples, her husky laugh, her auburn hair, and of course her fulsome figure. The girl didn't lack for shapeliness and he and his libido had certainly noticed. Randle recognized the signs of being "preoccupied," so he took the exceptional step of writing down the questions he needed to ask Charlotte when he saw her, pertaining to the case. His strategy was to come clean at the beginning of the meal, and then ask his questions over dessert. That girl loved desserts.

Not surprisingly, Randle found that Charlotte was already waiting in line when he got to Ruby Tuesdays. He had remembered to bring his lunch coupons with him too, so she would see he was a frugal man as well.

"Hello sunshine," said Randle. "It's so good to see you again."

"Likewise, I'm sure. Hope your hungry cause I had to skip breakfast this morning and I am famished!"

"Whoa . . . that word is above my pay grade. I'll have to look that one up."

"Rightttt . . . " said Charlotte. "Don't play dumb with me mister. I know you've got plenty of smarts in that head." The chitchat continued while they stood in line, and when the host called Randle's name, Charlotte took his arm and they went inside together.

The sweet tea was on the table, and when Randle reached across it, he took Charlotte's hand, swallowed hard, and said, "Charlotte, I want to check in with you about something, sort of true confessions time. Originally, when I contacted you on the basis of our previously knowing each other and even dating, I was just using a previous contact to try and gather evidence on an important case I was working on. In other words, pretty much a strictly professional inquiry, and you were very good about it. It never crossed any lines between personal and professional boundaries as far as I was concerned. We were just old friends consulting on something of mutual concern."

"BUT, and this is a big but . . . I want to come clean now and tell you, that increasingly, I've had feelings for you and about you, and I don't want to take advantage of you just for the sake of gaining insider knowledge. I really don't want to do that. So I decided the best thing was just to admit I like you and would like, with your permission, to actually date you and see where our relationship might go, in addition to whatever happens on the professional exchange of information. I wasn't intentionally sparking you before, but as they say, feelings happen!"

Charlotte sat there listening to all this quietly, and had been looking down at the table towards the end of Randle's speech like she was thinking. What she was thinking was, "Well, finally he's made his intentions and motives clear."

Then she said, "Randle, I've always liked you. And so when you got in contact with me, I realized that it might amount to nothing on the personal level, but one part of me was curious to see what was going to happen. I tried not to get my hopes up, or act too enthusiastic about our meetings, but the more often we met, the more I got vibrations from you that something besides trading info or reminiscing was definitely happening."

"I'm glad it has dawned on you as well, and I especially appreciate the integrity of your coming clean. That's something I would expect of a person with Christian values, or at least open to Christian values. Which reminds me, that I don't really know where you stand on or with Jesus, but that will be something we should talk about on a future occasion. For now, I'm happy to have an open ended relationship to explore further, and this may be the start of something special—Who knows?" And then she squeezed Randle's hand. "And by the way, I appreciate that you spruced up for this meeting. It suits you."

Relief was written all over Randle's face, and he added, "Well I'll know we've really crossed over into a personal relationship when you start calling me 'honey', since that's the Southern thing to do."

Charlotte just laughed and said, "And now a word from our alternate sponsor, business. I do indeed have some important stuff to share with you, but let's order first."

When the waitress with the teased up bouffant hairdo showed up, Charlotte ordered a petite filet mignon with braised vegetables, and Randle ordered his usual cheeseburger with fries.

"O.K. down to brass tacks now," said Charlotte. "The Mayor, just this morning had a meeting with his low life brother Vernon, and I could hear a good deal of what they were talking about, though I have no idea where it transpired. He apparently threatened somebody that might be getting in the way of the construction project, and the Mayor, quite rightly blew up at him. Called him an idiot. And besides all that, he looked like the devil—big scratches on his head, an air cast on his arm, and he was dressed like the slob he is. I'm surprised the Mayor didn't send him home to get changed and come back later. He rolled into the parking lot on a dirty ole Harley Davidson looking for all the world like an aging Hell's Angel. Anyway, Vernon has done something stupid, maybe even criminal, and his brother has told him in no uncertain terms to lay low."

"Hmm . . . I'm going to have to sniff around and see who he's been messing with, or trying to mess with, but from what you say, it sounds like he got the short end of the deal when it came to the confrontation."

"Yeah he looked like something the cat dragged in. . . ." Little did she know just how *right* that description was.

Chapter Twenty-One

Cementing Their Relationship

Liz Lanceford had heard quite enough from her mother over the last few days about the misdeeds of Vernon, her estranged father. At this point she was especially angry about the late alimony payments, and had decided she was going to go and surprise Vernon and confront him, maybe even in front of his workers, hoping that that would shame him into action.

Vernon Lanceford, while a big man who knew how to use his size and a rough demeanor to bully people, was actually not really all that brave when it came to real abuse and violence. He would leave that to the "goon squad," and preferred not to know how the goal was accomplished. Out of sight was out of mind. On this morning, doing anything violent or stupid was the farthest thing from his mind.

Vernon had signed the contract for the road job and returned it by mail to the city, and the "stay" on construction was only temporary. Vernon had absolute confidence that his lawyers would be able to deal with the impending lawsuit with dispatch, maybe even settle out of court, and then he could get on with making his millions. To that end he was already making lots of preparations for construction, including the making of large cement pillars and blocks for the bridges for the bypass, and large cement sewer pipes as well.

Salvo Sand, Gravel, and Cement was well out of town on Highway 51. In fact it was closer to Matthews than it was to Pineville, but it had a Pineville RFD mail delivery. When Vernon's grandfather had started the business, it had been way out in the country. Not so much any more.

It took some thirty minutes for Liz to go from her mother's condo in south Charlotte to Salvo, and when she got there, all of the workers were off on a job. Not Vernon however. The site included a huge garage where the cement mixers and other trucks were parked, a smallish office complex, and a gigantic gravel pit where the stone had been dug out of the ground for many years, leaving a huge gaping hole in the ground, almost like the entrance to an underground cave. Vernon didn't mess with the big mixing and pouring jobs, but he did like to keep his hand in on some of the smaller projects. On this morning, he was making some small concrete elbow joints for pipes using Quickcrete to expedite the process, a form of concrete that dried within mere minutes. It took only ten minutes for it to set with a large batch, and much less than that for smaller batches. These small joints were going to be used to fix a problem in Matthews where a small water main had burst, and an emergency call had come in for some help ASAP. The process was pretty simple—mix the quick drying cement and water in a large vat, then take a pourer and pour it into the molds for the pipes. The molds were interesting because of course one needed a hollow middle to the pipe so one had to pour around a form that looked like a long cigarette with a filter in the middle that was not attached to the tube, with a space of about six inches between the one and the other.

Liz had come prepared for anything, and the closer she got to Salvo, the more her anger rose. She was really going to give her father a piece of her mind, and if necessary threaten to expose him, presumably by going to the press. Just for safety, she brought her personal weapon, an old Army issue handgun she had bought at an Army Supply store in Fayetteville. Knowing enough about her recent fits of rage after nightmares, she decided she would not load the gun this morning, lest something really stupid happened between her and her father. But of course, he would not *know* she had an unloaded gun. Wearing her army fatigues she looked ready to rumble, ready for whatever transpired. She might be small, but she was much less squeamish about personally resorting to violence than her father.

It took her a good fifteen minutes of combing the Salvo site to spy her father in the distance mixing concrete near the gravel pit. He had just stirred up a fresh batch in his three feet deep vat, and was ready to take his scoop and pour some into the molds when suddenly he looked up and there was a familiar face he had not seen in a couple of years.

"Liz?" he said quizzically.

"Yeah, that's right. And I did not come to give you a hug. I came to give you a warning."

Vernon laughed his big deep laugh, "You came to threaten me you little pip squeak?"

"Something like that," she said with a big frown on her face. "You need to stop missing those alimony payments. My mother didn't send me out here, I came on my own, but I'm tired of hearing about your ways, tired of learning indirectly my father is a world class jerk, tired of hearing first about your cheating on Mom and then your attraction to bimbos. Just sick and tired of it. So, from now on, you had better walk the straight and narrow. Am I making myself clear?"

Vernon was taken aback by this verbal onslaught, but his protective reflex was to not take it too seriously due to the size of his daughter, so he continued to have a stupid grin on his face, and he began to snicker . . . "And what exactly are you going to do about it if I don't pay on time?"

With this retort, something snapped in Liz, and whatever last shred of respect she had for her father and his authority as a father, disappeared. She went into military mode, drawing her pistol, and she said, "I'm going to make sure right now that you will do the right thing going forward." Aiming the gun right at Vernon's feet, she said, "Step into that vat right now, or I'll shoot."

Vernon of course knew about Liz's military training and had even heard about her earning some marksman awards for shooting, so he could tell she wasn't joking. But he froze.

"I SAID STEP INTO THE VAT OF CONCRETE RIGHT NOW. NO MORE DELAYING."

"But, but . . ." Vernon sputtered.

"DO IT!!!"

And so finally Vernon stepped into the vat of already solidifying Quickcrete.

"Now, what is going to happen is while you are standing there for the next five or so minutes, you are going to make me some promises. Right here, right now, and if I so much as suspect you are reneging on your promises, I'll be back and will be much less lenient the next time. I want a promise you will pay Jane every month—got it?"

"Yeah, O.K., she must have really been whining lately. She ought to go out and get a real job."

"Shut up! Next, I want a promise that you are going to stop trying to cheat your way to the top. No more shady business deals that besmirch the family name, and cause your brother and the rest of your family no end of shame and grief. Have you got it—NO MORE!"

Vernon was silent for a minute trying to calculate how he could satisfy Liz without actually promising anything on that score, so he just said, "I hear you."

"That's not good enough. Say you'll promise to forsake your illegal ways."

Trying to make a joke, Vernon said, "Next you'll be breaking into song with that old Santana classic 'You've Got to Change your Evil Ways.'"

"This is not a joke. Say I swear . . ."

"Alright, I swear," (but he was thinking, I didn't tell her what I swore to do).

"Next, I want you to quit frequenting sleazy strip tease lounges. Your brother is coming up for re-election and all he needs to mess that up is a headline about your low life activities. Swear it!" and again she pointed the gun at him.

"Alright, alright, alright . . . I swear. You need to stop waving that gun around. It could go off accidentally."

"Wouldn't that be a shame. Pineville would lose one of the pillars of the community! Course if you stand there long enough, you could literally become one of those pillars. I'm not foolin' around Vernon. You're a poor excuse for a father, brother, husband, and it is now time to clean up your act before you end up in jail for the foreseeable future. Am I clear?"

"Crystal. Can I get out of the vat now?"

Liz looked at her military watch, and said, "In a minute or two. One last thing. I hear there's going to be a lawsuit. If you end up testifying you better make it crystal clear that your brother had absolutely nothing to do with your misdeeds—NADA! Got it?"

"Got it. My precious little white sheep of the family brother, whom Mom always liked best, and who never took a beating from Pop like I did, needs to keep his lily white reputation in tact. Oh yes, I get it. It's always been that way. I do the dirty work, and if something good happens, he gets the credit." Vernon said this with some venom, and then spat. "Can I get out of this vat now?"

Looking again at her watch, Liz said with a sly smile "Well now that our agreement has been cemented in concrete . . . you can try."

And sure enough, enough time had elapsed that the Quickcrete had begun to harden around Vernon's big ole working boots. He could just barely slide his feet a bit on the bottom of the vat, which was some three feet deep. He was up to just below his knees in Quickcrete, and began to panic.

"Liz, honey, I know we've not been close, but you can't just leave me here. There's no one else around. Help me out of this before I'm really turned into a statue!"

"Ah, bless your heart," said Liz with sarcasm. "Can't I just leave you here like the way you abandoned Mom and me and left us without a means of supporting ourselves for two years? Oh, I think I can . . . and I will. Maybe I'll call your office after I cool down and let them know that you were in a pickle. Maybe . . . but I want to hear you say one more time, and this time with as much sincerity as you can muster . . . 'I'll do what you demanded!' SAY IT."

Now Vernon was in a total panic, because it was almost to the point where he couldn't move at all. "O.K. I PROMISE, REALLY. SWEAR ON A STACK OF BIBLES. Now help me out of here."

"Like I said, I gotta be going, but you look scared enough now that I'll give your secretary a ring and tell her about how our agreement has been cemented in concrete . . . so to speak."

"Liz . . . Wait . . . Liz . . . don't abandon me . . . Liz . . ." the voice trailed off as she walked slowly back to her car, muttering to herself, "Well maybe that will finally teach him a lesson. Maybe." And as she drove off, she did indeed call the Salvo office, and said, "Word up. Your boss is out there near the gravel pit and needs some immediate attention."

"Who is this calling please? Is this a prank?" said Sally the secretary.

"Nope, I'm serious as a heart attack. This is just a word to the wise, and you'd better go see what I'm talking about—pronto!" On the drive back to Charlotte, Liz began to whistle a tune she had learned in the Army and which went through her head when a mission had been accomplished—the tune was "Another One Bites the Dust. . . ."

Chapter Twenty-Two

The Law Shows Up

Masey was still shaking when Benji arrived on the run, and rang the front doorbell not wanting to disturb the evidence on the carport door. Peering out the window in the front door, Masey threw open the door and immediately wrapped her arms around Benji and had a good cry. "Thank you so much for coming. You're such a good son. I have to admit I don't normally get this shook up, but that sign in my own carport really did it to me."

"It's alright Mom, it's alright. The police will be here shortly and things will start moving in the right direction again." Benji gently guided Masey over to the sofa and they sat down together, holding hands. Benji handed her his handkerchief saying "I never use this thing, so maybe you can get some use out of it today."

In about twenty minutes there was a knock on the screen door that shielded the front door, and two good-sized men in blue suits came into view.

"I'll let them in," said Benji.

When Miss Perkins saw two large, unfamiliar men enter the house, she snuck under the sofa for safety. She did not like disruptions to her tranquil home life, and was on guard even now in case she needed to protect her turf, not to mention Masey.

"Ms. Bumgarner we are sorry to have to disturb you, but we will need to gather as much information as we can. We view this as criminal trespass. Is there any indication of forced entry into the house? Was there anything disturbed inside?" asked Joe Delany, a tall thirty-something police sergeant.

"No sir, when I got home the doors were both still locked and had not been fiddled with either. All's well on that front. But you need to attend to what you can discover in my carport. Benji, would you back my new car out for these officers so they can have a thorough look under there?"

"Thanks mam," said the other officer. "I was just about to ask you to do that." This officer was carrying a big box to take samples, and hopefully find things like hair or finger prints or footprints."

"Be sure to check the splat in the grease spot where apparently the intruder fell. This is the first time I've ever been happy there is a grease spot in my carport."

"O.K. mam, we'll go about our business now, and try not to disturb you too much. We promise to do our best to catch this person. We'll check back with you once we're done, and let you know if we have any more questions, and then we will go back to the lab and see what we can figure out."

The work in the carport went on for most of the afternoon, between photographs, taking down the sign after taking photos, dusting for fingerprints, checking for footprints, and the like. These policemen were nothing if not thorough. They took samples from the small blood spatters they found as well, and when they were done they returned to the house for a few final questions.

Joe Delany led the questioning: "Mr. Moore, what is your shoe size, just for elimination, since you come to this house pretty regularly—right?"

"Yes, I do. My shoe size is 9.5."

"And your blood type?"

"The most common type—O+."

"And you Ms. Bumgarner—your blood type?"

"AB–, though nobody has asked me that question in a long time, and I haven't spilled any blood in the carport."

These sort of routine questions went on for about another five minutes, and then came a surprising one—"Ms. Bumgarner, do you have a pet dog or cat?"

"Why yes. Miss Perkins is my cat, and I believe she's still under the sofa here. Ya'll seemed to have freaked her out."

"Could you please entice her out from under there. We want to check her claws for possible blood traces. We think the villain may have been clawed by your attack cat" and with this suggestion, which lightened the mood, everyone laughed.

"Benji would you go in the kitchen and get Miss Perkins one of her favorite treats—one of those cat chews?"

Benji obliged and came back with two of them. Masey then said,

"Here kitty, kitty. I have your favorite treats Miss Perkins."

The cat didn't need to be asked twice, she sauntered out from under the sofa, and had just eaten the first one when Masey picked her up and held her on her lap, while the forensics man checked, sticky-taped, and photographed Miss Perkins front claws.

Looking at the image of the picture on the back of his Nikon, he showed Miss Bumgarner the enlarged picture of her front left paw, claws extended. "See that little pink bit on that side claw? You have one brave cat. She seems to have jumped on the man from some height as he came to the door, I reckon from the air conditioning unit in the kitchen window."

"Lands sakes! She does like to sleep up there in the breeze, especially during the hot summer months. Miss Perkins you did a good job of protecting our house, and here's another treat for you!" And then she rubbed the cat and everyone could hear her big purr.

"That's all for now Mam, but be on the lookout for strangers of any sort, including ambulance chasing lawyer types."

"Don't you worry Mr. Delany, I've got the only lawyer with an all-access pass to me and my house sitting right here beside me," and she patted Benji on the knee.

Once they had gone, she said to Benji. "That went well, but I wonder what they will discover from all this? Do you really think it will provide any real leads?"

"Maybe if there are partial finger prints on the sign. We'll soon see. Those boys work fast. I'll bet you hear from them in the morning."

"Speaking of in the morning, could you manage to spend the night here just for tonight so I could have some peace of mind? This really rattled my cage."

"No problem," said Benji, "I'll just call Mary Lynn and tell her my plans. How's about we go over to the Longhorn Steak House for supper, I'm sure you're not up for cooking."

"It's a deal. I've eaten nothing since breakfast," and she gave Benji a hug.

"Son I don't know what I'd do without you." The rest of the evening was passed with a nice meal, a little TV watching of *Wheel of Fortune* and *Jeopardy*, and then a welcome good night's rest.

Chapter Twenty-Three

Hightowers And Firm Foundations

The offices of Jason Hightower and associates were impressive, sitting as they did on the twentieth floor of the Bank of America building near the corner of Trade and Tryon. Jason's personal office had a 270 degree view of downtown Charlotte, looking out on three of the four points of the compass. Jason was a rising star in the legal community, a Harvard Law School grad, and before that a Duke Phi Beta Kappa grad. Tall, blonde, with blue eyes, and a silver tongue, and only thirty-three years of age, he nonetheless already had several major notches in his belt when it came to the winning of major trials. He was supremely confident in his abilities in a variety of areas and ways, including confident in his ability to woo most any woman he found attractive. The stories circulating in the office about his "conquests" on that front were becoming the stuff of legend. Lately, he had been dating Miss North Carolina, or at least that's what the gossip column in the Charlotte Observer had intimated.

Hightower came from a "high cotton" family, quite literally, from Louisiana. His ancestors had owned a cotton plantation with many slaves, and Hightower had worked hard to distance himself from that whole part of his past, almost never referring to his upbringing in the Bayou state, nor for that matter to his parent's connections with the notorious Huey Long of *All the King's Men* fame, or infamy. He presented himself as a self-made man, which of course was a myth, but at least it was a pleasant fiction in his own mind. His one real mentor had been his main law professor at Harvard, Harvey Kravitz, who had taught him how to use the law to his client's advantage. Normally, he was an attorney for the prosecution, suing people that his clients wanted sued, but occasionally he had had to defend clients as well, and had done so with almost an unblemished record over the previous five years. It had brought him a boatload of money, and this penthouse office space near the top of the Bank of America building.

Sipping his small glass of Woodford Reserve Bourbon, Hightower was looking at his calendar, and what had recently been added. The most notable item was the circuit court case, very recently filed, and expedited at the request of the Mayor of Pineville, in regard to the bypass off of Highway 51. On the surface of things, the case to stop the project for a variety of reasons looked flimsy. There had been a rezoning hearing, there had been a vote taken, there had previously been a rule change that stated it was not necessary to have more than one hearing. Unless it could be proved that the outcome was rigged, Hightower thought winning this case was a slam-dunk. And of course it's hard to prove collusion or intent to bend the rules in regard to due process.

But Jason Hightower knew perfectly well that juries, and this par-ticular case was indeed going to a jury, could be fickle, and could be easily swayed by emotive arguments that hardly held any logical or legal weight. There was always an iffiness when one had to deal with both a judge and a jury—more people, more variables, more things that could go wrong, from a defender's point of view.

Picking up his phone, Jason dialed 3231, the extension for his legal secretary, Latoya Harrison. She was a sharp cookie, very good at her job and Jason needed something specific from her:

"Latoya, I need to find out more about the plaintiff, one Ms. Masey Bumgarner, and also about her lawyer Benjamin Moore. I don't really re-call meeting him before, but then there is a surfeit of lawyers in this town. Could you send out our investigative man, Guy Franks, to do a little spade-work for us? And while he is at it, I need to know a bit more about Vernon Lanceford, and what has been going on in his life. Yes, he retains me as his lawyer, but there are still some unanswered questions I have about him. Specifically, I want to know what sort of business dealings he has had lately in regard to the bypass project. I want to know if he offered any golden handshakes to anyone, etc. Can you ask Guy to make this a rush job? For some reason, this case has been given priority, at the request of the Mayor."

"Why certainly Mr. Hightower. I will get Guy going on this this morn-ing and ask him to report in regularly."

"Thanks so much," and then Jason finished sipping his bourbon, put the glass down, and looked out the window. "This case should be a slam dunk, but something tells me there are important things I don't know yet which may make it more difficult. We'll see what Mr. Moore sends us in the discovery process soon enough."

Chapter Twenty-Four

A Statue Of Limitations

Vernon was wincing. His man Vinny was trying as hard as he could to break the concrete gently so Vernon could extract himself from it, without also breaking his boss's feet. Vinny, it should be noted, was no Rhodes scholar, but he did have a couple of redeeming qualities—namely he was loyal and he did what he was told. He never questioned Vernon, never crossed him, and always tried his best to please. He was rather like a dog whose trip to obedience school had been a big success. But there was one thing niggling at Vinny. He had been named on the witness list for the coming trial in regard to the bypass. He was worried that his boss might ask him to lie and he be caught in a lie, which would be perjury. Vinny had been to jail once, and he had no desire to repeat that mistake.

"Work a little faster," Vernon insisted. "I got things to do this afternoon."

"Boss if you don't mind me asking . . . how in the world did you end up in a vat of quick drying cement?"

"Well, as they say Vinny, it's a long story But I'll tell you this much, it involved someone sticking a gun in my face until I stepped into the vat and thereafter, until it hardened, which didn't take long. We'll leave it at that."

"You want I should deal with this person who did this to you Boss?"

"Nope. It's a private matter. We have bigger fish to fry just now. Kapish?"

"Yeah, o.k. just asking."

"And I appreciate your asking. Your loyalty over these years has been key to our getting things done."

"Thanks Boss. I'm worried about something though, what am I going to say if I get put on a witness stand and the lawyer asks me about the money and those envelopes?"

"We'll talk about that later. Let's break some rocks now shall we?"

Finally, after what seemed like an eternity, Vernon was extricated from the cement, after which he took off his ruined boots, washed down the bottom of his jeans, and padded into the office looking for all the world like a child who had been caught doing something wrong and had been sent to his room. It was all the secretary could do not to snicker when he went by into the bathroom. Once he closed the door, she mumbled to herself, "Sometimes men are just ridiculous and they make fools out of themselves."

"I heard that Sally," said a voice behind the door.

Sally smiled and said, "Well boss, I would say if the shoe fits wear it, but I can see those shoes don't fit any more."

There was an audible groan that emerged from the bathroom in response to that comment, and then, "Good one Sally. Gotta give you credit for that retort."

Chapter Twenty-Five

Things Heat Up

Charlotte and Randle had become something of an "item," and the friends of both parties had noticed. All of a sudden, Charlotte was sending and receiving texts right, left, and center, and even during work. The girl was distracted by "love." Things had gotten steamy of late in Charlotte's dating life, after a long dormant period. While the old cliché *men are like microwaves, and women like irons,* was just that, a cliché, it was fair to say that both Randle and Charlotte were both "hot" for each other, and were beginning to wonder about "how far was too far" in their physical relationship, since the last two dates had involved a good deal of passion without any genital consummation. As the NASCAR boys in Charlotte liked to say, "they were all revved up with nowhere to go."

Trying to keep her mind on her job had become increasingly difficult, as she kept rehearsing in her mind what a good Christian girl should be thinking about all of this. One thought that had crossed her mind was to draw the line "south of the border"; that is, below the belly button. North of the border passion, o.k. South of the border, not until marriage. Of course maintaining that rule was another thing. And how, with hormones raging, was one supposed to differentiate between being "in love" and merely being "in heat"? Inquiring minds wanted to know.

And not surprisingly, Randle was hoping for more. Where was the line between playing hard to get, and being too loose? Charlotte did not want to lose another chance at a relationship that might lead to a wedding. After all, she was not a spring chicken any more, and the biological clock was definitely ticking. Soooo . . . Charlotte finally decided that she would need to be sticking to her newly devised rule, and would explain it to Randle the next time they were together. There was courtship intimacy and then there was marital intimacy, and she was only o.k. with the former in the current state of their relationship. But she too was hoping the relationship would develop in the direction of marriage bells. But first things first. "Stay in the moment" she told herself.

Charlotte nearly jumped out of her skin when she looked up and there was her boss staring at her from about two feet away.

"Earth to Charlotte, come in Charlotte, and I don't mean the city," said the Mayor.

"Sorry boss, I was uncharacteristically preoccupied."

"Would you like to explain that remark," said the Mayor with a grin.

"Umm . . . boyfriend issues."

"Thought so," said the Mayor. "It happens, but try to stay focused on what's in front of you. And . . . congrats on the new beau."

"Thanks." And just then a phone call came in on line two, which of course was not the boyfriend line. "This is Guy Franks and I work with the Hightower law firm in Charlotte. I need to have some time with the Mayor to take a deposition for the up-coming trial, and I was wondering if there was a good time in the next few days when we could get this done, as the trial has been set for an early date?"

Charlotte looked through the Mayor's calendar and replied, "Certainly. The first appointment of at least an hour's length is next Monday. Would that work for you?"

"Well, I was hoping for this Friday, but I guess that will have to do."

"O.K., I'll put you down for that day, at 10 a.m. and I would suggest being here a bit earlier to be on the safe side. The the traffic around here is bad during and even after morning rush hour."

"Will do. Thanks for your assistance."

It dawned on Charlotte that when the trial actually got going, there was not likely to be much free time, and she was betting she would be called as a witness at the trial as well. This caused a little anxiety attack, as she did not want to lose her job, but on the other hand, she was definitely not going to lie under oath, not that she believed in swearing oaths on the Bible, since Jesus said "let your yes be yes, and you're no be no." Anyway, it was time to concentrate on work for the next little while because the beau was coming to pick her at high noon and she could hardly wait.

"Oh wait, what time is it?" she asked herself, and for the second time this morning she nearly jumped out of her chair because someone came up behind her and put his hands over her eyes.

"Guess who?"

"Alright lover boy, just a sec. Let me add something to the Mayor's schedule page here on the computer, and then we're out of here for lunch."

Chapter Twenty-Six

Brad Sweats The Details

Brad Street was by nature a worrier. The phone call had come from Guy Franks about a deposition and he was troubled about what he would say if asked about the money. His wife knew something was eating at him but she had not been able to pry it out of him no matter how hard she had wheedled and cajoled him. Brad finally decided that the smart move was to plan out in advance what he would say, which including anticipating, and then preparing an answer to any and all questions that might be asked. As it turns out, this was going to take a lot of time and thought, and so when he got home from Belk's each evening, right after supper, he would go to his computer and work on his own Q and A sheet, over, and over, and over again. He still had not had the courage to come clean to his wife about his drug habit.

On this particular evening, his wife Jillian snuck into the man cave and peered over his shoulder and asked, "Whatcha working on?"

Startled, Brad responded, "Oh, just some stuff trying to get ready for an interview that is coming up. All the city councilmen have to give a deposition for this coming trial in regard to the lawsuit stopping the bypass projection. I'm just working on my possible responses, and trying to anticipate questions I may be asked. That's all."

"So why so secretive about all this the last few days? I'd be glad to rehearse you with the questions, if that would help," said Jillian stroking her husband's hair, and trying to calm him down.

"I sure do appreciate that honey, but I think I'd best just go over this myself. There are some aspects of the questions that will involve confidential council matters and I don't want to violate confidentiality."

"O.K. suit yourself, but let me know if there's any way I can help, and I'll certainly be praying for you about that deposition."

Brad at this point was sweating—sweating that his wife would find out about his drug habit, sweating she would find out about the money, sweating that he would be turned in for theft of the money. Just sweating. He had decided it was better not to tell her about the drug habit just yet, because he needed her full support, and he was already too nervous about the deposition. Heretofore, the money had been hiding in the locked glove compartment of his car, which is also where he hid the cocaine in the past. This impending ordeal had stressed him out, but oddly it had put enough fear into him that he hadn't had a snort of cocaine all week. He was afraid of being discovered. He was afraid that all that he had worked for would crumble, and that he might even lose his family in the process.

Fear can make a person do all kinds of things, illogical and sometimes just plain stupid. Fear-based thinking is understandable for a person who has returned from a war zone and has PTSD in some form and to some degree. What it had done in Brad's case is drive him to his knees, whereas before he had not much been a man of prayer. He had left that to his wife, who was "more religious" than he was, especially after what he had seen in war zones.

But going forward, he realized he would need all the help he could get, including from "Above" and so he was trying quietly and secretly to mend fences with the Almighty, and the first step was giving up the drugs. He figured he might need some divine intervention before too long, and so he was trying to get back into God's good graces. He was uncertain however, how much repenting would be required to accomplish that goal. His prayers had been more of a negotiation than a series of penitential prayers, or even petitionary prayers. Time would tell whether it was "mission accomplished" in terms of "getting right with God."

Chapter Twenty-Seven

Sheri's Shock

Vernon came into his house looking totally out of sorts. He looked beat up, and tired. Not to mention he was in a truly foul mood. Sheri had just come in from shopping, thoroughly enjoying riding around in the "Little Red Corvette" (yes, she had been listening to the old Prince song while driving), and her mood was quite good.

"So what happened to you sunshine?" was her opening gambit.

"It's been a bad day, to say the least! Don't even get me started. I'm headed straight to the hot tub, and we can talk there. I'm getting into my trunks, you should come. I'll pour us a couple a drinks and we can relax."

"Sounds like a plan. Wait until you see this new bathing suit I bought today."

"You know, that's the first thing that's gone right today—I can't wait."

After pouring two gin and tonics with two olives in each, Vernon went into the bedroom and changed into his bright red (as in N.C. State Wolfpack red) swim trunks, grabbed the drinks, and headed onto the back porch, where the hot tub was. He set the drinks down, took the cover off the hot tub, turned on the bubble maker, sat in a chair sipping his drink, and waited for both the water to heat up and Sheri to appear. When she did it got Vernon's attention immediately . . . his eyes nearly fell out of their sockets.

Sheri somehow had managed to buy a bikini with less material in it than went into a pair of men's socks! "Now baby that's what I call a tiny weeny polka dot bikini!"

"Thanks tiger . . . I figured you'd approve. Let's get in the water and let our cares float away for a bit. And you can tell me all about your troubles."

"Well . . . it all started with me being attacked by a wild cat, who scratched me up pretty good."

"Do tell. Did the cat ambush you from a tree? I mean it's your head that's all scratched up."

"Not exactly. The cat was sleeping on top of a window air conditioning unit and pounced on me from there."

"You must have aggravated it somehow."

"I guess, but then you won't believe what else happened."

Taking a long sip of her gin, Sheri, trying hard to look interested replied, "Yes . . . "

"Well I was minding my business . . . "

"Vernon, when have you ever minded your own business? You're all about minding somebody else's business."

"O.K. fair point, but as I was saying, I was at Salvo, mixing some concrete, and my crazy daughter showed up, threatened me about my wife's alimony checks, pointed a gun right in my face and forced me to step into some quick drying cement."

Sheri couldn't help herself, and she began to giggle. "She did what!?"

"It's not funny. She just left me there high and drying, so to speak, and it took a while before Vinny could get me out of that mess, which is why I need to go shopping for a new pair of work boots."

Sheri smiled and said, "Honestly, I never thought I'd hear the words Vernon and shopping in the same sentence. You continue to surprise me."

"Well you can't say I'm boring you."

"No sugar, you're not boring, dangerous maybe, but not boring."

So the patter went for a while, and, after the alcohol began working, there was snuggling and other sorts of extra curricular activities. One thing that Vernon and Sheri had in common, they were almost always ready for some action. But the kind of action Vernon was about to face did not involve fun and games with the girlfriend. Just then the phone rang, and Vernon hopped out of the hot tub, grabbed his landline phone, and said impatiently "Yes. What do you want?"

"Mr. Lanceford, this is the Pineville police department, Officer Delany speaking. We need you to come in for some questioning please, at your earliest convenience."

"What? Can I ask what this is about?"

"Yes sir, its about criminal trespass, threatening a little old lady, and maybe a few other things. We'd rather you come in voluntarily, rather than us coming to your place with a warrant. So how about it?"

Vernon thought for a moment, and then replied. "Alright. I'll be there in the morning, but I'm calling my lawyer as well. He'll come with me."

"That isn't really necessary at this juncture, but if you insist, it's your right."

"Darn straight it is. Tomorrow then." And he hung up.

"Sheri, just when I thought this day was going to get better, the Law called."

"What did you do? Kill somebody's cat?"

"Naw, nothing that drastic. But I'm off to visit Pineville's finest in the morning. So if I'm gone when you get up, don't be surprised."

"Alright. No problem," but she was thinking "and if I'm gone when you come back from the station, don't be surprised." Sheri could smell trouble a mile away. She sighed, realizing this meant she would have to give up her sugar daddy, and give back the Corvette as well . . . in due course. Maybe she could string Vernon on a little longer until the gravy train really left town.

Chapter Twenty-Eight

Masey, The Minister, And The Garcias

Jesus and Maria Garcia were also residents on Buttermilk Lane. They were the closest neighbors to Masey Bumgarner, and over the course of the last four or five years, they had become friends. The Garcias had moved to Charlotte from Texas when Jesus had gotten a job with a major Charlotte company, the Lance Cracker Company. The Garcias were of Catholic background, but with Masey's encouragement they had attended and then joined Grey's Chapel Church. They especially liked their minister, Taylor Sampson, who had been so welcoming, and indeed had made a point when the Garcias joined the church to take the occasion to make clear, using Galatians 3:28, that the Christian Church was supposed to be ethnically inclusive. From time to time Masey had helped out the Garcias by looking after their two youngest children when they both had work to do on a weekday, and Masey had grown very fond of them. Maria cleaned houses for a living, three to four days a week. They were a very close and attractive couple, diminutive in size with olive colored skin, in their mid-thirties.

On this particular day these neighbors and friends were meeting with Taylor because it had dawned on the Garcias that they could not afford to buy another house, and yet if they were reading the published blueprint right, their entire front yard would become part of the highway and sidewalk complex, because their lot was in the major bend in the road as it turned South. When this dawned on them, they had panicked and talked with Masey, and she told them about the lawsuit being filed. They were praying about joining the lawsuit but wanted some spiritual guidance from their pastor. Unfortunately, when Masey had called other neighbors, they had declined to join in, being basically too frightened to join a lawsuit which they feared may come back to bite them later if all went wrong in the trial.

The conference room in Grey's Chapel was small, but since there was only four people meeting, it was adequate. The secretary had brought in coffee and doughnuts to fuel the discussion, and Taylor himself had been in prayer in preparation for the meeting. He had begun to see this trial as potentially life-changing for various members of his church, not least because some of them actually worked in the City Council office, some of them worked at Salvo, and some of them were in the predicament Masey and the Garcias found themselves in. This trial could actually split his church, depending on how it came out.

Jesus was the first to speak up, "Father Sampson I have been praying about our situation and it seems fragile to me. On the one hand, Maria and I are new citizens of the United States, we became such in part because of my service in the National Guard in Texas for some years before we moved here. As such, we feel a bit timid about sticking our noses out by means of a lawsuit, though we know we have a right to do so. We are not eager to draw attention to ourselves. On the other hand, we really cannot afford to lose our home. Maria cleans houses and my landscaping job does not pay enough for me to be able to build a house, or buy a better one with the money we would get when the land is condemned. So, what should we do? We know what Masey has already decided to do, but is it right, is it o.k., would the Lord bless our joining this effort?"

"These are excellent questions, and I can see you've given this whole matter a great deal of thought already," replied Taylor with a smile. "I think that you must make this decision on the basis of faith, and not on the basis of fear of possible negative consequences. If the lawsuit is successful then you don't lose your home and things go back to normal. If you lose the lawsuit, then we will all help you make other plans. You know, I think, we have a realtor who is a member of this church who can help if need be. If I were in your position, I would join the suit with Masey. It shows that this is not just the complaint of a single person, but a more general problem has been created for the community by this paving project, and the Judge and jury will have to take that into consideration."

There was silence for a bit while Jesus and Maria, now holding hands, processed this. Then Jesus looked at Maria and she said "Si," nodding her head. "O.K., we will join Masey in this, but would you pray over this situation now for us?"

Masey interrupted: "Before you do that, I know you've been told about what happened at my house, and that sure rattled my cage a bit, but I'm feeling better about it now. Would you also pray for protection for the three of us going forward please?"

Taylor said "sure" and then reached out and took the hands of Masey to his left and Jesus to his right and said: "Dear Lord, we know that your plans for these believers are for good and not for harm. We claim your promise that you work all things together for good for those who love you. Masey and Jesus and Maria do love you. We know there will be some difficulties along the way, but we ask for a fair outcome to this trial but we ask that you will protect and guide them in this venture. We ask that justice and mercy will prevail here. You have called us to be especially concerned about widows and those at the margins of society, and surely this is such a case. And God, give me guidance to know how to be of good support and help as this all transpires. We ask this in the name of the Father, and the Son, and the Holy Spirit, Amen." And Jesus and Maria crossed themselves as the Trinity was named, and opened their eyes on a new stage in their lives. This would be their first testing of their rights as United States citizens. It was both exciting and at the same time frightening, but such is always the case when people step out on faith and do things beyond their comfort zone.

The ride back home with Masey involved Masey encouraging her friends and saying: "I must tell you I am feeling much more comfortable about all this now that you've joined me in this mission. We need to call Benji as soon as we get home, and alert him to amend the affidavit so all our names can be on it. Whoever put that sign up on my door didn't know who he was messing with. He certainly couldn't have known he was even messing with Jesus, and now we have the proof right here in this car." This produced a laugh all around, relieving the tension.

Chapter Twenty-Nine

Not On Easy Street

Sweating bullets. Waiting in a long polished corridor outside the law offices at the courthouse to give a deposition is rather like being in purgatory. You're not sure if you're going to ever get out alive, and meanwhile you are just in agony. Finally a PA came out of an office down the hall and called for "Mr. Street."

On the one hand, Brad was glad to get this ordeal over with. He had actually prayed (something he didn't do a lot) that they would not ask him any questions about money. In fact, he had gotten down on his knees and begged for such an outcome. It remained to be seen how efficacious his pleading was. One thing he knew was he was not a rhetorician or lawyer, and he wasn't sure that an almighty God (whom he did believe in) was subject to manipulation through prayer.

After being ushered into a private room, he was seated at a little table, on which sat a recording device with a microphone. The equipment was already on and ready to run. The PA in question was a young woman, tall and thin with short straight black hair named Suzanne. Arousing him out of the thoughts that were rattling around in his head, Suzanne said, "Thanks for coming. Shall we get to it?"

"Yes, that's fine."

"O.K., to start with please state your name and address, and the role you play in Pineville city government."

"My name is Bradley Street, and I live at 4422 Heathcliffe Lane in Pineville. I've served on the Pineville City Council for the last two years."

"Mr. Street, would you please state for the record your own description of the closed-door meeting that was held by the council regarding the contracts for the possible upcoming highway project. Did you notice anything unusual or irregular about the meeting?"

"Well now that you mention it, I did," said Brad to his own surprise. "For one thing, why were we deciding on contracts before we even had one public hearing or vote on the proposed project? I supposed that the Mayor simply wanted to get his ducks in a row, so that at the hearing people would know that once the vote was taken at the public meeting the project would be green lighted and would begin thereafter. I'm not saying we don't need a bypass desperately, because we do, but it seemed a strange procedure to me. I also supposed, after the fact, that the Mayor was in a rush to get this done. He wanted the project under way before he had to run for office again, so, I imagine, he could point to it as evidence that he's getting things done for the city of Pineville." Brad paused at this juncture, quite proud of his candor, thus far. He had been told that these depositions would be read by both the defense and prosecuting attorneys, but that they would be otherwise confidential.

"Mr. Street, in regard to the various bids for the project, would you please state how many there were, and how much discussion went on about the various bids, and also whether the Mayor made a pitch for one or another of the bids."

"In regard to the latter, the Mayor did not try to influence our deliberations. We had some five bids for the project and we evaluated them carefully as we always do. This is a fiscally conservative council on the whole, and so we regularly choose the lowest bid, unless someone knows a good reason not to do so. In this case, no one objected to taking the lowest bid, not least because we are talking about a multi-million dollar project, and a savings of a half million is a lot of savings. I'm just saying, we went with the lowest bid."

"Mr. Street, before the decision was taken, did anyone try to offer you, or to your knowledge, other city councilmen, some kind of incentive or bribe to vote a particular way."

"Absolutely not."

"And did you know in advance that the owner of Salvo Sand, Gravel, and Cement was in fact the brother of the Mayor?"

"To be honest Mam, I did not. The bids themselves were part of legal documents and the only names on the documents were from that Hightower law firm downtown. So, no, I did not know that."

"Let's move on to the hearing itself. Was there anything that struck you as odd about the hearing?"

"Yes, indeed. Just when the public debates were heating up someone in the audience, I don't know who that man was, called the question, and when the council was asked if we were ready to vote, we said yes. In truth our minds were already made up, and we could see a storm coming from some of the residents who would be most affected by the decision, and we were of a mind to dodge that storm if possible. So when the chair asked us if we were ready to vote, and get out of that uncomfortable situation, we said yes. I mean there was some obvious hostility and anger in the room."

"Now let's move on. After the vote was taken, and the project was given the go ahead, was there anything unusual that transpired thereafter?"

Brad laughed a nervous laugh, and said "What do you mean by unusual?"

"You know, people coming around thanking you for the vote, or even some unexpected gifts coming your way, things like that."

"Well Mam, that is actually normal. People send thank you notes and the like if they stand to gain from the project. That sort of thing. Obviously if something like that comes after the fact, it's not a bribe."

"No, but it could be seen as a kick back, an attempt to smooth out any further possible obstacles to the project happening."

"I suppose, but I can assure you that nothing illegal happened after the fact so far as I know."

"Mr. Street are you certain about that?"

At this juncture Brad laughed that nervous laugh again and said, "Mam, I'm not a lawyer, but I don't know of anything illegal that happened after the public hearing."

"Nothing about envelopes of money that magically appeared in councilmen's mail boxes?"

At this point Brad shifted in his seat and got a little irate, "Look Mam, things are put in our boxes all the time—letters, thank you notes, gift cards, and once in a long while, money, and if we are running for office again, then those sorts of things are considered campaign contributions, particularly if they involve money. Not personal gifts, but campaign contributions. That's all."

"That's all you have to say on this matter? You realize of course that you have to keep a record of such donations if they are to be considered tax deductible campaign contributions?"

"Yes Mam. Of course I do."

"One final thing. The city council changed its rules when it came to hearings last spring. Only one hearing would be required before a vote, not two. Didn't that strike you as a bit odd?"

"Well at the time, I presumed it was simply a cost cutting measure. Nothing had been said then about development plans, so I had no notion this might be to grease the wheels of what has now happened in August. Our city council has operated with a deficit the last several years, and it mounts up. So I figured we were just trying to save money, that's all."

"O.K. that's all for now. I'm sure there will be further questions for you later during the trial Mr. Street, and I thank you for your co-operation thus far."

Brad notice the perspiration was dripping from his armpits and had beaded up under his nose, but he tried not to look uncomfortable when he asked "Am I free to leave now?"

"Yes, you may go."

As he was walking out of the building, he was not sure whether he had had a narrow escape, or had actually opened himself up for far more difficult questions. Either way, he needed some Mallox about now. But then another thought came to him . . . what about just a tiny little bit of cocaine instead, just to make him feel better and give him a little high? He had been on the wagon for a little while, but he still had one little packet in his glove compartment. Stopping at the drink machine, which was just outside the building next to the parking lot, he got himself a Coke Zero. "Coke Zero goes well with coke!" he joked, and then laughed at his own joke.

He got in the truck, popped the top of his drink can, turned on the CD player to his favorite Eric Clapton Greatest Hits CD, skipped to the fourth song entitled "Cocaine" opened the glove compartment, got out the little white packet, shook it into his drink, and smiled, and said "Ecstasy, here I come . . . " and as he swallowed, he revved the engine while still in park and sang along to the second verse—"If you got bad news, you wanna kick them blues, cocaine/ When your day is done and you wanna run, cocaine/ She don't lie, she don't lie, she don't lie, cocaine." It felt good to feel powerful and still in control of one's life, or so he told himself.

Chapter Thirty

"I Fought The Law, And The Law Won"

Vernon was out of sorts. He woke up groggy, with a big headache from too much drinking the previous evening, and then after taking two aspirins, his headache got worse when he remembered he needed to call his lawyer, and then go down to the Pineville police station. Sheri had mysteriously disappeared before he got up, and as he was shaving he was trying to figure out what to say to the Law about that sign, if, that is, they asked. He was not volunteering any information he didn't have to volunteer.

Having cleaned up, he put on what his mother used to call his Sunday-go-to-meeting suit complete with a clean tie, and he rang the Hightower office. After waiting what seemed like an eternity, he was put through to Josh.

"What's cooking Vernon?"

"Well Josh, I reckon I did something stupid. I put a threat note on an old lady's house who has filed suit against the highway project. Dumb, I know, but I was angry. The Pineville police called yesterday and told me to come in. So what's my best move?"

"You are absolutely right. That was real stupid, and could even be used as evidence against your company at the trial. I don't think I need to come in on this one. Here's what you do. Firstly, you don't admit to anything voluntarily. Nada. Secondly, if they say they've got you dead to rights because your fingerprints are on the sign. . . . Vernon, are your fingerprints on that sign?"

"Nope, I don't think so, I was careful about that."

"Good. So if they don't have any proper evidence, don't admit to anything. Look exasperated if the proceedings go on too long, and then tell them that if they have any other questions on other matters to take it up with the Hightower firm. Got it?"

"Gotcha. But supposing they have some kind of flimsy evidence, then what?"

"Well misdemeanor trespass and threatening is not a major offense. They both result in fines. I would say just pay the fine and get it over with. Don't drag things out. You don't want to go through two legal procedures at once."

"Nope, I sure don't. O.K. I got a strategy in mind. Thanks a bunch. I'll call you if I need you, but hopefully not."

"Yes, hopefully not, because I've still got a ton to do to prepare for the trial."

The ride to the Pineville police station only took fifteen minutes. Vernon had done the drive-through at Starbucks, and after inhaling one of their muffins, he was now sipping his "flat white"—which had two shots of espresso in it. That ought to keep him fully alert during his powwow with the Law.

The Pineville police station was like many other such places, a bee-hive of activity on this morning. There were calls coming in, officers going out and getting in their squad cars, people being shuffled in and out of the local city jail, files being filed, secretaries answering phone calls, EMT people hanging around waiting for the next emergency, and so on. Vernon marched into the station feeling rather confident that he was ahead of the game. He was met by Sergeant Shultz.

"Mr. Lanceford, thanks for coming in. If you'll just follow me to this little conference room down this first hall here, we'll get started."

The so-called conference room was actually the coffee and dough-nuts break room, and it had all the smells one would associate with such a place—the smell of bad over-cooked coffee, both caf and de-caf, and all the usual stir sticks, napkins, cups, artificial sweeteners, etc. After grabbing a cup of coffee and offering one to Vernon which he turned down, already having a good buzz, the Sergeant sat down and beckoned Vernon to do likewise across the table. He set his small digital audio recorder down on the table and turned it on. Gone were the days when he scribbled notes on a yellow legal pad with a pencil.

"Mr. Lanceford, we have recently been called to the home of Ms. Masey Bumgarner, do you know her?"

Vernon scratched his chin and said, "No sir, I can't rightly say that I do. Don't believe I've ever met the woman."

"Were you aware that she filed suit, and now a couple of other people have been added as plaintiffs, against the building of the very bypass your company Salvo has been contracted to build?"

"Well I was aware somebody filed suit, but I leave those things in the hands of my capable lawyer downtown, Joshua Hightower."

"Yes, well, we will have to speak with him in due course. Two days ago a sign was left taped to Ms. Bumgarner's door threatening her if she didn't drop the law suit. Were you responsible for that sign?"

Vernon smiled a cheesy grin and said in a patronizing way, "Now officer, do I look like the kind of person who would be afraid of a lawsuit filed by a little ole lady, so afraid that I would do something stupid like that, especially when I have one of the best lawyers in Charlotte?" And he paused for dramatic effect.

"Sir, I'm not here to psychoanalyze you and your motives. Just answer the question."

"Well, I've got one for you—did you find any fingerprints or incriminating evidence that I might have had something to do with this?"

"Fingerprints—no. The few partials we found were too smudged to be helpful. But incriminating evidence, yes."

"And what evidence might that be?" said Vernon, his temper rising.

"Oh we've got blood samples that we tested for DNA, and low and behold it matched yours from your previous escapades, like the DUI you got last year where we took a DNA sample from a mouth swab."

"I see," said Vernon taken aback. "And where exactly did you find that blood sample?"

"Oh on the floor of the Bumgarner carport. And how exactly could it have gotten there if you hadn't been there?"

Vernon thought for a minute or two, and then said, "O.K. I admit I went over there to talk to the woman. Not to threaten her, just to talk. Her darn cat jumped on me in the carport, and scratched the hell out of my head, leaped on my head no less, and I reckon some blood splattered from that. I should just sue her for having an attack cat."

"I don't think so Mr. Lanceford. I don't think so, and since you were not invited over to have a little chat, you could be charged with criminal trespass."

"Just for driving in somebodies drive way, and never seeing them and never threatening them?"

"So you're denying you left that sign?"

"Damn straight I am. It might have been one of my over-zealous workers, and so I apologize and I'll talk to them. I just wanted to talk to her. Wasn't no sign there when I drove in the driveway."

"So you are saying it must have been put up later?"

"I reckon. I didn't hang around. I went home and licked my wounds. Damn cat!"

"Alright Mr. Lanceford, we can't prove you put up the sign, but I 'spect you did. So here's what we're gone do. Firstly, I am going to issue you a ticket for trespassing, which you'll need to pay on the way out. Secondly, I am warning you that we've issued a protection order for that property and we will be watching it, and I am warning you further that there must be no contact with Ms. Bumgarner going forward—no email, no phone calls, no nothing! There's a restraining order issued for you and any of your employees going forward. Am I clear? Furthermore, this whole conversation will be admissible as evidence at the coming trial, and it will not cast you in the most favorable light, to say the least."

"I understand," said Vernon trying to look contrite, "and I apologize for my over zealous behavior."

"Uh Huh. Well, duly noted. You are free to go now," and the Sergeant handed him a ticket. "Pay that as you leave please."

Vernon took the ticket, and saw that it said $1,000 and he nearly swore, barely stifling a few four letter words, as he left. He handed his credit card to the secretary who took money for tickets, and she smiled and said, "Sorry sir, we don't take credit cards, but there's an ATM right outside the door you can use." So Vernon went outside muttering to himself about getting this money back when Hightower won the trial, and then paid his fine and left.

As he got into his Ram pickup, and turned on the radio to the classic rock station, what was playing but an old familiar tune by the Bobby Fuller Four. The name of the tune—"I Fought the Law, and the Law Won". As he drove off down Highway 51 he said to himself, "Ain't it the truth. Ain't it just the truth."

Chapter Thirty-One

Masey Deposed And Indisposed

When it came time for the deposition from Masey Bumgarner, it was interesting to note the different demeanor the recorders took in her presence. For one thing there was her pleasant demeanor, and then there was her diminutive size, not to mention her Southern drawl and Christian manners. She seemed like everyone's epitome of a Grandma, and it took an exceedingly obtuse or cynical person not to see the goodness and sincerity simply oozing out of her pores. You just couldn't be stern with her, or mean—rather what happened was that one became deferential and polite, even if one wasn't customarily that way.

Margaret Diffenderfer was the main recorder in Judge Martin's office, and among her many skills, she was a world-class typist, who could keep up with just about any speed of talking. Just to be on the safe side she also did a digital recording to double check her work. Tall, angular, fifty years of age, and wearing bifocals, she just looked every bit the legal secretary she was in her gray business suit and black high heels. Because Masey was the main plaintiff (though the Garcias had now been added to the lawsuit), her deposition was taken in the Judge's office, with copies sent to both the plaintiff's and the defendant's lawyers.

"Now Miss Masey, if you would just sit over here near the digital recorder, in this more comfortable chair, we'll get this necessary task over with so you can get on with the rest of your day."

"Bless your heart, I appreciate you're making this easy."

"Can I get you anything to drink or eat before we get going? We have nice Danishes in the other room, and some good tea and coffee, whichever you'd like."

"That's so kind of you, but honestly my stomach is a nervous wreck about this whole deal, so I'd best not eat or drink anything until I get this over with. My son Benji, who is also my lawyer, is out there in the hall if any technical questions arise which I can't answer. Goodness knows I don't have much familiarity with the law."

"No problem. You'll do fine. So shall we get started?"

"By all means."

"First, state your full name and age for the record."

"Well everyone calls me Masey, but my full name is Jewel Mays Bumgarner and I'm embarrassed to admit I'm already sixty-three years old."

"And would you please state for the record, what exactly prompted you to file your lawsuit?"

"Let me first say, as a Christian person, I really wrestled with and prayed about this, and talked to my pastor as well. I got back from a once in a blue moon holiday to discover that it had already been decided that by using the provisions of eminent domain, that a good eighteen feet of my front yard was going to be lopped off so that a four lane bypass could be paved down Buttermilk Lane, and even worse, my neighbors the Garcia's were basically going to lose their whole front yard, and they have young kids. All without us even having a say in the matter. We would have to just accept it, and accept whatever compensation was offered without so much as a peep or a how do you do! It wasn't fair, and it only got worse when I talked to a local realtor and she said I would probably just need to sell my house and move if I didn't like the idea of living next to a dangerous thoroughfare like that, and of course sell it for about half it's current value in light of the development about come down this road. You can see my dilemma. So, with some hesitation, I filed suit."

"Were you not aware there was a rezoning hearing earlier in August?"

"No Mam. Notice for that was not sent out soon enough, and I was already gone on vacation. It should have been, by rights, sent out at least a month prior to the event, but it wasn't. I found it when I picked up my mail when I got home and sorted it all. Again, this was not fair."

"Did you not receive an earlier email about this event?"

"Mam, I'm not much on the email, but I have since gone back and checked, and even checked all the email in my junk email box on Hotmail, and there was absolutely nothing. Nothing at all. In short, I was not properly notified."

"Is the aim of your lawsuit to force another hearing?"

"Well, I have now learned, much to my chagrin, that the law was changed about the number of hearings required before something big like this can be voted on and approved. So no, that is not the aim of the lawsuit, since what was done was not, strictly speaking, illegal. No, the nature of my lawsuit is to stop the building project dead in its tracks, by demonstrating collusion and malfeasance and injustice and several other big lawyering terms which my son told me to mention, but which have now gone right out of my head."

"You have listed not only the construction company head, Vernon Lanceford, but his brother, the Mayor, and the whole city council in the lawsuit, is that correct?"

"Yes Mam. It seems to have been a team effort to pull this off, while pulling the wool over the public's eyes."

"And you are claiming there was under the table money given to the council members after the fact?"

"Yes Mam, I suppose to make sure no obstacles would arise to stop the construction once it was approved. They didn't realize they might run into an irate widow along the way. In fact it is more than suspicious that it is the brother of the Mayor who got the contract. That cannot be a mere coincidence. No way Jose, not with all the construction companies we have in the Charlotte area!"

"I see. And I see you are not asking for monetary damages? Why is that?"

"Because I'm not suing to take somebody else's money. I just want to be left alone and live out my life on Buttermilk Lane in peace and quiet for the rest of my days. It's bad enough I lost my husband a couple of years ago, I just can't lose my home and tranquility as well."

"Still it seems highly unusual that you aren't asking for compensation for all the stress you are going through."

Masey at this point began to tear up. "I've done told you, I just want to be left be. Leave me be. I don't want to damage or hurt anybody else or their livelihood. I can't afford a big city lawyer anyhow, so my son is helping me. I just want this to go away. The sooner the better."

Margaret could see how upset this woman was. She was sitting there shaking and holding her little handkerchief and dabbing her eyes, and trying to maintain her poise, with difficulty. Margaret's heart went out to her, but she dared not say so, as she was supposed to be the emissary of the impartial arbiter of the case—Judge Martin—and so instead she just said . . .

"Ms. Bumgarner, I'm sorry for all your trouble. You are free to go now."

As Masey picked up her pocketbook, and slowly walked out of the room, Benji was right there in the hall sitting on a padded bench, drinking his latte, and he got up immediately to help her.

"So how did it go Mom?"

"As well as could be expected. The lady interviewing me was alright, not stern or abrupt, and with good manners, but she sure asked a lot of probing questions. I'll tell you about it on the way home. I'm sure glad that's over. Maybe you and me could stop at another favorite place, Joey Noble's Steak Restaurant, and find some comfort food for lunch. What do you say? I'm paying."

"Well, as the Godfather once said, 'You've made me an offer I can't refuse.'" And they both laughed as they went out into the parking lot.

Chapter Thirty-Two

Jane And Liz Explode

The paperwork came quite unexpectedly to Jane's mailbox. It came in a formal looking black folder inside a large manila envelope. It came from the Hightower law firm, and looked very official. Jane had a premonition this was about to make this a bad day indeed, but she decided to wait until Liz woke up to open it. Liz had been out carousing the night before, exploring the nightlife in Charlotte and finding it somewhat to her liking. Jane sipped her coffee at the breakfast nook table and reminisced about when she and Vernon used to prowl around on Friday nights in Charlotte. Those were much better days, days without rancor, or lawsuits, or damaged emotions.

It was not until almost ten in the morning that Liz got up, yawned, stumbled into the shower, and could be heard singing some pop song she must have heard in a club the night before. She kept singing "shake it off, shake it off." Oh to be young, thought Jane. But on the other hand she recognized that Liz, though young, had plenty of baggage, and sometimes she even carried weapons in that baggage. Liz was an accident waiting to happen as a result of her war experiences and her refusal to spend any significant amount of time in the free counseling services provided by the military.

When Liz came walking in, still drying her frizzy hair, Jane said, "We got an envelope from Vernon's lawyer, and that can't be good. But before you start reaching for the Tums, what would you like for breakfast?"

"Oh I thought I'd just scramble a couple of eggs, and maybe have some toast and jam and juice. That ought to feed the beast for a while."

Jane knew better than to try and do breakfast for the ever independent Liz. So she bided her time, sipping her coffee, and they ate quietly together after about ten minutes of cooking up breakfast.

"Sooo . . . what's in the envelope? I'll bet it's not the Publisher's Clearing House Prize."

Jane laughed, "No sugar, I'm sure it's not that. Shall we open it now."

"Might as well get it over with."

When Jane slipped the folder out of the envelope, she noticed it was even sealed with tape, as if the document held some closely guarded secrets. When she slit it open with her butter knife, and went to the first page, it said "Revised Will."

"Oh boy. I've got a bad feeling about this."

Vernon, it seems, had had enough of his rebellious daughter, especially after she had humiliated him to the point that he had to be rescued by his employees from cement. So he decided to cut her off, entirely, in the new will.

"Well honey, what it says here is that you'd better stay in the military a little longer, as Vernon has written you out of the will . . . completely."

"What?" said Liz, her eyes getting big. "I'm gonna get that SOB for this."

"Careful darlin', that's your Grandma you're talking about in that B word."

"O.K., but that's the last straw, truly, the very last straw. I hope he gets taken to the cleaners in this trial."

"Well," said Jane, "yes and no. The will does not mention any change for me, and I want that boy to continue to have to suffer and pay the alimony, so it won't help if he goes broke or to jail—it won't help at all. That'd just be cutting off our nose to spite our own faces, but don't you worry. If you need help down the road, I'll take care of you. Momma still loves you."

Liz began to cry. "How did it ever come to this? How did such bad blood get stirred up between you two?"

"Oh, about the time I got pregnant with you, and Vernon found out sex was going to be less frequent and less fun. You may remember me telling you that I had morning sickness something terrible when I was pregnant with you. It was not pretty, and I wasn't in any mood for a romp in the hay. That's when Vernon started the pattern of frequenting the ladies of the night, which has continued until now."

Liz balled up her fists and said, "I despise him, I really do. I'd just as soon never see him again."

"Never is a very long time darlin', and besides if you let him get to you like that *then he wins*. You've got to get beyond him, like I did. You hear?"

But Liz wasn't listening too closely, she was thinking instead of how she might get revenge for yet another deep wound inflicted on her by her father.

Chapter Thirty-Three

The Mayor Prepares

It wasn't exactly a summit meeting, or a strategy session, but on this Saturday morning it had that kind of feeling. Tom Lanceford had summoned his brother to his palatial mansion off of Overbrook Drive to clear the air, and make sure Vernon understood that he needed to maintain a low, very low, entirely low, profile between now and the end of the trial, if he wanted to be able to build that bypass.

After the two men had settled in, and the maid had fixed them a breakfast of champions—ham, eggs, sausage, grits, toast, jam, juice, coffee—the Mayor looked his brother right in the eyes and said, "Listen up Vernon. There cannot be any more shenanigans. Zero, zilch, nada. No more incidents that lead to little trips to the police station. The prosecution is watching, and gathering evidence, and is ready to pounce. And I want to review one more time with you—What the heck did you do, in regard to giving kickbacks to the council men? Did you really give them all little brown envelopes with lots of dough in it and a thank you note? Seriously? For real?"

"Yeah. The note was impersonal though—it said from the workers, which I think I mentioned before."

"Except, here is where I tell you that I've interviewed some of the councilmen and they say no such benefaction showed up in their city mailboxes. Nothing."

"What?"

"Nope. I made discreet inquires of five of the councilmen I know the best, and nothing. No little brown envelopes, no gratuities, and no notes. Nothing."

"I'd better find out what went down in detail from Vinny."

"You think?"

"O.K. I'll check on that, but suppose for a minute it went missing for another reason. Suppose the money did get into all those boxes, but some opportunistic person that was in your building, took the money and ran."

"But how would they know it was money?"

"Because they opened one of the envelopes and saw it was money, and then saw all the other envelopes?"

"But that would mean it was one of my fiscally conservative, always worried about the budget councilmen who came in to get his mail, discovered the windfall, and saw the other envelopes and took the money and skedaddled. It doesn't sound like them to me."

Vernon laughed at this point and said, "You don't suppose it was that prissy do-gooder secretary Charlotte do you? You never know about women. You can't trust them."

"Speak for yourself. It's you who is hanging out with low-lifes, and that's another thing. Your sex life is your own business, but for now, I'd say you'd better ditch the bimbo, and be clean as a whistle until the trial is done. If the Observer gets hold of your carousing and the like, never mind your misdemeanors, you can forget about the paving project, even if we win the trial. You'll be too hot to handle, especially since I intend to run for re-election."

A glum Vernon looked at his brother and said, "I guess I'm just a perpetual screw up."

"Except for now you're not. It may be boring, but you are going to be a good citizen for the coming months."

Silence reigned over the remainder of breakfast as the brothers were lost in their thoughts. Finally Tom said . . .

"You'd better track down that money, and make no mistakes. We can't afford for it to show up as a surprise late in the trial."

"You're right about that. I'll take care of it."

"Why is it," Vernon thought to himself as he was leaving, "that when I make mistakes it always comes back to bite me, but when golden boy makes mistakes, it's no big deal, and soon sorted out?"

Chapter Thirty-Four

Sheri's Debate

It was Sheri's birthday, and naturally, Vernon had forgotten, even though she had reminded him just last week. But of course Vernon was preoccupied with many things and what she said to him, other than "let's have sex" went in one ear and out the other. She had been going back and forth, debating whether it was time to move on, or not, and find another boyfriend, of which there were plenty of candidates, rich and poor, at the Platinum Club. But, for one thing, Sheri had become very attached to her little red Corvette, and couldn't afford to buy it; and for another thing, she wasn't getting any younger. At thirty-eight, though she looked about thirty and kept herself in good shape, she was nearing the upper limits of pole dancing productivity, as far as the owners of the Platinum Club were concerned.

So, Sheri debated back and forth in her mind about whether to leave Vernon or to stay. To her knowledge, he had never once cheated on her since they had been together, and honestly he had been very sweet to her, and generous. Why mess with a good thing while it's going, she told herself. She was resilient enough to believe that even if the party with Vernon was suddenly over, she had had to start over from scratch before. She could do it again, although the older she got, the less she thought that was a good idea. So for now, she decided she was in a "wait and see" mode, especially waiting and seeing what happened with this impending trial and construction project. If that all turned out well, Vernon could be "flush" with money for a while. "Wait and see," she told herself.

In the meantime, she seemed to have developed a nasty rash in the nether regions. She figured she'd better get some penicillin from her doctor, and be checked as well for STDs, which she had done regularly, and thus far she had been clean. And of course, being a smart girl, she had always used protection anyway.

The drive down Highway 51 to Matthews was a stop-and go-drive, what with all the stoplights and traffic. Sheri didn't really care, because she was in no hurry. She had the top down, the summer breeze was blowing in her hair, and all seemed right with the world. Her doctor's appointment in Matthews was not for another forty minutes anyway, and besides, once you get to a doctor's office, they are hardly ever on schedule with their patients anyway. Granted some of their patients lose patience and just leave before being seen, but still, they seem to always be running behind. Sheri felt sure that her check up would resolve the rash issue, and in the meantime, she resolved not to do anything rash in regard to Vernon.

Chapter Thirty-Five

Randle And Charlotte Reach A Crossroads

It had certainly been a whirlwind romance the last few weeks between Randle and Charlotte, but now that the calendar had turned the page into September, Randle had decided action was called for, and totally surprised Charlotte over dinner by offering her an engagement ring. It was quite beautiful, a chocolate diamond from Zales, and definitely not cubic zirconium. Charlotte broke down and cried, and said "I didn't think this day would ever come," and then with Randle staring at her waiting with bated breath, she said, "If you really want me, then the answer is yes. But I'm in shock Randle. We've only dated for a little less than a month."

Randle himself had realized he wasn't getting any younger, and honestly, after years of playing the field, he had never found a nicer girl, and one more compatible with him, than Charlotte. With both of them being thirty-something, it was time to get on with marriage and possibly family, if it was ever going to happen. Of course Charlotte had barely mentioned Randle to her sister or parents thus far, only in passing actually, so they were going to have to cross the threshold of the "meet the parents" thing much sooner than Charlotte had thought likely.

One part of Charlotte was of course thrilled. The last few days, she had done almost nothing but daydream what it might be like to be married to Randle, and now—look what just happened!

Randle had thought this out over the course of the last week, and he was sick and tired of playing the dating game at bars and clubs and ending up with desperate, or overly paranoid, or too fragile, or too self-conscious women. And besides, he really had always wanted to marry a good

Christian girl, and this was his opportunity. All week he had been pumping himself up for this moment with the phrase "carpe diem." He'd get up in the morning and give a pep talk to himself in the mirror while shaving, saying things like "Randle my man, its time for you to be brave, stop sowing your wild oats, and really settle down. Charlotte is the perfect mate for you, and in fact, she'll keep you on the straight and narrow. You need to get back into church and 'get right with the Lord.'" Randle's family had gone to church, but when he got into law enforcement it had become basically impossible as he often worked on Sunday mornings. He finally had thought of a line to use on Charlotte, and he had saved until this very moment.

"Charlotte honey, like you've been suggesting, I guess it's time for me to lay down the law, and take up the Gospel again. We need to get ourselves into a good church, and then some pre-marital counseling, and then some wedding bells."

Charlotte's "WOO HOO" could be heard right across the whole floor of the Country Club dining room where Randle had taken her to propose. Then she said, "If you don't mind, I'm going to text my Mom and sister with a picture of the ring on my hand, with the little phrase 'Guess what????'"

"Go right ahead," said a beaming Randle, "knock yourself out. As far as I'm concerned you can text your whole Baptist church if you like!"

Life for these two had definitely taken a turn for the better.

Chapter Thirty-Six

Vinny's Vendetta

Vinny was getting sick and tired of being the gopher and the bailout guy, with little or no money to show for it. For the last five or more years of his life, he had worked for Vernon and never once gotten a raise. He had cleaned up Vernon's messes, called the goon squad occasionally when Vernon wanted to seriously threaten someone, planted money in people's pockets to grease wheels, covered up his infidelities, did troubleshooting with his brother . . . you name it, Vinny had done it. And he had decided it was time Vernon gave him a raise and better appreciated his many services, including breaking him out of concrete just this last week. Vinny's job had no job description at all, he was just expected to be up for anything, legal or not—to be a jack-of-all-trades. He had decided it was time to have a meeting with the boss, when he came in this morning.

Vernon finally shuffled in at about 9:30 in a grumpy mood. He had not yet been able to figure out what had happened to the money, but he needed to get to the bottom of that. After grabbing a cup of coffee from the pot in the secretary's office, he looked up and saw Vinny and said, "We need to talk."

"I was just about to say the same thing boss."

"Good, let's go into my office and close the door."

Sitting down about five feet apart, Vinny's opening salvo was, "Boss, don't you think it's about time I got a raise. After all, I've done all kinds of things for you over a long period of time."

Suppressing his anger, Vernon retorted, "May I remind you, Vinny, that you are an illegal alien in this country, and without a green card. You're real name is Vincente Lorenzo and you are not a U.S. citizen. Under those circumstances, you are very lucky to have work, and may I also remind you that I rescued you from a very bad situation where you were about to be deported, and my lawyer did his magic and saved your butt."

"True boss, true," said Vinny himself getting angry, "but you owe me quite a lot."

"O.K. so let's call it even, and I'll think about a raise for you after the trial is done and we're back to normal work, am I clear?"

"Crystal," said Vinny in disgust. "So what did you want from me?"

"About that money we gifted to the councilmen, it seems to have disappeared. Know anything about that?"

"What? I did the job, and then left in a hurry. Whatever happened after that I neither know anything about it, nor do I have anything to do with it. Is that why you aren't giving me a long overdue raise? Because you think I pocketed some of that money when I didn't? Come on boss, you know me better than that. I've been a good foot soldier."

"Yeah, you have, I confess. So how do we track that money down?"

"Well, I suppose I do a little work and figure out which councilman might have absconded with it?"

"Yeah, you do that, and when you find him, sweat him, and get the money back, and I'll tell you what—if you can get it back, I'll give you a thousand dollars of what you recover. How's that for motivation?"

"Alrighty. That's more like it. I'm off as soon as you print out for me the list of names and addresses of the councilmen."

"Yeah, just ask the secretary for that, and get to work. We need that money back."

"We sure do, and by we, I mean *me*, and also you," said Vinny as he ran out the door.

Chapter Thirty-Seven

Benji Prepares, And Brad's Scare

No matter how much time he spent looking over the various affidavits and depositions, looking for clues that he did not otherwise have, Benji still had a hard time finding a smoking gun—that slam dunk piece of final evidence which would put the final nail in the defense's coffin. He needed to track down what happened to the money, and he thought that maybe the way to do this was to go over the depositions one more time. The one that bothered him the most was Brad Street's. He seemed evasive towards the end of the interview. He never denied receiving money— he simply said that if he did it would be used appropriately for campaign funds, not for personal finances.

"It's time to get to know Mr. Street a bit better, and step one is to go to his Facebook page." Brad Street indeed had a considerable Facebook page, regularly updated. It, along with tweets, was how he communicated with his constituency far more often than on the phone. Street had found that social media was a good buffer between himself and the public. On the Facebook page were endless pictures of Street in uniform, receiving a bronze star from the President, with his loving wife and young kids, and then at Belk's as a new employee. Scrolling down through the comments it all seemed exceedingly normal and above board. Except for one thing . . . some of the comments by several of the war buddies seemed a little weird.

For one, there were comments about getting together more regularly, and one comment said, "You would not believe the new 'stuff' I've found.

It's prime quality." Now "stuff" was an all-encompassing term, but it seemed like the buddy, this one was named Roy Vanelli, was trying to entice Brad into getting together with the reference to the "stuff." This seemed like more than just a casual comment. He needed to talk to Mr. Street, the war hero, and pronto.

––––––––––––––

The momentary ecstasy that Brad experienced was quickly followed by the agony, because the cocaine that Brad had used was not the usual stuff. Like most cocaine that comes into the U.S. through Mexico, this batch of cocaine had been diluted with the drug levamisole,[1] a drug which in itself is used in veterinary medicine to de-worm horses. But if there is too much of the diluting drug in the cocaine, it can cause severe illness, and even death in human beings. Brad almost immediately had difficulty in breathing but he had the common sense to open his window and yell "Call 911" to someone walking into the court building. The shakes that followed, and then the stroke like symptoms, left Brad lying on the front seat of the car, gasping and sweating. The person who called 911 was Jillian Parks, and she came over to the truck when she saw something was terribly wrong, turned the truck off, waited until she saw the ambulance coming, and then pointed them in the right direction.

The EMT crew went right to work, taking Brad out of the truck, and putting an oxygen mask on him as they laid him on a stretcher on wheels. His pupils were very dilated, his pulse racing, and he was rapidly losing consciousness; so the race was on to get him to Mercy Hospital as quickly as humanly possible. This took all of ten minutes, and Street was raced into the emergency-room operating theater.

The emergency room doctor yelled—"propofol, stat! We need to put him under as quickly as possible to stabilize the situation, stop the heart from racing. Susan I need you to take a little blood as well, and find out ASAP what is in his system that produced this reaction. Hurry." One of the EMT workers who had done a quick look in the truck said to the doctor— "this may provide a clue, I found this little paper sleeve in the passenger's seat. Looks like a cocaine packet to me."

––––––––––––––

1. See the article at http://www.sfgate.com/health/article/Most-cocaine-diluted-with-unsafe-livestock-drug-3277375.php.

"O.K., Susan have the lab analyze that as well. We are in a race against time. Fortunately this man is in good physical shape. And by the way, who is he?"

The EMT worker replied, "His wallet indicates he's Brad Street, the one who was on the news a while back, something of an Iraq war hero. He's got a VA card in his wallet. He seems to now work at Belk's here in town, as he had a Belk's work schedule in his pocket. Shall I call his wife?"

"Yeah, right away. Get her down here. We need some answers, especially if he regularly takes any medicines or is allergic to any."

The phone call to Mrs. Street went straight through and Jeremy Bender, the EMT worker, tried to keep Street's wife as calm as possible with his questions. She was hysterical within minutes, and racing to the car.

"Mam, you need to be careful when driving here. It won't help if you get hurt on the way here."

"Yeah. He's still breathing you say?"

"Yes Mam, and the doctors are sedating him to help the situation. They know what they are doing and will do their best. Does Brad have any allergies, especially allergies to medicine that you know of?"

"No, not that I know of. He has mild hay fever, but even that is not a big deal. I'm on East Boulevard now, I'll be there soon."

The EMT worker asked a few more questions and then hung up and went outside to look for the Blue Honda Civic that Mrs. Street was driving. In about five more minutes a Honda came racing into the ER parking lot and a tall young blonde emerged looking like she had just heard an air-raid siren.

"This way Mam, just come with me. I've already told the doctor what you said."

"Thank you so much, and if you need any more information I've got our insurance cards and the like with me."

The initial lab report, both from the testing of the blood, and the testing of the white packet confirmed what the EMT suspected—Brad Street had indeed taken cocaine. It was not clear when the lab report came back to the doctor, whether he could act fast enough to counter the effects of the drug levamisole, as Brad's breathing was becoming more and more shallow. The anesthesia had calmed his body down and relaxed his muscles, but the drug had been completely ingested, and it was too late to induce vomiting and stop the damage.

"I want a saline drip, right now!" said the doctor. "We're going to try and dilute the cocaine and the levamisole, it's our best bet at this point if we are going to save him."

Meanwhile, Street's wife looked in the window of the ICU and watched the beehive of activity around Brad. She started saying a large number of Hail Mary's while fingering her rosary beads. Though she currently attended a Baptist Church, she had grown up Catholic, and this was the only way she knew to pray in an emergency. She was hoping Mary was listening.

Part Two

Consequences

Chapter Thirty-Eight

The Trial Begins

On September 6th, on a morning when there was a little chill in the air, betokening Fall was coming, the court of His Honor Judge Sawyer Martin was filled to the brim with litigants, court employees, and lots and lots of spectators. The Charlotte Observer had done a full page spread in the Sunday papers, turning this case into a David vs. Goliath match—an old widow and her Hispanic neighbors vs. the juggernaut of city government and wealthy contractors. Even CNN's Ashley Benfield had heard about the trial and had flown to Charlotte to report on the case. While it might not reach O.J. Simpson proportions in terms of its fame or notoriety, it still was going to be an interesting trial, putting to the test various key aspects of America's credo, including protection of the tired, the poor, and the huddled masses yearning to breath free so that they would not have their fate imposed on them by greedy contractors and big government. Both sides, it would seem, were prepared, if not spoiling for, a fight. The Charlotte Observer had called this "a little parable or test case of whether our democracy still works to the benefit of everyone."

Mayor Tom Lanceford, accompanied by his wife Amber, and his staff, including Charlotte Tate, who had indeed been subpoenaed to be a witness, arrived early. He was represented by the very same firm as his brother's company, since they were all co-defendants in this trial—the firm of Hightower and Associates, who came looking like something out of a Brooks Brother's suit catalog. They had no less than four lawyers on their team—three men, and a short but well-dressed woman, not to mention three more PAs who would sit behind them taking notes and providing briefs.

Vernon, not surprisingly, arrived late, looking somewhat disheveled, but nonetheless he had shaved and put on his best suit. He sat down next to his brother in a chair that squeaked under his bulk whenever he moved, and settled in for a long ordeal. His breath smelled of bourbon, but he whispered to his brother, "Don't worry, I just had a little nip to steady myself," to which his brother replied, "At nine in the morning?"

On the other side of the aisle sat Benji Moore, and his sole partner, Thomas Lessing. In addition to them, there was Mary Lynn, Benji's secretary playing double duty as PA, and Benji's personal investigator, Randle Radcliffe. Benji's junior partners were involved in another case and could not be present. The rest of the front row on their side of the aisle was taken up by Masey, sitting next to Benji and looking very smart in her blue dress with her gold cross around her neck, and the two Garcias, who were clearly frightened out of their wits and wondering why in the world they let themselves get talked into this ordeal.

The courtroom itself was large, but Judge Martin, being a no nonsense judge, was not allowing any TV cameras in the courtroom, and the news media was relegated to the large balcony that hovered over the back third of the seats in the courtroom. There would only be still cameras and sketch artists allowed as far as the visuals were concerned, and if one or more of the court appointed security guards saw cellphones recording the trial, they were instructed to confiscate the phones, tag and label them, and not return them until the trial was over.

One estimate had it that there were fifty people from the media, and the first floor of the courtroom was filled as well. Everyone was expecting sparks to fly in this case, and the bookies in Charlotte were even taking odds on who would win the trial, with the current line being 2-1 in favor of the big boys and the Hightower Law Firm. The inside skinny was that the sympathy vote would go to the widow, but the jury would side with the rhetoric of Josh Hightower.

Suddenly the bailiff announced, "All rise for Judge Martin," and the audience obliged. With camera shutters going off in the balcony, Judge Martin entered the courtroom, and then all were told to be seated. The Judge took care of housekeeping matters first, announcing there would be a break for lunch about noon and that the days proceedings would end at about four in the afternoon. After making sure the court appointed recording secretary was ready, the Judge said to Benji Moore, "Counselor, you may proceed."

Benji quickly quaffed his last swig of bottled water, arose, his legal dossier in hand, and marched to the podium in front of the jury. The jury selection had gone rather smoothly with both sides excluding three or four candidates for a variety of reasons. The result of the selection process was a jury of twelve persons, six women, six men, with three of the men and one of the women being either African American or Hispanic. Benji felt good about who was on the jury, not least because Judge Martin had not allowed the Hightower firm to stack the jury with people who would be inclined to favor the construction project—shopping center owners who wanted to build on the new bypass, employees of Salvo, the Mayor's college buddies, and so on.

Clearing his throat, Benji looked straight at the jury, surveying them from left to right and then began:

"Ladies and Gentleman of the jury, the case that is before you is very clearly a case of David vs. Goliath, or in this case, a widow vs. a very large construction company and the City Council of Pineville, with their high priced, Cadillac law firm. It took some real guts for my clients, Ms. Masey Bumgarner, a widow sitting right over there, and her neighbors the Garcias, to go to court against such large forces in our community."

"Common sense might have suggested not even trying to head off the bypass at the pass by filing a lawsuit against those who had already decided to build one, and had awarded the contract to do so to a local firm, Salvo Sand, Gravel, and Cement, because what chance *really* did vulnerable citizens with very limited means have against all the forces that those that were favoring the development could marshal? What hope could those who sought to stand in front of the steamroller, that was already cranked up and ready to start paving two days ago, have of avoiding being run over in this lawsuit? On the surface of things, the odds seemed slim that Masey and the Garcias could win their case. Shoot, even the local bookmakers have given 2 to 1 odds against their doing so."

"But ladies and gentlemen, this is America, and one principle we hold dear is 'justice for all,' a system that was set up to protect the weak from the powerful, those with little influence from those with much, and the good from the wicked. In America, justice should not be for sale, and the law should not be bent to satisfy the powerful at the expense of the lives and livelihood of the weak. During the course of this trial you are going to hear the defense's lawyers make a variety of arguments about the legality of the proceedings at the rezoning hearing, the legality of the proceedings when the bids were evaluated for the construction project, the lack of nepotism involved in which company got the bid for the contract, the good character of the Mayor and the City Council members involved, and so on."

"Again, on the surface of things, all might seem to be perfectly legal, and without collusion or prejudice against any of the good citizens of Pineville and the surrounding communities. Ladies and Gentlemen, I predict their presentations will be polished, their arguments reasonable on the surface, their rhetoric will be emotive, and their conclusions clearly and precisely drawn. And unfortunately, it will mostly be a façade covering up the real truth of the matter."

"I intend to show you a very different side of the story, a side that involves the contract for the paving project going to the brother of Mayor Lanceford, a brother who at this point is rather infamous in the community when it comes to his behavior and conduct, as the police will be able to confirm under oath. I intend to show that the proceedings about the number of zoning hearings and votes was deliberately altered last Spring as part of the scheme to pave the way for the railroading of this paving project through the Council and then the public hearing."

"I also intend to show that there was not proper discussion or debate about the project allowed, and indeed that the person in the audience who 'called the question' and forced an early vote by the council was in fact an employee of Salvo Sand, Gravel, and Cement. Further, I intend to show that the city council members were in fact given a kickback after the vote passed at the public hearing from Salvo, Sand, Gravel, and Cement, and in fact worse than that there was bribery of a key person in advance." There was a gasp from the gallery at this point, and Benji noticed the Mayor and his brother looking a little uneasy.

"But lest you think that's all, I'm prepared to show that Mr. Lanceford over there, the brother of the Mayor, personally undertook a trip to Masey Bumgarner's house and sought to threaten her unless she dropped this lawsuit like a hot potato. There is an old saying 'if you keep acting like a skunk, people will eventually get wind of it.'" This produced general laughter in the courtroom, and even the Judge could be seen trying to suppress a smile.

"In this case, all of these proceedings stink to high heaven, and present us with anything but a fair process that led to Salvo getting the bid for this highway project. Justice is what we demand, and a redoing of the whole process that led to this outcome. My client desires that this project be stopped dead in its tracks, and if it is to be undertaken at all, it be done somewhere that does not ruin a whole batch of people's yards, and lives, endangering children and animals who live on Buttermilk Lane. That is not too much to ask. I would have you know, that unlike some litigious persons, my clients are asking for no compensatory monetary damages for emotional distress. *None.* They only want to be left in peace to live out their lives on their lane without losing their yards, their peace of mind, and frankly the real value of the property they currently own."

"As you will likely know, the laws of eminent domain can take private property and condemn it and pay the owners far less than the fair market value for the land in order to undertake a paving project like this one. And that is precisely what is going to happen, if the defendants are not found guilty of collusion, malfeasance, and gross injustice to my clients. It is my hope, ladies and gentlemen of the jury, that you will see through the smoke screen that the defendants' lawyers will seek to put up, a smoke screen that hides the truth about what has happened while we stood helplessly by and watched a rigged good ole boy system yet again get what it wanted at the expense of 'the least of these our brethren'. Thank you for your attention."

There was brief applause from some in the gallery, which Judge Martin gaveled into submission and then said, "Counselor Hightower, it's your turn."

Buttoning his suit jacket, Josh Hightower, he of the blonde shock of hair, handsome facial features, and tall angular frame strode to the same podium and began. "Ladies and Gentlemen of the jury. What you have just heard is masterful rhetoric, but sadly as the Bard once said, it is 'full of sound and fury, signifying nothing' when it comes to the issue of legality. My clients have done absolutely nothing illegal in the proceedings that led to the awarding of the contract to Salvo, Sand, Gravel, and Cement. Nothing at all. This trial should not be about human personalities, or general consideration of what is really fair. We are in a court of *law* here ladies and gentlemen, not a court of public opinion, and not even a morality play. The issue in a court of law is not what seems generally fair, or most popular with the general public, the issue is whether what was done was *legal*—pure and simple. We intend to show that the Mayor of Pineville, a man of impeccable character, had nothing to do with the choosing of his brother's firm for this contract. He did not recommend it, he did not counsel the city council members to do, he did not twist any arms, and when the decision was taken, a unanimous decision I might add, he was not present. In fact we will show the decision was made on the basis of a perfectly normal criteria—it went to the lowest bidder on the contract. Pure and simple, and no collusion at all."

"Furthermore, despite the obfuscations of Counselor Moore, we intend to show that there were no bribes offered for the votes of the city council members, and that the law says that any citizen of Pineville has the right to attend a public meeting and raise their hand, and 'call the question' when debate has gone on for a sufficient period of time. That is the way the law reads, and that is what happened. Furthermore, we will show that Ms. Bumgarner and the Garcias have been offered a very fair price for their land, which is hardly prime real estate."

"All this and more we will prove in defending our clients in this case, and I contend that fair minded persons, who stick within the bounds of the law, and do not pay attention to emotive arguments about prejudice, will agree with us—fair minded persons like all of you, ladies and gentlemen of the jury. Thank you so much for your time and attention."

Benji was sitting in his chair with his notes rolled up like a newspaper in his hand, and he was squeezing it hard. He knew he had his work cut out for him. At this very moment, a court appointed runner came into the courtroom, rather breathless, a runner that Randle had sent on an errand. He handed Benji a note which read: "We have found Mr. Street finally. He is in Mercy Hospital, heavily sedated, and in no condition at present to attend the trial. Seems he had a drug overdose." With this Benji rose and said, "Your Honor, may I approach the bench?"

Judge Martin summoned Benji and Josh Hightower forward with a wave of his hand. "Your Honor, I have just received notice that one of the key witnesses for our case, one of the city councilmen who can best shed light on the facts, is unfortunately sedated in Mercy hospital, and not likely to be able to be present for some days. I therefore must ask for a continuance until he can appear, as his testimony is critical to our proving our case."

Josh chimed in, "Surely your Honor this is not necessary. We have the six other council men here present who can testify to what happened at the meetings."

"True," said Benji, "but your Honor, none of them know anything about the kickback money, because Brad Street not only found it, he took it all, likely because of his drug habit. He is in the hospital due to a cocaine overdose he took after he was deposed. He is the one who can prove the attempt to grease the wheels of this process by Vernon Lanceford."

Judge Martin frowned, looked at his witness list, and said, "Ordinarily, I would not agree with you Mr. Moore, as this usually appears to be a typical stalling tactic of someone not fully prepared to make his case, but in this instance, I'm going to allow a one week continuance and hope and trust you can get that man into court. Isn't he the Iraq war hero?"

"Yes sir, he is."

"Very well, you may have your continuance. Step back from the bench please." With this the Judge stood and explained to all those present that one of the key witnesses, Mr. Street, needed some time to recover in Mercy hospital from "something that went wrong" and so the trial would be continued in a week's time. The reporters raced out of the courtroom to find out something more about Mr. Street and his condition at Mercy hospital. The clock had been rewound by a week, but it was still ticking.

Chapter Thirty-Nine

Not So Street Smart

Brad Street was no longer at death's door, but he was not in great shape either. He had been moved from ICU into a private room at Mercy Hospital once he had gradually come out of his toxic shock condition. His wife had been fully informed of the details of how he got into that condition in the first place, and it was fair to say that she was in as much shock, of a different sort, as he was. She had had no inkling her husband had a cocaine habit, but now that she thought about it, it certainly explained some of his mood swings and secretive behavior. Her concern now, going forward, was to get him completely clean of drugs, and then find an appropriate rehab center so he could stay that way, while hopefully not losing his job at Belk's. They needed the income. Biding her time, she also wanted to make sure that there was not another shoe that was going to drop, related to the drugs, for instance like some kind of drug dealer being after him, and he had not warned her about it. A frank conversation was on the horizon as soon as he was up to it.

Randle found himself waiting in the family waiting room at Mercy, flipping through the old magazines that lay here and there, hoping for a moment to talk with Brad, or his wife, or the doctor, to get a prognosis as to when he might be fit enough to appear in court. Brad's wife certainly knew about the trial and his plans to be there to testify, but that was the furthest thing from her thoughts at the moment. Randle had been tasked with discovering a certain date when he could appear at the trial. Thirty minutes went by, then forty, and finally, Samantha Street emerged into the waiting room, and Randle approached her.

"Mrs. Street I'm truly sorry to bother you, but I am an emissary from Counselor Moore and I am wondering if you could give me a prognosis in regard to when your husband might be well enough to be released from the hospital, and then at least give a taped response to questions for the trial that is going on, and has been put on hold because of his medical difficulties?"

Samantha looked exhausted, and really in no mood to answer questions, but she had been raised to be polite, and so she said, "Well, as luck would have it, the doctor says he is going home in another day or so as long as he continues in the current direction, and then maybe a couple of more days of recover will be necessary. He needs to regain his strength, and we will have to schedule him for some counseling and rehab with the VA. But he wants to get his part of the trial over with, I can tell you that, so we can get on with our lives. So, I would guess, early next week perhaps? It's just a guess at this point. Do you think his testimony could be scheduled early in the proceedings so he could have that behind him?"

"We are all glad he has taken a turn for the better, Mrs. Street, and I'll not trouble you again. I will ask Counselor Moore to try and put your husband at the top of the witness list. If I may give you a little advice, since I saw reporters downstairs, I suggest you make no comment to them one way or another, that is, unless you want to do so, or they will hound you and follow you around."

"Thanks, I'd managed to suppress my memories of the press, so you're right. Mum's the word for a while, at least until the trial."

Randle beat a fast retreat so he could go report to Benji, who in turn would inform the Judge. It looked like next week was when the trial could resume.

Chapter Forty

The Come To Jesus Meeting

While Charlotte realized she had already gotten on the roller coaster and was strapped in for the ride called engagement, and then likely marriage—nevertheless before her car got too far up the first hill and started going fast—she had resolved she had to have the faith talk with Randle. She was a little bit nervous about it, but nonetheless hopeful, since Randle had professed he needed to get back into church. But Charlotte was smart enough to know there was a difference between dating behavior and marriage behavior, and she wanted to sort out the Jesus and church thing long before the wedding invitations were being created and a church for the service had been chosen.

Randle rang the door of her apartment, knowing from the text he had received from Charlotte that they were going to have an "important chat," and he had a good feeling he knew exactly what it would be about, and so he had been thinking ahead about his responses.

Charlotte invited Randle into her small living room/dining room/kitchenette area, which she had spruced up before he arrived, and had sprayed some floral air freshener to make the place smell nice, covering up any possible leftover cooking odors. Charlotte was a good cook, and liked to cook, but now was not the time for those sorts of distractions.

"Come in come in," Charlotte said, as Randle stepped in the door and gave Charlotte a little peck on the cheek. They had settled into a nice little courtship routine, or so Charlotte told herself.

"Want some coffee or Coke or something?"

"Just water thanks. What did you think of the first day of trial?"

As Charlotte was returning from the kitchen with two cold bottled waters she replied, "Well, it ended rather abruptly, and so do we have any idea when it will commence again?"

"Yes, we do. I just came from the hospital, and Street should be back on the streets by next week. Drug poisoning I reckon was his problem."

"Well let's get down to it," said Charlotte. "Randle, I do indeed already love you, but I also love my Lord Jesus, and I honestly need to know where you stand with the man upstairs."

"Well, we've not really talked about my religious history, but here goes. I was baptized as an infant in the Methodist Church. So I don' t have a big dramatic baptism and conversion story to tell you. I have always believed in God and Jesus, and until I went into police work I attended church almost every week. Since then, it's been more sporadic, but I want to get back to it."

"If you are wondering, I do pray pretty regularly, and a lot more recently, since we've gotten serious about our relationship, which I have no doubt is true of you as well. I would say I'm not a *mere* nominal Christian, as I really do believe in the Bible and the Christian faith, but I need to learn a lot more about the Bible and about the faith. I won't have any problems with the vows for Christian marriage at all, and in case you are wondering, I'm definitely not, hand on the Bible, saying all this just to 'get the girl' as we used to say."

"When you meet my Mom and Dad, when they come to town next week (you remember they live in Greensboro now) they can confirm I've spent plenty of time in church, was confirmed in the Methodist Church, regularly attended and so on. I've even been to Christian summer camps when I was younger. That's about all I need to tell you, I think."

Charlotte listened eagerly to all this, and replied, "Randle, I appreciate your candor about this. I think we have a good starting place, and if we join the young couple's class, I think we can begin to have a faith journey together. I really like the lively praise worship service at 9:45, which is followed by Sunday School, so I was going to propose that this coming Sunday we start putting our best feet forward when it comes to having good church habits, if you are good with that."

Randle said, "Of course, but I was kind of waiting for you to give the signal on this. Honestly, I'm fine with attending the Baptist Church, since the Baptists and Methodist around here at least are kissing cousins and pretty similar as Protestants."

"Good, then that's settled. So let's hold hands now, and have a prayer together, and if you don't mind, I would like to pray first and then you chime in as you feel led."

"Sure, go ahead."

"Lord we present ourselves to you as an engaged couple in love, and we confess we love you, and need your guidance, and your Spirit to bind us together. We know we are not perfect, and have a lot to learn, and we know that the journey into and beyond marriage will have some challenges along the way, but we ask you to be with us in all this, and we will give you the praise and glory. Thanks for bringing us together once again, after many years. We claim your promise that all things work together for good for those who love you."

Randle cleared his throat and added, "Lord I echo what she said, and I would ask in addition that you make me the man you want me to be, so I can be a good husband to Charlotte, and a good provider too. Lord we are not young people any more, so we ask we might grow in love and in the faith at a more rapid pace than some, since we are now engaged. Bind us together with bonds that cannot be broken, and thank you, Thank you for helping us find each other once again. In your name we pray," and then they both pronounced the AMEN in unison and had a good hug and kiss. Charlotte looked at Randle, and felt both relieved and excited. Things were going well, so far.

Chapter Forty-One

Masey And Miss Perkins

It's always good to be home, after a trying day, and Masey had had quite enough of her stomach jumping around like it was on a trampoline during the first day of the trial. Her senses had been heightened by the drama, and she figured she would have a hard time getting the image of Vernon Lanceford out of her mind. What seemed to bother her even more was his brother, who on the surface seemed like a solid citizen, and a decent human being, but then he was the one who was really behind pushing this construction project with no thought as to its possible effect on the residents of Buttermilk Lane, or if he knew the effects, he certainly didn't care.

Masey had taken off her pretty blue dress, and put on her nightgown and robe and slippers, and was enjoying eating a light supper, after which she and Miss Perkins would retire to the TV room, and watch *Wheel* followed by *Jeopardy*. Of course sometimes Miss Perkins would get tired of sitting on Masey's lap, usually during *Jeopardy*, which frankly was too highbrow of a show for Miss Perkins, whereas the wheel show at least had action to her liking.

Normally, what would happen during *Jeopardy* is that Miss Perkins would jump down, go back into the kitchen to see if any more food had magically appeared in her dish, and if not she would amble off to one or another of her favorite places to park herself. One such place was the window at the back of the house, which overlooked the backyard. Masey had two bird feeders in a nearby oak tree, and Miss Perkins would watch the birds with rapt attention. Miss Perkins had never been much of a birder, never left a carcass on the back doormat for Masey to inspect, but she seemed to imagine herself a mighty hunter as she looked out the window and watched the birds come and go, and sometimes hiss at them if they got too close to the window.

Having watched *Jeopardy,* normally Masey would then go visit her old desktop computer and check her email on her Juno account, get a little joy out of deleting a bunch of spam and advertising email, and then read and respond to one or two recent emails from friends. About half way through composing the second email her phone rang, and since she had a cordless phone right there on the desk, she picked up immediately, "Yes, may I ask who is calling?"

All she could here was voices in the background, and breathing on the line, so she tried again, "Hello, who is calling?"

This time someone actually spoke but it was muffled, it sounded like a handkerchief was over the mouthpiece, "You're going to lose this case, why don't you just quit now?"

Masey had the presence of mind to write down the number that was appearing on the caller ID, for Benji to check out. She then made up her mind to speak, "Whoever you are, and whoever you work for, God is watching you, and you'd better repent. I am not about to withdraw from this trial, so GO AWAY," and then she hung up and immediately called Benji.

"Son, I just had a threatening phone call, or at least a call that was trying to encourage me to quit while I'm ahead in regard to the trial. I have no idea who it was, but here's the number on the caller ID 704-364-5175. Would you please check that out for me? I suppose it might be a call from one of those disposable phones, but still, it might not if the person was about as smart as he or she sounded, I couldn't really tell the gender of the caller the voice was so muffled."

Benji scratched his head, "Mom, you know these things happen in a high profile case, and I'm sorry it just happened to you. It does mean you need to be careful going forward, but knowing you, you're not about to back down."

"You would be correct of course, but harassment is harassment and the Judge ought to know about it, and see if he can't put a stop to that nonsense. It ain't gonna work anyway. Bit between my teeth if you know what I mean."

"I certainly do. Get a good night's rest Mom, looks like we'll be back at it on Monday."

"Night night, and Miss Perkins says good night as well."

"Purrrfect," said Benji, and Masey giggled and hung up. "That boy is too much fun, and I love him."

Chapter Forty-Two

Jimmy Grimes

Jimmy Grimes was appropriately named. He was good at doing the dirty work, and he had done plenty of it for Vernon Lanceford, but lately Jimmy had not been getting paid, and when Jimmy didn't get paid, he got angry—very angry. The fact that he had a rather uncontrollable temper was one of the things that had made him so useful to Vernon. He would go and rough up people that owed Vernon money, and almost always it would produce results.

Vernon of course, left the dirty work to Jimmy, so he could not be blamed. It was indeed Jimmy who had worn his one and only leisure suit to the zoning meeting, had politely raised his hand and "called the question" when the debate about the highway project was heating up, and Brad Street had noted this and reported to Grace who was chairing, that the question had just been called. Yes he had been doing dirty work of all sorts for Vernon, and for fun and profit. Jimmy was one of those sadistic persons who got pleasure out of causing others pain. Perhaps it was his abusive upbringing that had conditioned him this way, or perhaps he was just a nasty piece of work, but either way he had no problems being brutal. Along the way he had made plenty of enemies, to say the least.

Jimmy had been informed he was on the witness list, and at the moment, he was so ticked off with Vernon, as opposed to being paid off by Vernon, that he was seriously contemplating spilling the beans on Vernon's various nefarious deeds. He had already been interviewed once by Randle Radcliffe, and had a phone chat with Benji Moore, and was instructed to keep his mouth completely closed until he testified, something that was difficult for Jimmy because he was a big talker. It was especially difficult for him to keep anything from his buddy Vinny, who also worked at Salvo, as Vinny was good at prying things out of people without much effort. He just had the gift of getting people to talk to him when he put on his friendly and understanding act.

Jimmy's hobby on the side was rhythmic talking, otherwise known as rap music. He was the lead rapper in a Charlotte band called Beast Mode, named after the football player Marshawn Lynch. Vernon had not cared nor had he explored what Jimmy did in his spare time. Vernon was one of those people who evaluated others on the basis of their size, and so in Vernon's mind, anyone who was a small as Jimmy or say his own daughter Liz, was unlikely to be any real threat to him. He could not have been more wrong.

Jimmy was happy to have a few more days away from the pressure cooker of a trial, so he was basically just hanging out at Salvo, and doing whatever odd jobs the foreman asked him to do. Vernon had not been around the business much in the last few days as he was busy being prepped for the trial by both Josh Hightower and also his own brother. The one time Jimmy had seen Vernon, he seemed glum, playing his cards close to his vest, which was so not the normal M.O. for Vernon.

Then he got a phone call, unlike any phone call he had ever had before. The voice was muffled, as though the mouthpiece of the phone was covered with something, and the gruff voice simply said, "You'd better not think about ratting out your boss Vernon. You better put that thought right out of your mind, because there will be consequences if you do, no matter how the trial goes." And then the person hung up. Jimmy didn't recognize the number on the caller ID screen on the phone, nor the voice, but it sent a chill up his spine.

What was he going to do now, now that he had already spoken with Benji and done a taped interview with Randle? He decided he would simply wait and see how things were going at the trial, and then make a mid-course correction if need be. Honesty was not as high on his list of priorities as self-preservation.

Chapter Forty-Three

Tete A Tete With The Tates

The meeting with the parents came on a bright Saturday morning where most folks were out shopping, playing golf, and the like. To say the least Randle was sweating it. It was a hot day anyway, but there was not enough men's deodorant in the world to keep him from sweating on this day. Randle had led the rather carefree bachelor's life for a third of a century, and he honestly had not seen this coming. Today he was wishing he had had a warning about how the time flew by between engagements and marriages rather like the one written in his side view mirror—"Caution: objects may appear to be farther away than they actually are."

The Tates were high society Charlotte, part of the elite Country Club set, as well as being quite active in Grace Baptist Church—Charles, the father, was a deacon in the church. The Tate house was palatial, and bordered on Quail Hollow Country Club, and was part of a gated community. If Randle had not felt intimidated before now, he certainly did at this moment. His anxiety rose in proportion to the length of the driveway, which wound around and finally presented the visitors with a view of a southern mansion looking rather like Tara in *Gone with the Wind*, which is precisely what Randle muttered to himself as the house came into view. He saw that title as all the more fitting as it matched his feelings about his chances of getting through this without a major faux pas.

Charlotte, sensing that Randle might be a bit overwhelmed, tried to reassure him saying, "Don't worry honey, they are bound to like you, since I do. They trust my judgment, because I've never brought home 'the boyfriend from hell.' Never."

"Thanks, that's very reassuring. Glad to know that I'm at least one step up from a demonic boyfriend!"

"Oh, silly, you know what I mean, you'll do fine."

"Not so sure about that. I'm not only out of league, I'm out of my income bracket as well!"

"Oh my parents are old softies, you wait and see." And just then a car pulled up under the canopy on the front circular drive, and they were met by the butler, who offered to park the car for Randle.

"Thanks by all means," and then he whispered to Charlotte, "Should I tip him?."

"No silly, just relax." Suddenly two people looking rather like something out of *Southern Living Magazine* appeared at the open door, beckoning them into the house. Randle guessed Charlotte's parents were in their mid to late fifties, but they both looked in reasonable shape, and were tanned and well dressed. Charles came down the steps to meet them and said, "Welcome Randle, we've heard so much about you. We've been looking forward to this time together."

"Thank you sir, likewise. Charlotte speaks in glowing terms about you both."

"That's probably because my wife is the heiress to the GE light bulb fortune." And then when Randle didn't laugh Charles added, "Only joking, Suzanne is just naturally radiant."

After having been ushered into "the sun room" which was decorated in pastel colors and had the sort of wicker furniture you might expect to see on an old veranda in the South, the butler magically appeared again, and asked, "What will you two be having to drink?"

Charlotte without hesitation said, "You know me Sidney, I want my iced mango margarita, made with Cuervo Gold please."

"Certainly, and for the gentleman?"

"Could I have a dry martini, shaken, not stirred, two olives?"

"Excellent choice sir," said Sidney, who then retreated somewhere into the back of the house.

"So." said Suzanne, "Would I be right in saying that I may have met you before, some time ago?"

"Yes Mam," said Randle, "If you remember, Charlotte and I went to Myers Park High together, and even dated a little bit. I took her to one of the dances over at the Country Club once, but after High School we lost touch for a while."

"And now you're in the fascinating field of private investigation!"

"Yes Mam, never a dull moment, and especially not now since I'm involved in this whole Salvo case."

Charles butted in at this point and said, "And here I thought at first Charlotte was telling me you were like Ace Ventura, Pet Detective . . . just kidding!" And then he laughed at his own joke, while Suzanne frowned at him.

Randle could tell Charles was trying hard to break the ice—trying too hard, frankly— and Charlotte was feeling a bit uncomfortable, so she changed the subject. "Randle is here in fact to do something very traditional, and old school Southern . . . And so I'll hand it over to Randle."

Randle gulped, and said, "That was quick. O.K., Mr. and Mrs. Tate, I would be grateful if I could have your permission to have your daughter's hand in marriage. Rest assured I plan to strive to be the best husband I can possibly be, because your daughter deserves it."

Before Suzanne could answer, Sidney returned with the drinks, including two Maker's Mark bourbons for the parents, and Randle said spontaneously, "Excellent timing, I could use that drink about now!"

After they had taken their drinks Suzanne said, "Randle, you've just shown us you have good manners and are a proper Southern gentleman, and if Charlotte wants to marry you, we will be delighted to have you as a member of the family, and of course Charlotte has already told us in no uncertain terms 'this is the one!' So I propose a toast . . ." and they all stood up and raised their glasses.

"To the future Mr. and Mrs. Radcliffe." But just after the initial drink, Charlotte said, "Well, Randle and I talked about this, and are in agreement that we would like to do the hyphenated thing so we can share our two names as we share our two lives, so, going forward we will have a proper posh British name—the Tate-Radcliffe's. I hope you approve."

Charles chimed in, "Why of course. That way, we won't be losing a Tate, we'll be gaining a Tate and two Radcliffes, so to speak." The foursome sat down and had a long chat about everything, including what the couple was thinking about the timing and nature of the wedding.

"Ya'll are both old fashioned and new fangled at the same time!" suggested Suzanne.

"I was hoping for a Christmas wedding, if that's o.k. with you Mom, and not too rushed," said Charlotte.

"Wow, we will have to call the wedding planner tomorrow, or even today while ya'll are here. This is very exciting, even if a bit quick. Randle are you good with a Christmas wedding in Grace Baptist Church?"

"Absolutely. At this point, I would go to the ends of the earth for the ceremony if that's where Charlotte wanted it to happen."

"Well actually, that gives me an idea," said Charles. "We just adore Hawaii, so why not let us book you a proper honeymoon in Hawaii?"

"Holy smokes," said Randle, "I always wanted to go to Hawaii someday, how does that sound to you Charlotte?"

"Perfect! Just perfect. Of course the danger is, we may like it so much, we may never come back," a comment which produced some laughter. At this point in the conversation Randle had calmed down, and was no longer having an anxiety attack, since things seemed to be going smoothly, and when the butler summoned them to their lunch a little later, Randle felt quite comfortable with Charlotte's parents, even in spite of the Pet Detective joke.

Towards dessert, Randle's phone began to vibrate in his pocket, and he discreetly took it out and looked at the screen which had a text message from Benji saying, "We Have a Problem. Call Me." Randle figured a problem was not the same as an emergency, so he decided it could wait until he and Charlotte were headed back to her condo.

Another hour passed, another text message, this time saying "Urgent," and Randle felt forced to say, "I'm terribly sorry, but I need to call Counselor Moore, if you will excuse me for just a minute," and they did.

Once he got through to Benji, the first words Randle heard were, "I think they are going to call this 'the Case of the Vanishing Witnesses.'"

Chapter Forty-Four

Brad Confesses

It is never easy to confront the truth about oneself when that truth is not pretty. It is even more difficult to admit the truth to those whose opinion you value the most. On the ride home from the hospital Brad sat in stony silence while his wife drove them both home. The man she thought she knew very well turned out to be not the man that was sitting next to her in the car on this morning. Trying to think how to break the ice on perhaps the most critical conversation of their marriage, she simply said,

"It's time you told me all about the cocaine habit."

Brad could not look directly at his wife. He stared across the dashboard at the traffic in front of them and pondered where to begin.

He said, "It started in Iraq. I, and several other guys were looking for something to gear us up for the coming sweep operation in Anbar province, and somebody had cocaine. I don't know where it came from or how Howie got it, but we had it. You have to understand those were very difficult and dangerous operations. The point of snorting the cocaine was to take the fear away and heighten our senses so we would be completely alert and able to do our jobs."

"So you are telling me cocaine helped you win the bronze star?"

"In a sense yes. Otherwise I would have been too afraid to run across that field and grab a couple of wounded buddies and drag them to safety. Most people are not naturally brave under those circumstances. Self-preservation is the natural instinct, not 'ooo raa' bravery."

"So what happened when you got home, and were turned into Mr. Hero? I would have thought that would be enough of an adrenaline rush right there to last you for a good while."

"You're right. It did, that is until the thrill wore off, and it became apparent I was going to have a difficult time finding a good job so that I could support my family, so that I could be the breadwinner."

"No one asked you to shoulder that burden all by yourself."

"True, but that was how I was raised in a good ole Southern home. I felt like I was supposed to do that, to be the man in the family."

"When did you start using when you were back in Charlotte, and how did you find the stuff?"

"It actually happened quite by accident. One of my platoon mates showed up one day in Belk's and we got to talking, and before we were done, he had given me the number of a guy who could get me some powder. I should have said no thanks, as I had been clean for a couple of months, but there was some stress in dealing with both the job and the city council part time job, and I started using again. Only, it was a lot more expensive over here than in Iraq. A lot more. And I fell behind in my paying the dealer. It was at that point that desperation set in."

"So is that's when you added one problem to another, by taking a huge pile of money that wasn't yours?"

Brad didn't answer this question; he just hung his head, and began to cry. Then he asked a question, "Did you find the money, or did the authorities?"

"You got lucky. I found it first after they carted you off to the hospital, and put it away in the house. The authorities don't know about it . . . yet. They did find the cocaine packet you had on the seat of the car. This is likely the result in some kind of drug charge, I reckon."

By this time the Streets were home, and were met by Chloe at the door, their cute little three-year-old daughter with the brown curly hair. She came running out the door hollering "Daddy" and grabbed him around the legs.

Suzanne added: "We'll continue this conversation later, but for now, I'm supposed to tell you that you have to take the aversion medicine, which should help prevent you going astray again."

"Thanks," he said. "Thanks for sticking by me."

"You need to rest up for the trial which begins again on Monday, and think hard about what your testimony will be. I'm going to pay the babysitter and send her home now."

Brad carried his overnight bag into the house, his mind a jumble of images and ideas. *It seemed like the universe had been set up by God like a set of dominos—you make one bad moral choice, and this led you down a rabbit trail to others, which in turn led to a snowballing of bad consequences, again and again and again. Brad wondered what the world would be like if there were never consequences to bad moral choices. What if it was never true that "you reap what you sow?"* Brad reckoned the world would be in even worse shape than it is, if that were true.

And what made redemption possible was forgiveness, followed by a fresh start. This didn't mean there wouldn't be consequences to the previous bad choices, but still forgiveness was his hope, starting first with forgiveness from his wife, whom he dearly loved, and had let down. He would think about that over the weekend as well. Monday was going to come too soon.

After paying the babysitter, Samantha went straight to the kitchen cabinet where she had hidden the envelopes of money, and stuck them in a FEDEX overnight envelope, addressed to one Vernon Lanceford at Salvo Sand, Gravel, and Cement in Pineville with a note attached, saying, "Here's your money back from the city councilmen. Some deposit, some return." She called the FedEx man to come and pick up the envelope and told him it would be under the front doormat. She didn't want that kickback money in her house for one more minute, lest temptation overcome her husband again.

Chapter Forty-Five

The Judge Is Alerted

The first thing that Benji did once Masey called and told him about a threat over the phone was to call Judge Martin. He needed to know what was going on behind the scenes. The Judge did not like being bothered at home, but in this case, he was happy to take the call, because it affected the court case and forewarned him that something had to be done to stop the intimidation of witnesses. He wondered how many more witnesses had received similar phone calls, and who was making the calls. The list was pretty long of who might have done that, but it always led back to Vernon Lanceford, or even his brother, both of whom stood to lose a lot if the paving project didn't proceed.

"Thank you for your call Counselor, I will deal with the matter first thing when we resume on Monday, and in the meantime, you had best make sure all your witnesses on your list are good to go. We don't want any more interruptions now do we?"

"No Judge, we certainly do not, but I was sure you needed to know the sort of duress we are operating under. Miss Masey's nerves are shot, frankly."

"Tell her to muster up her courage, and we'll see this through to a just conclusion."

"Certainly. I'll tell her."

When he hung up and turned to Masey, she had that searching look on her face and said "Well?"

"The Judge will deal with the matter first thing when we resume. It's clear that this whole deal has rattled some cages, to say the least. Now we need to get some sleep."

"Yes we do," and turning to her boon companion Masey said "Come on Miss Perkins, its time to go to bed."

Chapter Forty-Six

The Goon Squad

The money had come in a Ziploc bag. It was fifties and hundreds in unmarked bills. The contract came with it on a single sheet of paper. The deal was half now, and half when the job was completed. The job had two parts, one more dangerous than the other. Threatening phone calls, on a burner phone that could be disposed as soon as the calls were made, was easy. The second part took more planning. It involved the kidnapping of two vital witnesses—Vinny Coletti and Jimmy Grimes, both employees of Salvo Sand, Gravel, and Cement. Since Desmond had many short-term clients, most of whom wished to remain anonymous, he was sometimes unsure who exactly was commissioning these acts, and that was especially the case this time. He had not recognized the voice on the phone that had made the initial call, and anyway the caller was disguising his or her voice, which made it doubly difficult.

The Goon Squad, as they proudly called themselves, had been operating in the greater Charlotte area for over fifteen years, and had a reputation for getting things done—getting the dirty work accomplished very efficiently, no questions asked. This was another such mission, and the pay was good, so, who was Desmond to argue? Shoot, this time it didn't even involve roughing someone up or killing them. This was child's play compared to some jobs they had executed, and *executed* was the appropriate word.

The contract specified the collecting of the two men on Sunday, and taking them to a remote location well outside the city. In this case, the location was in Kings Mountain, North Carolina, south of Gastonia and near the South Carolina border. These gentlemen would be entertained at an abandoned old Motel Six building until the trial was done. Chained with leg irons in both cases, and kept in separate rooms, they would have a large baby sitter watching their every move. The mission was not to starve or harm them, just to keep them under wraps until the all clear came.

"Piece of cake," said Desmond, to his right hand man Charlie. "Piece of cake. Let's get this over with quick, and collect the rest of the money."

What the plotter of this little scheme did not know is that without telling their superiors, both Vinny and Jimmy had been interviewed by Randle and recorded by him, just in case. Things were about to get lively.

Chapter Forty-Seven

Liz And Jane Meet Sheri

Though it was not quite an ambush, it felt that way when Sheri walked out into the parking lot at the Platinum Club, heading for her beloved Corvette, and found two women waiting for her in the dark beside the car. For a moment Sheri thought about going back into the club and getting one of the bouncers, but these two women didn't look too dangerous, so at first she thought they might be wanting to ask some questions about how one got hired at the Platinum Club. She could not have been more wrong.

"Miss Lavalier, I presume," said Jane, as Sheri approach the car, keys in hand.

"Yes, whom do I have the pleasure of addressing?"

"My name is Jane Smithwick, used to be Jane Lanceford, and this is my daughter Liz. I realize this is a bit awkward, but we thought you ought to know a couple of things about dear ole Vernon, and if you don't mind, we wanted to ask a couple of quick questions, without slowing you down too much. We know you've been with Vernon for a while, and that's none of our concern, but there are some 'collateral issues' shall we say."

Sheri was not comfortable with this exchange, but when she noticed that Liz had fatigues on, and even a pistol strapped to her waist, she thought, "Better not to argue, just get this over with."

Jane continued, "First, perhaps you do, or you don't know, but Vernon recently drew up a new will, and you are in it."

"Really," said Sheri. "Do tell. I hadn't heard."

"The other news about the will is he wrote his own daughter out of the will."

"That's bad," said Sheri. "I didn't realize that either. Vernon has not mentioned any of this to me. He's been too busy with trial stuff."

"Yeah, I imagine," said Jane. "We wondered if perhaps, at an appropriate juncture, you could ask Vernon about the will. It's really unfair to Liz, whose about to muster out of the Army, and may need some of the support he could give, even if he is a stinker when it comes to family."

Sheri thought about how to respond to this, and said, "I may be able to look into it, but it could take a while. Vernon doesn't want to be distracted now, what with the trial being complex, and likely to go on for a while."

"Understandable. We'd just ask that you try. Nothing may come of it, but we'd rather this be resolved without lawyers involved, if you catch my drift."

"Oh I understand that."

"One more thing, and this is definitely just a word to the wise. Vernon, even before we were divorced, was trespassing in other men's honeypots if you get my meaning. And the result of this is that he has some STDs that require ongoing treatment just to contain them. You can't ever get totally shed of it. I'm simply telling you this, one woman to another, cause I've had to take the medicines for a long time. Thought you'd appreciate a heads up."

Sheri was surprised by this revelation, not because she didn't already know this, but because it suggested that Jane actually cared what happened to her. "I'm much obliged for your telling me. I'm pretty careful, and I visit my gyno regularly, and yes, I'm already on that medicine as well."

"Ah good ole Vernon just keeps passing along the gift which keeps on giving," said Liz with a sneer that had some venom in it.

"Well thanks ladies for the info, and I will not forget. Liz I'm sorry about you and the will, and I'll see what I can do. Sisters need to stick up for each other—right?"

"Right," said Liz. "Glad you see it that way, especially since too many men are scum and take advantage of women."

Sheri was not going to argue, she got in her car, and drove off to Vernon's house, wondering even more, "Now what should I do?"

Chapter Forty-Eight

The Trial Resumes

When Judge Martin looked down his roster of who should be in court on this morning, two names stood out as unaccounted for—Vinny Colletti and Jimmy Grimes, both employees of Salvo. "Mr. Vernon Lanceford, would you please approach the bench," said the Judge with a huge frown on his face.

"Mr. Lanceford, where exactly are your employees who are expected to testify at this trial? Where are they? I will not put up with any shenanigans by you. Do you understand? If I find you are obstructing justice here I will slap your behind in jail so fast you will not know what hit you. Where are Mr. Grimes and Mr. Colletti?"

Vernon actually looked shocked, "Honest judge, I have no clue. I do know that Jimmy called me on Saturday to tell me he had received some kind of threatening phone call about his testimony, and I assured him it did not come from me. No way. I'm already having enough difficulties without adding to the pile. So, Judge I don't know where these two men are. I have no clue, honestly, hand to my heart."

The Judge looked up and called the Mayor and Josh Hightower forward, "Gentlemen, two of our witnesses have gone missing again, and it will not do! Can either of you account for the whereabouts of Mr. Jimmy Grimes or Mr. Vincent Colletti?"

After they both professed total ignorance, the Judge told them to go and sit down. "Very well, no one seems to know what has happened to a couple of our witnesses, so what we shall do is place them at the bottom of the pile of testimonies."

At this juncture Benji said, "Your honor?"

"Yes, you may approach the bench."

"Your honor, my PI, Randle has their testimonies on tape if it comes to that. They are digitally recorded and could be printed out if necessary. I shared this information with Mr. Hightower at the disclosure stage of things. He knows this. So worse comes to worse, we still have their very voices speaking if we need them, and no one has tampered with these recordings, in fact I would be happy to turn them over now to the court, just in case, if that would be preferable to you."

"Yes indeed," said the Judge. "Bailiff, will you take Mr. Radcliffe's recorder, and tag it and mark it, and lock it in the court safe in my office please."

"O.K. we're going to get started. Mr. Moore, call your first witness."

Benji stood up and said, "The prosecution calls Charlotte Tate."

There was a murmur in the gallery and, as Charlotte came to the stand, lots of still cameras clicked repeatedly. Charlotte was wearing a teal and black business suit (rather like the Panthers teal color), and looked very professional.

"Ms. Tate, state your name and occupation for the record," said the Judge.

"My full name is Charlotte Landry Tate, and I am the secretary for the Mayor of Pineville, and have been for the last seven years."

"Ms. Tate do you swear to tell the truth, nothing but the truth, so help you God?"

"Judge, I never swear, and certainly not on the Bible in which Jesus says don't swear, but just let your yes be yes, and your no be no, but certainly I do promise to tell the truth to the best of my ability."

Benji walked over and smiled at Charlotte, "Ms. Tate, tell us in your own words what the working environment is like in the city council building in Pineville."

"It's actually quite regular and normal most of the time. I'm the Mayor's personal secretary, so I take care of his incoming calls, mail, calendar, and other related matters."

"Very good, and if you were asked what you noticed of late that was definitely out of the norm or out of the ordinary day's business, say during the past several weeks since the rezoning hearing, what would you say?"

"I would point to one thing in particular, a man in a camouflage outfit coming into the office and putting pudgy brown envelopes into the mail slots for the city council persons and then leaving quickly."

"Did you get a good look at this man, at his face?"

"No sir, unfortunately, when I looked up he had just finished what he came for and was leaving. I was just finishing writing down something on the Mayor's calendar and I saw only the back of his head—he was short, had dark hair, somewhat long. Maybe Hispanic, I couldn't be sure."

"And since this seemed so irregular, what did you do next?"

"Since this person was not a mailman, and since I was in charge of the office mail, I went to check what had been placed in the pigeonholes."

"And what did you discover?"

"These were all envelopes stuffed with money."

"You are sure of that?"

"Oh yes, very sure. I felt them and checked it out, it was money alright."

"And then what did you do?"

"Well, had the Mayor been in town, I would have immediately reported this to him, but since he was on a business trip, I sent him a text message informing him, and asking him what to do next."

"And did he reply?"

"Not for several hours. Apparently, he was away from his cellphone, and when he did reply, the office was already closed, and I was heading home."

"So it is your testimony that those envelopes of money just sat there the remainder of the day."

"Not the whole day, because I had had to go to Kinkos to do some duplication for the Mayor about mid-afternoon, we were creating booklets about the highway project and needed professional help. When I got back the envelopes were gone."

"Nothing further your honor," said Benji.

"Do you wish to cross examine this witness, Mr. Hightower?"

"Yes your Honor," said Josh, striding to the witness stand with the cameras clicking once more. On this day he was wearing a Carolina Blue business suit with a white tie. He looked like something out of a Tar Heel apparel catalog.

"Ms. Tate, you say you were sure those envelopes had money in them? Did you open one of the envelopes and check to see it was money?"

"No Mr. Hightower I did not, I simply felt one of the envelopes very carefully. I'm a lady who likes to shop Mr. Hightower. I think I know the feel of money when I come in contact with it." This produced a laugh.

"Perhaps, perhaps, but it could of course have been coupons for Hardees couldn't it. That's at least possible—right?"

"No Mr. Hightower it could not. They are of a different size and shape and sheen, and they don't stack like bills do. I deal with money regularly in the Mayor's office."

"Still there has to be some reasonable doubt. I mean it could have been counterfeit bills you know—same size and shape, but counterfeit."

Charlotte went pale: "I hadn't thought about that."

"Well it pays to be sure, especially when it comes to money. Nothing further your honor."

"Mr. Moore, you may call your next witness."

"The prosecution calls Mr. Brad Street." After the swearing in of a chastened Brad Street, wearing his new Belk's suit, but looking very pale, Benji then asked,

"Brad I would like you to think back to the day Ms. Tate was referring to, that Tuesday when the money miraculously showed up in the councilmen's boxes. Did you come to the city council building on that day?"

"Yes sir, I did. I came to collect my mail."

"Were you anticipating what we might call, in colloquial terms, a golden handshake?"

"No sir. Nothing of the kind. But there definitely was real money in those envelopes."

"Is it your testimony that you opened an envelope on the spot, discovered money, and then took your envelope away?"

"Yes sir, I did do that. There was also a memo with the money, a thank you gift from the workers who will be building the bypass."

"Was it signed?"

"No sir, but it was on company stationery."

"I see. And do you have any idea what happened to the other envelopes in the other city councilmen's boxes? Ms. Tate says they were all gone by the end of the work day."

Brad hesitated, and then said, "Yes sir, unfortunately I do. The temptation was too great, and I took them all. I was way behind on some bills, and I took them, even though they didn't belong to me. I assumed, since they were surprises, that no one would miss them after the fact." There had been several gasps in the audience at this point and the Judge said, "Quiet in the courtroom."

"I'd like to add that I was ashamed of what I did, but I was desperate. My Belk's job, which I am very thankful to Mr. Belk for, nevertheless does not cover my bills, nor is the little stipend for being on the city council do so, nor does what I get from my military service. This is not an excuse, I know, just an explanation."

"Understood. Describe the money in the envelopes. What denominations were there, and how much was in each envelope?"

"It was entirely hundreds and fifties in each envelope, and all seven envelopes had a thousand dollars in them. Obviously, it was not a bribe, since it had not come earlier, nor been promised before the decision was taken to give the contract to Salvo. You could however call it a kickback I suppose."

"Yes," said Benji, "that's exactly what it should be called. And why do you think this was done?"

"I assume so that the city council would iron out any further possible obstacles in the way of this project being done and completed. I suspect they feared being sued. I suspect they feared precisely this kind of legal proceeding we are now in. I need to add that my wife has now sent the money back to where it came from . . . that is, all of it that we still had."

"Nothing further, your Honor."

"Mr. Hightower?"

Josh came to the witness stand this time without the usual smart aleck look on his face. "Mr. Street, I gather that you are an Iraq war hero, a man awarded a bronze star by the President himself. Am I right?"

"I did receive that honor sir."

"But that is not the only thing you received because of your time in Iraq now is it, Mr. Street?"

"I'm not sure I understand your meaning sir."

"Is it not true that this past week you were in the hospital due to a cocaine poisoning episode? Is it not true that you picked up a cocaine habit in Iraq, a habit which you continued when you came home? Is it not also true that the reason you needed to steal that money, was not to satisfy ordinary bills, but because you owed some drug dealer money, and were afraid of getting further behind? Isn't this all the truth?"

Brad began to shake and weep . . . and said nothing.

"Answer the questions," Judge Martin said. "Take your time if you need to do so."

Slowly, Brad, wiping tears from his eyes said, "Unfortunately, you have accurately characterized the situation. I have now begun rehab for the drug addiction. It is very difficult for a vet when he comes home to get adjusted to life here in America again. I would just ask that you understand that."

"No doubt. But why should we believe you about the note in the moneybags, when you've been lying to yourself, and presumably to your wife and others for a long time? Why should we think you were honest about this?"

"Because, I have the paper to prove it." And with this Brad dramatically pulled a letter out of his jacket pocket, and showed it to the judge, the jury, and all those in the court. "This is what I've been holding onto ever since, as it proves I'm telling the truth."

The Judge said, "This is irregular sir, the evidence should have been disclosed before now for both the prosecution and the defense to examine and verify. Nevertheless since you are voluntarily handing it over now, and since you could hardly have done so while under sedation in the hospital, we will allow it. Bailiff, would you take this and mark this piece of evidence item twenty-three—letter from Salvo. It has been a very full morning of testimony, so we will now adjourn for lunch. Will all the representative parties please be back here by 1 p.m. sharp."

Chapter Forty-Nine

The Mountain Hideaway

On Oct 7th, 1780, something big happened at Kings Mountain. The colonists won a significant victory over the Redcoats there, which was one more nail in the coffin of British control of the colonies. Since then, not much of note had happened in this little community, which today has about 10,000 residents. It is in so many ways a sleepy little Southern town, except for the visit of tourists who come to see where the Revolutionary War battle was fought. Even in the summer the town is mostly quiet. On the Southern end of town, at the end of a strip mall, which was mostly stripped of any profitable shops, and strapped for cash to make improvements, stood an old derelict motel. The building was not entirely falling apart, having been an active business until 2012, but it was closed and boarded up. The Goon Squad, as well as some drug dealers had been using the back end of the motel for their own purposes, under the cover of darkness to avoid drawing attention to themselves.

As the trial recommenced on Monday morning, Charlie had gone out for breakfast food for his "guests" Vinny and Jimmy, both of whom preferred a Mexican breakfast, so Charlie was trying to track down the local Taco Bell. So far, he had not been able to get his GPS to work very well, so he stopped at a gas station, and asked for directions.

"Oh yeah, that moved on down 74 Shelby way. It used to be right across the street here, but they move to where they'd get more traffic. It'll take you about fifteen minutes to get there, straight out this road and take 74 West," said the man behind the register at the Shell station.

"Much obliged," said Charlie, as he headed out the door. It was another twenty minutes before he got to Taco Bell, ordered, picked up his order at the take out window, and headed back to King's Mountain. "They're gonna be right hungry by the time I get there," he opined.

The Goon Squad leadership prided itself on doing the job right, collecting their money, and keeping a very, very low profile. This was one of those businesses where word of mouth was everything, and actual visible publicity would be a disaster, leading to investigations by the police. Indeed, the Charlotte police had for some time been trying to track down the members of this criminal group, thus far with no success. What none of the Goon Squad knew is that the court had granted the police the right to listen in to phone calls to and from the Lanceford residences and businesses. And Officer Delany was busily collecting as much information as he could from those sorts of phone calls. Of course in addition to landlines, he really needed the data that came from cellphones, but Vernon Lanceford, unlike his brother, didn't much use a cellphone, in fact he despised the contraptions. The less used the better, was his philosophy.

On Monday night, a phone call went out from Tom Lanceford's residence to an unknown cellphone, the locale of which was pinpointed to be in King's Mountain N.C. This seemed irregular enough to Delany, not least because the call lasted thirty minutes, so that he called AT&T and requested, with an implied threat of a warrant being issued for all kinds of data if the request was denied, the name of the cellphone owner to whom that call had been made.

It belonged to one Charlie Blackburn, a known criminal who had been jailed a couple of times ten years prior in Shelby for petty theft. Delany called up the chief, told him about what he had discovered, and asked for an arrest warrant to go track down Charlie Blackburn in King's Mountain, ASAP. The chief was happy to oblige, and Joe Delany took his new partner Officer Sally Benson, with him. Maybe finally, he had gotten a lead that would help him break up one of the gangs running the criminal operations in Charlotte.

Chapter Fifty

Vernon's Vexation

Vernon had been far from thrilled with how the trial had gone so far. Thus far his company had been fingered as offering money to city council members, and that in itself might be enough to void the contract he had with the city. It probably got Brad Street fired as well. But Vernon kept telling himself that all his lawyer had to do was to show reasonable doubt to win this trial, since they were the defendants. The prosecution was the one who had to show probable cause, and the likelihood of collusion, fraud, bribery, etc. So while he was vexed, and wished the whole thing was over with, for now he was able to avoid panicking. He was however very concerned about where Vinny and Jimmy had gotten to. How come they had completely disappeared? Were they afraid of testifying after what happened in the previous days? Hard to say. Neither of them was answering their cell phones, which was not like them.

Vernon heard the garage door opening, and went to meet Sheri to see what she wanted to do about dinner. Vernon was thinking about cooking steaks on the grill, his favorite thing to do when it came to cooking out. Sheri walked in and smiled and said "Hey sugar, have you made any plans for dinner? I'm not working tonight, and I thought we could do something special."

"You took the words right out of my mouth. I was just thinking of a cooking a couple of filet mignons and some veggies on a skewer on the grill on the patio, but after we hit the hot tub first, if your game."

"I'm always game and a got a couple of questions for you, and a small request, but it can wait until we start marinating in the hot tub, shall I blend us up a couple of margaritas?"

"Sure. Sounds good. I'll go get my suit on."

"Suits me, I'll do the same in a minute or two." Sheri first checked the mail on the kitchen counter, and then went to change. She chose here flaming red bikini.

Vernon was already settled into his favorite corner in the hot tub when Sheri came walking out with two margaritas on a tray. He looked up, grinned and said, "You know, someday you should enter a swimsuit competition."

"What you talking about, I already won the wet swimsuit competition at the club five times over, and before that at Myrtle Beach too. Been there, done that, got the winning wet T Shirt prize from Johnny T Shirt at the beach."

"Why am I not surprised? Here's to your figure!"

They sat and snuggled for a bit in the hot tub when Vernon began to fool around, and Sheri calculated that, after a few moments of that, Vernon would be open to most any kind of suggestion. "Vernon sugar, I have one question. I know you love me, but did you by some chance put me in your will?"

"As a matter of fact honeybun, I did. I had my will revised recently."

"That's very kind of you. You didn't have to do that, but I have a little worry. Vernon, you have a daughter. You're not neglecting her are you, just to make me happy, cause I would feel really bad about nudging her out of the will?"

"Well . . ." said Vernon, and hesitated.

"I'm going to take that as a yes, and so I have a small favor. Why don't you have a do-over? Instead of putting me in the will now (as opposed to later if we get hitched) let's just pay off the Corvette and let me have the car, and keep your daughter in the will. I'm serious about this. The car would really mean more to me and really tell me how much you care about me. So what do you say big man?" and then she tickled him in his vulnerable spot, in his right ribs.

Vernon flinched, laughed, and said, "Well, alright, but I wouldn't do this for anyone but you. I don't know why I should do this, since Liz hates my guts, but o.k., if it will make you happy, I'll get Hightower to fix it. Good thing I got that FedEx envelope today I reckon."

"And they say you're too inflexible! How wrong they are," said Sheri and giggled. "Now then, about those steaks . . ."

Vernon jumped out of the pool and grabbed a big towel to wrap around his big gut, and then he turned the starter switch on the grill, "Coming right up," said Vernon with a silly grin on his face. Vernon might be hard as rock with other people, but Sheri knew how to wrap him around her little finger.

Chapter Fifty-One

Amber Alert Part One

Amber Lanceford was a very hyper woman. She was hyper protective, hyper anxiety prone, hyper obsessive, and more. It didn't help that she drank super-caffeinated energy drinks either. When it came to her husband, there was very little she wouldn't do to protect him. Of course she drew the line at real violence, but short of that, if she thought something truly threatened her husband, she tried to dream up a way to make that threat disappear.

On the surface, she might appear like a vacuous blonde-haired trophy wife of a Mayor, but in fact she was clever, and a real schemer too. She thought it wise as well not to mention any of her schemes to her husband. That way if something went awry, he had "plausible deniability," which was important at this point. She however was very proud of her latest coup, which might just make it impossible for the prosecution to pin anything on the Lanceford's, or at least, her Lanceford. She knew how very important doing the bypass project was for her husband, as it was the key to further development in Pineville—development that would bring millions into the local economy.

Bright and early, Amber was on her treadmill in the basement of their gigantic home, when her phone rang, and she stopped to take the call. "Miss L, its Charlie. Just a note on the QT. The two packages are well wrapped up and secured, so you have nothing to worry about just now. Hopefully this trial will wrap up soon—due to lack of evidence."

"Yes, thanks for the report. But I told you not to call me here again. Next time, just send an email, got it?"

"Roger, over and out."

Amber turned on her Sirius satellite music channel again—classic country hits—and Tammy Wynette came blasting out of the speakers on the wall singing "Stand by your Man."

"Amen to that," said Amber.

Chapter Fifty-Two

Miss Perkins Visits With The Minister

It finally happened. Miss Perkins' girth had expanded sufficiently so that she could no longer shimmy through the cat door that was part of the back-door of Masey's house. Masey had been chatting with Benji who had come over immediately after the most recent threat on the phone, and had been busy calming her down. Neither one of them had taken notice when Miss Perkins sauntered off from the living room area and thought she'd check out the nocturnal wild life in the backyard. The problem was not when she exited—she managed that just barely—but the cat flap didn't bend as well inwards as it did outwards.

Rev. Taylor Sampson had also stopped by to reassure Masey that between his visits and Benji's efforts and the security rounds being made in front of the house by the city police, that she would be fine. He had held Masey's hand and they had prayed over the situation and she now had calmed down and had more of a peace about things.

"Think of it this way Masey," said Taylor, "phone calls like that are attempts at intimidation from a distance. If they were really serious about taking action against you and your house, they would be showing up here. But they probably have figured out you've got added security these days, so they are resorting to intimidation without direct confrontation."

Masey said, "Well I reckon that makes good sense. But it sure does jangle your nerves. You feel like your safe little haven is falling apart, but it's a mercy to have Miss Perkins with me here all the time. Speaking of whom—have either of you gentlemen seen her in the last thirty minutes or so?"

Then Masey went into her high cat calling voice, "Miss Perkins, where are you sweety? These men are your friends. Come out, come out wherever you are." There was no response at all at first, but then Benji heard a sort of low moan, the kind of sound a cat makes when it is really aggravated or about to pounce on something. He started running around the house with the flashlight looking under beds, behind the fridge, behind the night table in Masey's bedroom, and in general anywhere he thought the cat might be hiding or stuck.

Again there came that low moaning sound from somewhere in the back of the house. Benji went into the kitchen, and low and behold . . . there was half a cat in the kitchen, dramatically struggling to get her tummy and the rest of her into the room! Benji hollered to Masey, "Mom you gotta come see this, it's a hoot!"

Masey scurried into the room, quickly followed by Taylor. "Well I declare! Miss Perkins you have gotten yourself in a right jam haven't you. Haven't I been telling you, you were over doing the eating? Haven't I told you, you need to get out and chase more birds in the backyard instead of eating and sleeping all the time? Now look at you. You're just parked there half in and half out, unable to go either way. Maybe this will teach you a lesson, though I doubt it, since a cat's short term memory span seems to be about as long as mine these days." Benji and Masey and Taylor all broke out laughing, and Masey laughed so hard tears started rolling down her face. Meanwhile Miss Perkins had a harrumph look on her face, not grasping what was so funny.

Finally Masey said, "Benji would you go around to the back stoop and extricate the tubby tabby please?"

"Happy to oblige," said Benji.

"Miss Masey I haven't seen you laugh like that in a while. You know I think the Lord has a good sense of timing, not to mention a good sense of humor, and if I may get theological for a moment, despite appearances, he's watching out for you, so don't you worry."

"Thanks pastor, I appreciate that." About then Benji came in the kitchen door with a wiggling ball of fur struggling desperately to escape Benji's firm grasp. When Benji dropped her on the floor, Miss Perkins pretended like nothing had happened. She sat down, licked her paws and smoothed out her facial hair, and then waltzed off to the supper dish to see if there was anything more to eat.

"I suppose we're going to have to install a bigger cat flap, or alternatively, put Miss Perkins on a Weight Watchers diet."

"I'd pay good money to see you try the latter. I 'spect that will result in a cat-tastrophe!" quipped Benji. And laughter resounded through the house once more.

Chapter Fifty-Three

How To Grill Your Mother

No matter how many conversations or heated debates or arguments happen between a step-mother and her step-son, nothing can really prepare you to be examined and cross-examined before a circuit court judge, jury, and audience by your own offspring and the defense attorney. Masey was very nervous, but knew she would be called to the stand next. Her mouth was dry, her hands were fidgety, and her bladder and lower track kept sending her false alarms. As Judge Martin gaveled the morning's session into activity, and said to Counselor Moore, "call your next witness," without hesitation Benji called Ms. Jewel Mays Bumgarner.

Benji got right to the point: "Ms. Bumgarner, would you please explain to the court why exactly you filed this lawsuit."

In a soft voice she replied, "Yes, certainly."

The Judge interrupted and said, "Speak up please Mam."

"I have lived on Buttermilk Lane for the last thirty some years of my life. It has been home for me and my husband, and my pets, and my stepson for decades now. It has been a peaceful and safe place to live, and the older you get, the more you appreciate peace, tranquility, and safety, especially when the news on the Charlotte TV is so full of mayhem and car accidents. So, when I returned from my first holiday in many a year and discovered a notice on my door about a rezoning hearing that had already transpired, already come and gone, I was more than a little distressed. The accounts in the paper made clear that a new bypass had been authorized and it was going right through my front yard, whether I liked it or not. It would involve lopping off some eighteen feet at least of my front yard (that was just a best estimate, it might be more) so that a four lane highway and a sidewalk could be built."

"Now, I've lived in Pineville long enough to know that normally, normally when such a huge project will be undertaken, there are at least two rezoning hearings, and in addition plenty of time for discussion and debate before any final action is taken. But in this case, that did not happen. Indeed, low and behold a new rule had been passed the previous Spring, which I had no knowledge of, which made it optional to have a second hearing. In other words, it appeared to me that action was taken so that this building project, and subsequent ones (yes I've heard the news about a possible new Mall further up Buttermilk Lane), could sail through without a hitch."

She continued, "When I came and visited Judge Martin with my lawyer, he could only issue a temporary stay on this freight train that was moving down the tracks, and told me there was no hope, since it was not legally required, for a second zoning hearing. The only way I could stop the train was to file a lawsuit, which I was very reluctant to do, and went to my minster and had a good chat and prayed before I undertook this action. Why? Because I'm a Christian person and I'm not all about just doing self-centered and selfish things, when it might interfere with something that benefits the community as a whole."

"But now a lawsuit needs to assert that something illegal or possibly illegal and unjust was happening. When I learned that at the one rezoning hearing that: one, who would get the paving contract had already been settled in favor of the Mayor's own brother's company, Salvo, *even before the hearing* so that that could not be a subject for debate at the hearing, and then I learned that, two, the debate had hardly gotten started when someone in the audience called the question too quickly, but nonetheless the city council acted and voted to approve the paving project before those of us most affected could even raise proper objections, and then, three, I learned that the person who raised his hand was a current employee for Salvo, well then, I was very certain that, as they say, 'something is rotten in Denmark' or in this case 'in Pineville'. This had all the earmarks of collusion, nepotism, railroading, circumventing of due process, malfeasance, and a few other legal problems which my lawyer is better equipped to enumerate. And then, to top it all, four, I learned of the dispensing of golden handshakes after the fact to the city council members from and I quote 'the workers of Salvo Sand, Gravel, and Concrete.' If all this doesn't stink to high heaven like a dead skunk in the middle of the road, I don't know what does. Hence, I filed the lawsuit."

Benji then asked: "And Ms. Bumgarner could you please tell the Judge and the jury, what has transpired since you filed the lawsuit?"

"I have received a threatening message taped to my door, as well as evidence that Mr. Vernon Lanceford himself came to my house to try and argue me out of the lawsuit; and as recent as last night, I received a threatening phone call telling me I'd better drop the lawsuit quote 'like a hot potato' end quote. It's flat scared me to death and put me off my vituals, and I can tell you Miss Perkins, whom I believe made the acquaintance of Mr. Lanceford when he attempted to visit, has not been happy either."

"And just so we are clear, please tell the court who Miss Perkins is?"

"She's my big tabby cat who apparently jumped on Mr. Lanceford's head when he tried to beat on my door." This response caused general laughter in the room, which the Judge quickly stifled.

"No further questions at this point, but I'd like to come back with more depending on what Mr. Hightower has in mind."

"That's fine," said the Judge. "Mr. Hightower do you wish to cross examine this witness?"

"Why yes sir, absolutely I do," and he advanced quickly to the dock, and began,

"Ms. Bumgarner could you please remind us of your age?"

"I don't see how that's relevant, but I'm sixty-three, no longer a spring chicken."

"No Mam, you are not, and would it be fair to say that you've had your share of senior moments, especially since your husband passed away?"

"Yes sir, to be honest I've had a few. But on an irregular basis."

"But perhaps a few more when you are in a stressful situation?"

"Perhaps, although sometimes stress helps you focus on what is really important."

"Now Ms. Bumgarner, I am assuming you know the difference between when something is illegal, and something is immoral, right?"

"Certainly young man, but plenty of things are both immoral and illegal."

"True. So you are aware that it was not illegal, strictly speaking, for the rules to be changed about the number of rezoning hearings?"

"Yes . . . but . . ."

"No buts, Ms. Bumgarner, this is court of law, not a morality play. And you were aware, that any citizen of Pineville, even a Salvo employee, had the perfect right as a citizen to call the question when the debate seemed to be too contentious and not going anywhere—right?"

"I suppose."

"Well Ms. Bumgarner, I know for a fact that that is the case. It's the law. And did you also know that it was entirely at the chair of the city council's discretion as to whether to accept the calling of the question, or continue debate, as it was also at the chair's discretion as to whether to go ahead and vote?"

Masey was silent for a moment and then said, "Maybe so, but there is such a thing as the letter of the law, and the spirit of the law, and when you pile up a whole bunch of 'let's stretch the law to the max to serve a purpose' then it becomes unjust, which is what the law is never supposed to be. Never. The law is supposed to protect the weak, the vulnerable, the elderly, the disenfranchised. I imagine you know the inscription on the Statue of Liberty. And while I'm in a quoting mood, I've just been reading the biography of Martin Luther King Jr, and in it is this important quote: 'The arc of the moral universe is long, but it bends towards justice.' Something similar can and should be said about the law sir."

"Yes Mam, eloquent no doubt, but let's move on shall we. When you got home and found a sign on your door, did you also meet Vernon Lanceford?"

"No, he had skedaddled I reckon, after my attack cat gently suggested he was trespassing."

"So in fact you don't know for sure he was really there. It could have been someone else who put up that sign, couldn't it? There were no fingerprints found on the sign were there?"

"No good ones, no, but his blood splatted on my carport floor and it matched a previous test he had when the man got pulled over for a DUI, etc."

"Perhaps we'll discuss that some other time. The point is, Vernon never verbally threatened you, and it can't be proved he put up the sign. Perhaps it can be shown he was on your property, and in fact he already admitted this and paid a fine for simple trespass, not criminal trespass. That matter is legally over. Now Ms. Bumgarner, about that phone call. Tell the court truthfully did it sound like a man's voice, or a woman's voice?"

"Couldn't tell for sure as it was deliberately muffled with something over the mouthpiece."

"So in fact, you have no idea as to whether the call was even made by a man, or for that matter by anyone from Salvo, do you?"

"No, I reckon not for sure. But on the other hand, it can hardly be a random caller, now can it, since it was again a threat for me to drop the lawsuit?"

"Well it could have come from any interested party in fact, maybe an irate business man hoping for the new mall to be built. You never know. In any case, it can't be tied to Salvo directly, or clearly."

Then Mr. Hightower said, "Now let's turn the page and go in a different direction. Is there anything illegal or immoral about giving somebody a thank you gift after they have done something nice for you? I'll bet you have done that at some point in your life, being the good Christian person you are, right?"

"Yes, but what's that got to do with anything? I'm not on trial here, your clients are."

"True, but my point is, even if the Salvo employees after the paving project had already been green lighted, and without promising anything in advance, sent some money to each of the city council members, while it might *look* fishy, it might *look* bad, it couldn't meet the standard of a bribe now could it? There is nothing in the law about a voluntary kickback in connection with a public building project. If it was neither solicited, nor in fact received in six of seven cases, it's a moot point it seems to me."

"Not so moot, if its part of a pattern of foul play and dirty tricks, not so moot sir."

"Your Honor, I have nothing further at this time, but I reserve the right to question this witness again as things unfold in the trial, if you please."

"Alright Counselor Hightower, it's time for our lunch adjournment. We'll make it 1:30 this time since its now almost 12:15. Court is adjourned until then."

As Masey and Benji walked out of the court, Masey looked depressed. "I didn't do so well, did I son?"

"On the contrary, you did very well, but Mr. Hightower is slick, and he's done his homework. Not to worry, we have a couple of aces up our sleeve."

"Good, just so those cards up your sleeve are not jokers, and are actually legal to play in this game."

Chapter Fifty-Four

Hiding In Plain Sight

The good citizens of King's Mountain tended to read the Shelby newspaper rather than the Charlotte one, if they read a newspaper at all. So, it was not very likely that any of them would pay much attention to what was going on at the derelict motel on the south side of town. What was going on was a whole lot of eating, sleeping, and waiting, and not much else, and the captives were getting restless.

"So when is this ordeal going to be over?" asked Jimmy of Charlie.

"Not sure. Not until the trial is over or almost over."

"Who knows how long that could take, especially since we are not there to say anything and we are on the witness list."

"Well, that's the point isn't it? Our employer doesn't want you there."

"And are you free to tell us who this mystery man is?"

"Nope. No way Jose."

"Whatever. You realize of course that they know we are missing. Somebody is bound to be looking for us before long. Course they might not think of King's Mountain right away." In fact the captives had settled in to a routine and were not making trouble, since the food was good, and the sleeping accommodations adequate. Yes, they had had to use Raid to get rid of some of the cockroaches in the bathroom, but at least the shower worked, the portable TV had at least a few channels, and the Goon Squad member in charge of babysitting didn't really show any hostility towards Vinny and Jimmy.

Joe Delany had spent the morning figuring out the data about the phone call that had come from somewhere south of Charlotte to the

Mayor's house. Amber Lanceford's attendance at the trial was intermittent. She would be there when her husband requested it, to show he was a family man. Most of the time, she would stay home, and mind her own business, which is to say her recreational activities, which included ladies golf at Myers Park Country Club. It was there that Joe Delany managed to track Amber down as she was coming off the course and back into the clubhouse to change.

"Ms. Lanceford, may I have a word? It won't take long. Joe Delany here from your Pineville Police department."

"Why of course officer, how can I help?" she said as she wiped her sweating brow with a golf towel with the MPCC logo.

"You seem to have received a phone call a couple of nights ago from a location south of here, say near the South Carolina border. Could you enlighten me as to what that was all about? We aren't tapping your landline phones, in case you were worried, but we are monitoring the wireless services, including AT&T and Verizon and Sprint, with their permission. This phone call went on for a while."

Amber did not appear on the surface to be worried or nervous, she simply replied, "Oh that must have been our Frankie's call. Our son is at USC in Columbia and he comes and goes a good bit. He did call us that night."

"Are you sure about that, as it seemed to be a call from a burner phone, not any of the regular accounts at the providers?"

"Well, yes, I think so."

"You're sure you didn't receive a call from someone who might be harboring some captives who ought to be at the trial?"

At this point, Amber got huffy. "Seriously officer? What do you take me for? My husband has done nothing wrong, as the trial will eventually show. Why would I need to be involved in that sort of drastic enterprise?"

"Why indeed? I was asking myself the same question. Well, in any case we intend to check into this matter further. Thanks for your time."

No sooner had the officer gotten out of sight, then Amber asked to used the payphone, which still existed in the club house. "You can put the charges on my husband's running tab Sammy," she said to the golf pro behind the desk who was busily examining his tee time sheet.

Amber dropped some quarters into the phone, told the operator to reverse the charges, and dialed Charlie's number.

The phone rang a few times and then finally Charlie picked up, "Yep, who's callin?"

"It's me. It appears the police may be getting wise to our arrangement. Probably a good idea if ya'll think about moving tonight to somewhere. Let me know where. Just a heads up."

"Thanks, I'll tell the Boss and we'll take action."

In the parking lot, Delany was calling home base, and he was being regaled with the fact that that burner phone had just been used again, and they had triangulated the location. "King's Mountain," said the voice at the other end of Delany's cellphone.

"Right," said Joe. "Call Sheriff Jones down there and light a fire under him."

"Will do, right away Boss."

Chapter Fifty-Five

Im-Pressed By The Widow

There were story lines galore that the reporters at the Charlotte Observer could pursue from the bypass trial, but the line of approach that was determined to create the most "buzz" was the story of the harassed widow. In fact the editor of the Observer had green lighted a front-page article by Veronica Silva on Masey Bumgarner. The headline screamed, "The Widow Counterpunches." There had already been several stories about the trial, but this story, which appeared in the Tuesday morning paper was "trending" in the online edition, and in fact had been picked up by CNN, who had green lighted someone to interview Masey Bumgarner, no less than one of their legal experts, Ashley Benfield. Benji had told Masey that the Judge would not smile benignly at a litigant talking to the press during the trial, so Masey had turned down the opportunity to talk to the media until after the trial was over and done with.

The Charlotte Observer story recounted Ms. Masey's rebuttals and countering of Josh Hightower's lines of inquiry and cross examination, and the report had actually got right her quoting of Martin Luther King Jr. Now the black church community in Charlotte had decided to make Masey and her plight a major topic of prayer and conversation. Support was ramping up in several quarters of the city. The Observer had talked with Taylor Sampson, since he was not on the witness list. He had given a stellar rating to Masey's character and shared some anecdotes about her humor and personality. "I'll tell you this, those folks are messin' with the wrong widow. This one's just as persistent as the one in the parable in Luke's Gospel, and this widow has a much better judge to deal with as well." This sent Veronica scrambling for her New Testament to find the story about the widow.

When Benji took account of what the press was saying, he smiled, and said to himself sitting in his office in a gruff Mr. T kind of voice, "I love it when a plan comes together. Or to borrow another phrase from that ole TV show—'I pity the fool who messes with Masey.'"

Josh Hightower had also been impressed with the passion, pathos, and sheer feistiness of the widow, even though he thought he had done a good job of deconstructing the basis for her litigation. In terms of strategy going forward he figured he needed to concentrate on dismantling some of the supporting witnesses more than focusing on Masey, and next up would be the Garcias. He saw them as easy to bamboozle or at least make look inept, although he had a little bit of trepidation when he realized he was putting "Jesus" on the stand in the morning. Some Charlotte folks might not take kindly to that.

Chapter Fifty-Six

Jesus, Mary, And Joshua

The request from news agencies for credentials and seats in the gallery of the "widow" trial kept increasing, but there simply were not enough seats. So the court officials had to go to a rota system for all non-local reporters. It was becoming something of a circus. Speaking of which, some enterprising soul was actually selling T Shirts outside the courtroom, labeled "Trial of the Century," and another one said, "All my Trials Lord," with a picture of Jesus, and Masey, no less. Things were indeed getting out of hand, and the local talk shows were having a daily segment on the trial. It was fast becoming the talk of the town. And then of course came the news that "Jesus" would be the first witness in today's session. The press would have a field day with that.

Jesus and Maria had been holding up reasonably well thus far during the trial, though their sleep had not been as sound as they might like. Jesus was worried about his job, since he had to take time off from the job to appear at the trial. Benji had called his employer and explained the situation to Mr. Green of Lance Crackers, and he was understanding . . . for the most part. He asked when Benji thought the trial would be over, but Benji only gave a rough estimate. Much depended on when all the witnesses had made it into court and testified, and there were still the two missing witnesses.

Josh Hightower was becoming increasingly aware of the media attention to the trial, which normally he would have been thrilled with, except for the fact that the press was all too willing to portray him as "Slick Rick" the clever lawyer vs. the honest vulnerable widow. This was not the P.R. he coveted. One part of his brain was telling him to tone down the usual sarcasm and rhetoric, and just do his job, and live to fight another day, but another part was telling him to rattle the witnesses until they coughed up some damning admissions of some sort. On this morning he couldn't decide which approach to take with the Hispanic couple.

Once the court was in session, something surprising happened which Josh had not counted on. Tom Lessing, rather than Benji Moore, was taking the lead on this morning with these first clients, and with good reason—his Spanish was impeccable, a language Josh had managed a bare C in, in high school. So when Counselor Lessing approached the bench, he informed the Judge that he would sometimes speak to the witness in Spanish, and then repeat it in English, and if they replied in Spanish, he would translate if need be, all the while encouraging Jesus to speak for himself in English. His English was o.k., but he was not adept with some of the nuances of the language. Josh had not reckoned on needing a translator this morning, and so he was hoping he could catch a nuance or two of difference between what Mr. Garcia said in Spanish and what he said in English. Things were getting complicated, and if need be, he might ask for a court-appointed translator, so he wouldn't look inept compared to Tom Lessing.

Tom Lessing had been Benji's partner in law for the last five years, and he was an excellent colleague as well. He had legal specialities that complimented those that Benji had, and he was tall, dark, and handsome, something the jury would take note of. Tom was in fact from Texas, had some Hispanic blood in his family, and as a result had a slightly olive complexion. This worked well with his nice suede suit with the stripes and his dark brown boots. His slow Texas twang also was a nice change of pace at the trial.

Tom began slowly, once Jesus was seated: "Mr. Garcia . . ."

"Call me Jesus (pronounced Hey-Seus) por favor."

"Now then Jesus, can you tell me why exactly you decided at the last minute to join Masey Bumgarner in this lawsuit?"

Jesus tried English first, but stammered a bit due to nervousness, and turned to his native Spanish. Tom translated, "I am proud to be a U.S. citizen, not least because I believe in democracy, and the fairness of the democratic justice system. I am a first generation immigrant to the U.S. and my family came here precisely for this reason. We were living some years in Texas just after we came. When I got the job with Lance Crackers we moved here to Charlotte, only a couple of years ago. We bought a house that we could afford, just barely."

He continued, "When we learned that without our agreement, almost the entire of our front yard would be annexed due to the eminent domain rule, for this bypass, it was simply too much. We have bambinos, and they like to play in our front yard. Our yard will be ruined if this bypass is built, and surely we will have to sell our land at a below market value, and move. But when I have looked nearby at the cost of property, we cannot afford it. It is simply much too expensive. But the cost of apartments is not much better, and you get to build up no equity that way. So, I felt I had no choice but to protest the city council's actions. And like Ms. Masey, we are not asking for monetary damages, we simply wish to be left alone. I need to add it took a lot of prayer and talking to our priest to be convinced it was safe to do this. In the part of Mexico where my family is from, cartels and drug lords rule the courts and own the judges, and we were afraid. All the more so when we heard of the threats Ms. Masey has endured. But we are here, trusting in the Lord that he will work this out for good."

The speaking in Spanish and then the excellent and clear translation by Tom Lessing took a good deal of time. At the end, Tom said "we have nothing further at this time."

"Mr. Hightower, you are up to bat."

Josh hesitated a bit, and then walked slowly over to the witness stand. "Mr. Garcia, I have only a couple of questions for you. Firstly, how do you know that the bypass project will take all of your yard? Are you sure about that?"

Jesus looked at Tom Lessing and said "non comprende." Tom translated for Jesus, and Jesus responded, "I saw the pictures, the blueprint, I think it is called, which was published."

"And you knew how to read the blueprint?"

"Si, I used to work in construction."

"Tell me Mr. Garcia, did you or your wife attend the rezoning meeting?"

"No, I was working, Maria looked after the bambinos."

"Did you receive a notice about the meeting?"

"Si, but work got in the way."

"So, it doesn't sound like you much wanted to participate in the democratic process where you could have raise objections, that is until after you saw what was published in the paper."

Jesus did not know how to respond to this remark. "I could not."

"Isn't in fact true, that you had to be persuaded by Ms. Masey's lawyer to participate in this trial?"

"No. It was our priest who said it was a good idea."

"I see. Nothing further."

The courtroom had gone silent, in anticipation for what was next. And what was next was the examination of the principles in the trial. The Judge, as if sensing this was a crucial moment and was anticipating that a good deal of time would be required, quickly said, even before Hightower had managed to sit down . . .

"Call your next witness Mr. Moore."

"Your Honor it is now 1:30 p.m. Might we adjourn for the day? We've had a long morning session, and we are still awaiting the finding of a couple of witnesses, and besides the next two witnesses, the Lanceford brothers, will undoubtedly consume at least a whole day's worth of testimony.

"Counselor, you are thinking along wise lines. I will adjourn the court for today, and we will resume at 9 sharp, rather than 10 in the morning."

As Benji and Masey and the Garcias were leaving the courtroom, there were lots of cameras going off, and reporters shoving microphones in the faces of all of them. Benji stopped and said, "We have no comment now, or at all until the end of the trial, so take your pictures, but we will not be responding to questions." And then they proceeded in silence to the van which was waiting for them in the side parking lot, a van Benji had rented for the trial, since it had an unfamiliar out of state license plate and might help prevent them from being followed.

As they drove away, Benji said, "All of you did as well as could be expected. We have not made any major mistakes yet."

"Gracias," said Jesus. "I was too nervous."

Masey said, "Who wouldn't be under the legal spotlight? Even the Jesus we worship had trouble when he was on trial by Pontius Pilate who sneered at the truth. He warned his disciples would have to face trials like his. Let's go get some lunch. Taco Bell anyone?"

Chapter Fifty-Seven

The Crux Of The Matter

It was a rainy day in September, and Benji had gotten permission to park at the back of the courthouse to better avoid the media. He and Masey and the Garcias were let in by a security guard into the basement of the courthouse, and then led to the elevator that took them up to the main floor. They entered the courtroom by a side door, usually reserved for taking criminals in and out of the courtroom, and when they got there, at 8:45, the place was already mostly full. Randle came across the gleaming marble floor to Benji and whispered in his ear, "I managed to find the bank record. I've got it in hand."

"Excellent, good work," said Benji. The courtroom quickly settled down when the Judge entered, and after the first gaveling the Judge said to Benji, "Call your first witness of the day."

"I call Mayor Tom Lanceford."

Lanceford looked very official in his jet black suit with thin light blue stripes, his highly polished shoes, and his hair carefully combed back over his growing bald spot—hair that had been colored, except for allowing some gray at the area of the temples, which was meant to be a sign of distinction and experience. His facial expression was rather stoic, as if this was just another ordeal he needed to get through to get on with his career and life. One reporter was to call it later that day "his game face."

Benji had thought long and hard about how to approach this crucial witness. Because of disclosure rules, there was little that the Mayor would not know or intuit in advance about what was coming from the prosecuting attorney, except, that is, for late breaking news. Benji was going to save his ace up the sleeve, as a surprise for the end of the exchange.

After the preliminaries of identification, Benji went straight to the point, "Mayor, why exactly did you decide to have the city council vote to change the rules about rezoning hearings back last spring? Were you anticipating objections to the bypass project?"

"Honestly, the answer to that last question is yes. I had the rules changed because I had attended the Mayor's conference back in the spring in San Diego, and heard one tale of woe after another from Mayors about how building projects that were necessary to the growth and development of this or that city had been stalled or blocked, to the overall detriment of that city, due to a long lugubrious process of vetting involving several hearings and vote taking.

"In addition, I had lots of conversations with possible partners in development from Latin America, chiefly Mexico, who were interested in investing in a new mall and other job creating schemes in Pineville. It thus seemed prudent to urge the city council to review and revise the rules, which they were very eager to do, all of them being essentially pro-business. Of course, I had no vote in regard to that decision, nor was I present when it was taken, actually I was out of town. And before there can be any suggestion of undue influence, I'd say, if you've interviewed any or all of these city council persons, you already know they each have minds of their own. They were unlikely to simply vote the way I hoped, just to please me or go along with my desires."

Benji then said, "Let's fast forward to last month, when the sole rezoning hearing happened. August is of course a month when many people either go on vacation or are returning from vacation, and if they have young children are getting ready for school to start again. It would seem to me that if there was only going to be one hearing about the bypass project, then a considerable period of time would need to be allotted so your citizens could air all their concerns and grievances, don't you think? According to my calculations that hearing was over in less than two hours."

"With benefit of hindsight, I guess you are right. Debate may have been cut off too quickly. Robert's rules of order, I suppose, do not absolutely *require* the taking of an instant vote when the 'question is called' though that is the normal procedure. The chair could have asked if the audience was all ready for the question to be called, and if not, then the debate could have gone on for a while. But that didn't happen, and more to the point, it was not required that more debate be allowed, so it was what it was."

"And who was the chair on that day of the hearing?"

"According to my summary report, it was Grace McGhee."

"Were you aware at the time that she is the daughter of the former State Highway Commissioner, and a person who likely would not want anything to stand in the way of improving our roads?"

"Hmm . . . that consideration had not come to my mind, no."

"And were you aware that she volunteered to chair the meeting, which the other city councilmen were happy to have her do, since it meant they weren't directly in the line of fire, so to speak?"

"I had not heard about that, to be honest."

"And were you aware that your brother had had several conversations with her prior to that crucial rezoning meeting, and I am willing to bet they were not chatting about the weather?"

Josh Hightower stood up and said, "I object your Honor. Calls for speculation."

"Move to strike," said the Judge. "Be more careful in your questioning Mr. Moore, but do continue."

"Your honor, Mr. Radcliffe is now bringing to the bench a bank statement. As you know, Vernon Lanceford's business records were subpoenaed for this proceeding. He is presenting Exhibit R, which shows a transfer of ten thousand dollars from Salvo's main account to a trust fund, a private account at the Wells Fargo Bank in south Charlotte. The trust fund provides scholarships to students attending Charlotte Country Day School. Not incidentally it was a transfer on the day before the rezoning hearing, a transfer we believe which went to benefit Grace McGhee's daughter who attends that school."

The Mayor at this juncture looked quite alarmed. He spoke like a shocked man and said, "I knew absolutely nothing about this. Nothing!"

"Perhaps not," said Benji. "Let's continue. So the project got approved, and who do we suppose got the multi-million dollar contract? Why, it is Vernon Lanceford, your brother, and his company Salvo, Sand, Gravel and Cement. If this isn't nepotism, it's the first cousin of nepotism surely. Did you arrange this in advance Mayor?"

"No sir, I did not. I suggested nothing to the city council when they evaluated the bids. Nothing. I was not present at the meeting, and I did not give them any suggestions before the meeting. I did know my brother was putting in a bid, and I admit, I was a little concerned it might look bad, but then he had a right to bid on the contract. A right! He should not be discriminated against just because he is my brother. Anyway, he's a grown man with his own business, and I'm apt to ask, under those circumstances, as the Bible says 'am I my brother's keeper?'"

Benji chuckled, and said, "You do realize who made that remark in the Bible don't you? In case not, it was Cain, after he had killed his brother Abel, and was fending off the Almighty's questions. I doubt you really want to agree with Cain's approach. But let's move on."

"Before we do so," said the Mayor, who was getting angry, "the city council is very concerned about fiscal responsibility in an age where city finances are tight, and so they simply took the lowest bid on the contract, which just happened to be my brother's bid. It could have been someone else's but it wasn't. I suppose various members of the council knew Salvo was my brother's company, but that did not seem to trouble them, you'll have to ask them. In any case, nothing illegal was done in selecting Salvo to do the job. Nothing."

"Since we are quoting Biblical phrases, Mr. Mayor, perhaps you've heard about 'avoiding even the appearance of evil,' but I digress. Were you aware that the person who called the question at that rezoning hearing was in fact an employee of Salvo, indeed one of Vernon's close associates, Jimmy Grimes, whom as you know has now gone missing? How convenient. Fortunately at least we have a recorded testimony from him which we will no doubt get to in due course."

"I did not know that until after the fact, but Grimes is a citizen of Pineville, he had every right to be at the hearing and call the question."

"Maybe so, but you have to admit that it looks pretty suspicious and convenient for Salvo that he was the one who stopped the proceedings and forestalled any significant debate, just when things were heating up."

"I suppose. But again, nothing illegal was done."

"Mayor, let's move on to the money which mysteriously appeared in the mail boxes of the city council members after the day of the rezoning hearing. Money in unmarked envelopes, with a note in them from the workers of Salvo, supposedly. Did you have an inkling this was going to be done? When exactly did you find out about this?"

"My secretary, Charlotte Tate, alerted me to this, but I was out of town. Obviously I did not know about this in advance, and when I learned about it, I read my brother the riot act. Of course it was not a bribe, since the matter had already been decided, but it looked like a kickback, or a golden handshake after the fact, and I want nothing to do with that sort of slimy business. Nothing. I was very angry about that."

"You wouldn't happen to have discovered what happened to that money before this trial began did you?"

"No sir, I did not, and I was shocked I tell you, that a war hero like Brad Street, whom the city of Pineville honored in a ceremony last year, might be responsible for absconding with the money. But at least his testimony makes clear that the other city council members did not likely know anything about this farce, nor did they participate in it."

"No Mayor, perhaps not, except of course the chair of the rezoning hearing who participated in another apparent farce."

"Mayor, you've been in office now for some seven years. That's a long time. And nothing quite as extraordinary as these proceedings seems to have ever happened on your watch before, and not coincidently your brother's company does not seem to have been involved in any Pineville city projects prior to this time. Would it be a reasonable conclusion, in your mind, to say that your brother and his company have created unwanted headaches and problems for you and this particular project, headaches you had not anticipated?"

Josh Hightower rose again, "I object your honor. The Mayor's feelings, including his fraternal feelings on this matter are not relevant, especially if he learned about all this after the fact."

"I tend to agree counselor. Mr. Moore, let's move along shall we?"

"I have nothing further for this witness at this time," said Benji.

"Mr. Hightower do you wish to cross examine this witness?"

"No your honor, I think he has defended himself quite well, so I will pass for now." The afternoon's session promised to be equally as revealing.

Chapter Fifty-Eight

Amber Alert Part Two

While the press may have anticipated that Vernon Lanceford was going to be called up next to the stand, Benji Moore had a curve ball to throw, and he unleashed it first thing in the afternoon session of the trial. He called Amber Lanceford. When her name was called her head popped up instantly from what she was doing, which was looking at texts on her cellphone. Yes, she knew she was on the witness list, but she did not expect to be called so soon in the trial. Her right hand began to shake as she reached out to grab the rail in front of her and propel herself up to the witness stand. Suddenly all eyes were on her, and she could hear the faint clicking of cameras behind and above her head as she walked forward. Equally suddenly, she realized that this was not going to be a walk in the park.

Benji was standing waiting for her at the witness stand, holding a paper in his hand. Once she got seated and adjusted to where she was, she looked out at the rather large audience, and became even more agitated and nervous.

Benji could see this, and so be began slowly. "Ms. Lanceford would you please tell the court your relationship with the brothers Vernon and Tom Lanceford?"

Clearing her throat, her voice cracked and she managed to get out, "The former is my brother in law, and the latter is my husband."

"Very good, and how long have you known these men?"

"I've been married to Tom for close to thirty years, and I've known the Lanceford family for most of my life here in Charlotte. I suppose you could say I've known them for well over forty years."

"Excellent. And how would you characterize your relationship with Vernon Lanceford. Is he close family?"

"I of course know him well, but it is Vernon and Tom who are truly close to each other. Because of some of the things in Vernon's past, I've kept some distance from him and his activities."

"By 'things' I take it you mean his run-ins with the law, like his DUI conviction a while back?"

"Yes, that kind of thing. In my view a Mayor and his wife ought to be above reproach, so I've kept some distance from Vernon and some of his shenanigans."

"Would it be fair to say your husband also has avoided the activities of Vernon in so far as it involved 'a walk on the wild side,' to borrow a phrase?"

"Oh yes. You heard his earlier testimony. He knew nothing at all about the kickbacks and that sort of thing, and neither did I."

"I see. So, would it come as some surprise to you that there have been some phone calls to and from your own residence which seem to have come from some people who have something to do with associates of Vernon, people who can only be called shady, at best."

"I've no idea what you are referring to."

"You're sure?"

"Yes indeed," and everyone could see Amber was turning red in the face and becoming highly agitated.

"Your Honor, I request the permission to treat this witness as a hostile witness."

"Alright Counselor, but take it easy. One step at a time."

"The prosecution presents as Item 17 this print out of phone calls to and from the Mayor's house. What is notable about the receiving phone is that it is found in Ms. Lanceford's powder room, not a room, I would suggest, that the Mayor frequents all that much, and furthermore, it is a separate line from the main landline phone in the house. Furthermore, we have now tracked down at least one of the phones used for one of those incoming calls. It belongs to one Charles Blackburn, a known felon, and sometime member of a gang called the Goon Squad."

Benji continued, "Now Ms. Lanceford, refresh your memory, if you will please. Do you, or do you not recall receiving a phone call from a Charles Blackburn? A yes or no will suffice."

Clearing her throat Amber said, barely controlling her emotions, "I refuse to answer on the grounds that it might tend to incriminate me."

"But Ms. Lanceford, you are not on trial here. It is your husband and brother-in-law that are on trial."

Again she repeated her refusal.

"Your Honor I am prepared to show in due course that Ms. Lanceford herself has been taking a walk on the wild side. In fact, I suspect, though I cannot yet prove, that she has something to do with the disappearance of the two missing witnesses on our witness list." At this remark there were several gasps in the audience, and Tom Lanceford himself looked panic stricken—"No," he whispered. "It can't be."

"My suspicions are more than suspicions your honor, because as I speak, Sergeant Delany of the Pineville police is speeding down I-85 in the general direction of Kings Mountain and Shelby, as he has good intelligence that both Jimmy Grimes and Vinny Colletti were kidnapped by the Goon Squad. The question is—Who put them up to it? Who had most to lose if they 'squealed?' Surely the answer is the Lancefords, not just because Vernon might lose a vital contract, but because Tom is coming up for re-election as Mayor, and nothing could be allowed to get in the way of those things!"

Josh Hightower bolted from his chair and said, "Your Honor, this is highly irregular, it involves a bunch of, as of yet, unsubstantiated speculations, and putting of two and two together to make five. Anyone could have called the house of the Lancefords without solicitation. For all we know Mr. Blackburn may have called to threaten the Mayor or his wife. We simply do not know."

"Mr. Moore, what do you have to say to these suggestions?"

"Your Honor, we can prove that Ms. Lanceford herself made a call to this man. A twelve-minute call. I submit here the AT&T phone record of that call. This is item Number 12 for the prosecution, and I have circled the phone call in question. The phone number underlined is Ms. Lanceford's."

"Prove it!" shouted Amber.

"Why certainly. Mr. Radcliffe, it appears Ms. Lanceford left her cell-phone on the table over there where she is seated. We all saw her come up to the dock from there. Would you kindly go over, turn on the phone, and show us all the number of that phone?"

Radcliffe grinned, ran over, and brought the phone up to the Judge, and showed him, Josh, and Amber the phone.

"With your permission Judge, may I ask Mr. Radcliffe to bring up the call log on the phone?"

The Judge said, "I'll allow it, but this is rather irregular. Let's get to the point please Counselor."

Radcliffe was easily able to show there had been an exchange of not one or two calls, but *four* outgoing or incoming ones on the cell to the Blackburn number, including one voicemail. "Since we are going down this road already, shall I play the voice mail?" asked Randle.

"Go ahead Mr. Radcliffe, in the interest of clarity. Ms. Lanceford opened herself up to this line of inquiry."

It took a minute, but Randle found the message in question, turning up the volume on the phone, and everyone except those in the far reaches of the gallery could hear a man's voice say "Hi Ms. Lanceford, Charlie here. Just to let you know Jimmy and Vinny are o.k., they're behaving themselves and not trying to escape. We'll need a little more money to keep feeding them until the trial is over, so when you get a chance, send us some via FedEx. Be in touch when you can."

The Judge said, "Ms. Lanceford, I'm afraid I'm going to have to have you remanded over into custody as a flight risk on the basis of the probable cause rules. At a minimum we are looking at obstruction of justice, which I will in due course charge you with. And I am not setting bail, at least not for a while. Bailiff, would you come and get this lady and escort her to the friendly confines of the custody hall?"

It was a sad and pathetic sight to watch as she was escorted from the courtroom. She had lost control of her emotions, and at the same time her bladder, and you could see the big stain on her bright colored pants suit, as she was ushered out in shame.

It is safe to say that almost nobody in the courtroom had been prepared for these dramatic developments, not even Vernon or Tom Lanceford. Tom had his head in his hands and was weeping, and Vernon looking like he could chew nails, he was so angry. Hightower was quickly doing the calculus of how to recover from these revelations.

"The trial will resume Monday at nine in the morning. At that time we will take the next witness and his cross examination," said the Judge, who, in an aside to Benji said, "In all my years on the bench, I've never ever seen anything as reckless as that."

Chapter Fifty-Nine

Shelby's Finest

Joe Delany had gotten to the derelict motel just quick enough to see Blackburn and his captives leaving quickly in his SUV. It was, however, hard to get the two men in leg irons into the vehicle fast enough, and so as Delany was pulling up he got a clear shot of the license plate number (DW 4713, an N.C. plate) from about fifty yards away, and he called his counterpart Bart Johnson in Shelby and gave him the plate number and description of the vehicle. "I'm going to give chase and will let you know where they are going, but I'm going to try to keep sufficient distance so they don't suspect I'm tailing them. I can tell you now, they are heading west on 74, so they are definitely coming your way. Maybe you could set up a roadblock."

"Copy that. I'm calling in J. A. West and his boys to set it up."

The SUV was barreling down 74 at well over the speed limit, in fact going about seventy-four miles-per-hour and jumping from lane to lane to make quicker progress. Their destination was a shack in a field behind the old barbecue restaurant on the east edge of town. But the roadblock was set up for them right at the city limits.

Now Highway 74 is one of those old four lane roads that has lots of crossovers, and then about thirteen stoplights as one passes through the edge of Shelby. Sergeant Johnson had deemed it wise to stop the fugitives before they really got to the heavy traffic areas.

Charlie kept checking his rearview mirror but he didn't see any police cars behind him, and so he was not worried. What he didn't know was that Delany was driving an unmarked police car. It took about twenty minutes before Charlie got close to the edge of Shelby, and just before then he thought he saw a car that had stayed close for the last several miles, so he was dividing his concentration between what was in front of him and what was behind him, and when he came up over the hill and saw four squad cars waiting, blocking the right two lanes, he quickly turned a hard left into one of the cross over places, and prepared to turn around and head back towards King's Mountain. Johnson had anticipated that move, and had three more squad cars waiting on the other side of the road. The first one pulled in front of the SUV, the second one behind it, and the third pulled up beside the SUV, rolled down the window and motioned for Charlie to pull over. "It's over son, don't make it worse than it is—PULL OVER NOW," officer West said through his bullhorn. Charlie figured it would only make things worse to keep running, so he throttled down and pulled over to the right shoulder.

Joe Delany pulled around and parked behind the SUV. He sauntered over to the driver's side of the vehicle and said, "Son, you're in a peck of trouble, and as for your detainees, they have a date with destiny back in Charlotte."

Jimmy grinned and said, "I hope Destiny's good lookin' cause I haven't had a date in a while."

"You won't be so eager to see her when I tell you she's a bailiff in the circuit court, and your testimony is required at the trial."

"Darn," said Vinny. "I was just starting to enjoy this little camping trip. Free food, no jobs to do, hanging out. No Vernon yelling at me. It was all good, except the leg irons. Speaking of which, can we get these suckers taken off now? They're a pain."

Joe smiled and replied, "Just as soon as we get back to the circuit court, get ya'll cleaned up, and on the witness stand. And as for you Mr. Blackburn, you will not be rejoining the Goon Squad, trust me."

The ride back to Charlotte in the back of Delany's cruiser, with all three men handcuffed behind their backs, was deathly quiet. Delany called ahead and informed the Judge that the witnesses had been recovered. Since it was a Saturday morning, both Vinny and Jimmy were given the hospitality of the Pineville incarceration center for the weekend, lest they run off before they testified. Monday was going to be an interesting day.

Chapter Sixty

All Things Lanceford

Sheri had never seen Vernon this depressed before. He was always feisty—full of vinegar, as they say in the South. It was like all of his sins had accumulated over the years, and now came the payback . . . in spades. Sheri actually began to feel sorry for Vernon, it seemed to her that all this turmoil, while much of it of his own making, had humanized the man, turned him into something of a more loveable, tragic figure. The truth about Sheri was that Vernon was the only man who had ever treated her half decently, and with a little love and respect. Yes, of course, he had his biological urges, but there was more to Vernon than that. At this point, from what she had heard and read about the trial (as she could not bear to attend it), it was not looking good. At this moment, they were sitting alone at the house watching TV quietly, and sipping their beverages of choice. A gloomy mood had descended on the place.

"Sugar, I was thinking when this trial is over, maybe we should just go on an extended holiday," said Sheri.

"That's a great idea, if, that is, I have any resources left after this trial is over," said Vernon grumpily.

"Oh you're a survivor. That's for sure. You haven't killed anybody, you haven't robbed anybody, so how bad can it be?"

"Yeah, you have a point. Maybe you're right. We'll see how it goes. But honey I appreciate your sticking by me. I realize this is a funny time to mention this, but honestly, I do love you, and with your permission, I'd love to make an honest woman out of you some day if we can get through this mess."

"Vernon, that's the sweetest thing anyone has said to me in a while. We can talk about that after the trial is done, meanwhile how about if you come over here and let me love on you a bit, so you'll feel better about things?"

"You do not have to ask twice," and he bounded out of his chair and found the waiting arms of Sheri.

The mood at the other Lanceford house was one of shock. Tom was not a totally naïve person, nor was he blind, but he really hadn't seen coming that his wife would pull some tricks like she did. On the one hand, he realized she was trying to protect him and protect his future. On the other hand the sheer daring, and at the same time stupidity, of it was stunning. Who was this woman whom he had been living with for decades, a woman who had never ventured much beyond her country club set, a woman who was a member of a bridge club, and did charity work, and attended church regularly? Tom could only imagine this was an act of sheer desperation. She saw things falling apart, and tried to prevent the collapse. That was all he could figure out. He would have to go visit her tomorrow, since Sunday was the day when there were visiting hours at the jail. And he would have to talk with Mr. Hightower this evening to see what could be done on her behalf, sooner rather than later. "No matter how you looked at it, this whole debacle was likely to end badly," thought the Mayor.

"Either I'm seen as innocent but oblivious to what is going on around me, or I'm seen as part of a pack of wolves. Either way, it's not good."

Liz and Jane had been enjoying themselves of late. Liz had calmed down, and was in fact reading about the trial and how badly it was going for Vernon, and this had positively cheered the girl up. She wanted him to get what was coming to him, make no mistake. Jane had continued to temper such thoughts and comments with remarks like, "You realize of course without those alimony checks I have to go get a real job, and cannot continue to entertain you in the style in which you are rapidly becoming accustomed."

"Yeah, all good things must end at some point, but hey, if I muster out, and get a local job, we could manage together. I am really almighty tired of the military, now that's for sure. Enough of that macho stuff, that 'ooo raa' chest thumping. Enough. I'd like to develop my more feminine side for a while, find somebody nice to date, and get on with life in the real world."

"That's my girl," said Jane. "I like the way you're thinking. Well, let's just see how things at the trial go, and we'll make plans from there. Somehow, in the past, Vernon has always managed to land on his feet, though it's hard to see that happening this time. Nevertheless, time will tell."

Liz and Jane had settled in to a nice pattern of domesticity, and things were looking up from their point of view. As for the rest of the Lanceford clan, not so much.

Chapter Sixty-One

The Trial Resumes

Charlotte Tate had been watching Randle's action at the trial with increasing admiration and pride. He had been the go-to-guy and real helper to Benji Moore, and had been able to provide the key evidence when it was needed. It seemed to her that he had a real knack for this line of work, and a good future in the field, even if her father had made a crack about him being like Ace Ventura. Things were looking bright from her point of view. She had seen the Sunday paper with headlines about the recovery of the lost witnesses, and she was anticipating some interesting revelations in today's session.

Judge Martin had of course remained silent about how things were going, but if he saw trouble on the horizon he wasn't giving any indication of it. He was approaching things in the business-as-usual, even-handed manner he always did. On this morning his one concession to fashion was a bright red bow tie, peaking out of the top of his black robes. When he entered the courthouse rapidly, the bailiff asked all to rise, and those still taking their seats scrambled to get to their places.

Notable for their addition to the front three rows were Vinny and Jimmy, who had shaved and been given a fresh set of clothes courtesy of their employer Vernon, who had visited them at the jail the day before, producing a certain amount of heartburn in the two men. Vernon had said nothing about their coming testimony, knowing that there were cameras rolling in the jail cell. Instead he had been all sweetness and light, "Glad you were set free, I was getting worried about you. We'll see you in the morning in the courthouse."

Benji was feeling pretty buoyant about the coming proceedings, and had once again shuffled the deck as to who would testify next.

"Call your next witness Counselor Moore," the Judge said, sounding all the world like James Earl Jones doing an Arby's commercial. He had that good deep baritone voice that conveyed authority and decisiveness.

"The prosecution calls Vinny Colletti."

Once Vinny got settled in his seat, Benji leaned over the dock at Vinny and said, "Looks like someone wanted to prevent you from being here at all. Did you know who that someone was?"

"Well, I read the papers yesterday and learned it was the Mayor's wife. I was stunned, and had no idea who it might be. Honestly at first I thought Jimmy and I were done for. That Goon Squad doesn't usually play babysitter. But that is what happened this time, thank goodness."

"Mr. Colletti, tell the court please how you came to work for Vernon Lanceford, and how long you have been employed by him."

"Certainly. Vernon actually found me through a temp service. I had been working odd jobs, including some construction and landscaping jobs, and I worked for a while for Carolina Door, and Vernon was looking for such a person, and I reckon I fit the bill."

"And would you say your relationship with Vernon has been close? Would you say you were his most trusted employee?"

"Umm, maybe. I mean Vernon and I got along well, the pay was o.k., not great, and the jobs were interesting to me."

"And had Vernon ever asked you to do anything illegal in the past?"

"Illegal? No I don't reckon so, unless you count warning people about the consequences of their actions illegal."

"Did you by any chance have anything to do with putting up the threatening sign at Masey Bumgarner's house?"

"Nope, had nothing to do with that. I was working on a paving job in Matthews when that went down, apparently."

"Were you at the rezoning hearing which was so important to your boss's future job possibilities?"

"Nope. Wasn't there either."

"Mr. Colletti, do you own a camouflage jacket?"

"Yes. Weird question, but yes, I do."

"And was the man in the camouflage jacket who was seen in the city council office by the secretary Charlotte Tate, you? Were you the person who put the brown envelopes in the city councilmen's boxes?"

"Well sir, I can't lie, that was me. But I did not know exactly what was in the envelopes. I figured it was just some thank you gift to the councilmen, Vernon was so thrilled to get the paving job for the bypass."

"You didn't stuff the envelopes, and you didn't write that little message about thank you from the employees of Salvo?"

"Nope. I just took them over and put them in the boxes and left. Maybe the secretary did the stuffing and writing, but I don't know for sure."

"Nothing further your Honor," said Benji.

"You may cross examine the witness Mr. Hightower."

Josh seemed all business this morning, and with a frown on his face came up to the dock ready for a confrontation.

"Mr. Colletti, do you have a criminal record?"

"I have a few speeding tickets, if that's what you're referring to. I've never been in jail before this past weekend if that is what you mean."

"Never?"

"No sir, not as I remember."

"Well let me jog your memory a bit. Back in 1993 were you arrested for passing bad checks?"

"Umm . . . you know I was, and I had managed to repress that ugly episode in my past. I'm sorry I forgot about that."

"Right . . . you forgot about that. I'm sorry Mr. Colletti but you don't seem old enough to be having senior moments. Tell me, is it true that you threatened my client, Mr. Lanceford, that something bad would happen if he didn't give you a raise?"

"We discussed the raise, but no, I did not threaten my boss. No way."

"The fact is, you were tired of doing some of the things Vernon asked of you, weren't you?"

"Well everybody gets tired of the same ole jobs over and over again. I mean shoveling sand, gravel, and laying cement is not exactly riveting work, now is it? It's not exactly brain food."

"No Mr. Colletti, I suppose riveting work would have to actually involve rivets."

This produced a giggle in the audience.

Mr. Hightower continued, "Tell me Mr. Colletti, have you ever told a lie when you were in a tight spot before?"

"I suppose so. Why?"

"Might you be lying about whose idea it was to give the golden hand-shakes to the city councilmen once they approved the bypass project and awarded it to Salvo?"

"Now you're not making any sense. Firstly, I don't have a pile of money. Secondly, why would I want to give a kickback to those folks? You've got to be kidding."

"Let's try another line of inquiry. Do you have any dealings with the Mayor?"

"I've run a few errands for Vernon to the Mayor, but done nothing for the Mayor."

"Have you had any previous relationship with the wife of the Mayor?"

"Absolutely not. I've only laid eyes on her a couple times in the last several years. To say the least, we don't gravitate in the same circles."

"So why do you suppose she was so eager to have you not testify in this case?"

"Well, I suppose she thought I might know something that would in-criminate the Lanceford boys."

"And do you?"

"No sir. I don't honestly believe that giving a thank you gift, after something has already been determined, counts as a bribe, nor is it illegal. So, no. I don't think so."

"Thank you your Honor, nothing further with this witness."

Despite great expectations from the press and others, this day's testi-mony had not lived up to the expectations. But as Scarlet O'Hara once said, "Tomorrow, is another day. . . ."

Chapter Sixty-Two

The Visitors

The Mayor had requested of the Judge that he be allowed to visit his wife Monday night, as she had been so exhausted he had found her asleep in her cell on Sunday, and did not want to disturb her. He had already been in shock, but seeing his wife in an orange prison jump suit, her hair all disheveled and without make-up really worried him. Amber was a high-strung person. He honestly did not think she could cope with being in this environment.

He was buzzed into the facility and escorted to the small clean cell where his wife was sitting and reading a magazine. At least she looked a bit more normal than she had looked previously.

"Hi Honey," was Tom's opening gambit.

"Hello dear, nice of you to come by," said Amber.

"I did come yesterday during visiting hours, but you were sound asleep, so I thought it best not to disturb you after all the trauma of the previous day."

"Yes, they informed me this morning. How is the trial going then?"

"I'd say right now that things look pretty shaky, and they've retrieved both Grimes and Colletti, so all the witnesses are now in place. Colletti didn't budge much or offer much, but Grimes is yet to come up to bat."

"Well, I'm still hoping for the best."

"Me too. I hear they are going to move you from here to the corrections facility in Pineville later tonight."

"Yes, well that may make some things a bit easier. So far, I've been treated alright. Other than the fact that I'm now a nervous wreck, things are o.k."

"Are you sure? Is there anything I can do, anything they'll allow me to bring you that will make you feel a little better or more normal?"

"Yes, bring me my makeup case, if they'll allow it. At least I can try to look presentable. I've got some orange gloss lipstick that might go with this jump suit." And they both tried to laugh.

"Is there anything I need to know, anything I need to do to help this situation?"

"We shouldn't be talking about that here. Just send me Mr. Hightower sometime when it's convenient. There isn't a real rush." Of course there were various things Amber would like to say to her husband, but she was sure there were cameras on them, and she was playing her cards close to the vest, or in this case, close to the jump suit.

The Mayor had to talk to his wife through the bars, and before he left he took her hand through the bars and kissed it. He could not really fathom what had driven her to have two of his brother's employees kidnapped, especially after he had now heard the lackluster testimony of one of them, which did not seem so damning to him. Maybe Grimes' testimony would be different. Tom Lanceford left the facility in a somber mood, not really daring to reflect on the future.

Two hours later, when all was quiet, there was a change over of personnel in the facility. Mrs. Lanceford was to be moved, and the usual procedure was going to be followed. Two guards, one on either side, would accompany her out of the facility and put her in the armored police truck to take her across town to Pineville. The guards were young, and had not really encountered any difficulties prior to this night.

Meanwhile, the Goon Squad had their own plans. Not only had the Lanceford woman gotten one of their chief "operatives" arrested, she had not made good on her last payment for the job they were doing for her, a payment of some $10,000 which should have been in their greedy little hands the previous week. The truth was, Mrs. Lanceford had run out of cash to pay them with, and had not remembered to go to the bank before the day she testified.

The Goon Squad had a reputation to maintain when it came to payments and personnel, and in view of the fact that Charlie Blackburn was the brother of the head of the gang, the more easy-going affable brother of

Desmond, or "Gonzo" as he was called using his nickname, something had to be done about Mrs. Lanceford. "Gonzo" figured retaliation was in order, and he also figured that with the woman in jail, she was never going to pay up. What would the other gangs and thugs of Charlotte think if the famous Goon Squad *got stiffed by a mere high society lady*? This would ruin their reputation.

So it was that Gonzo had ordered a hit on Mrs. Lanceford as she was being transferred to Pineville. He knew that his brother was unlikely to get out of jail any time soon, if ever, and revenge was on his mind. As far as he was concerned it was all the fault of Amber Lanceford and she must be made to pay, especially if she was likely to spill the beans about Charlie, and share her knowledge of the Goon Squad.

The best shooter in the gang was an older man named Rasheed Winter. Rasheed had won marksmen awards in the Army years before, but now he was the heat for the Goon Squad.

The night was dark, cloudy, and there were few lights in the parking lot behind the circuit court jail entrance. The two young men emerged from the facility, the door closing shut and locking behind them automatically. Each of them had one hand on the upper arms of Amber. About two feet before they reached the vehicle, two shots rang out from behind a huge bush at the edge of the back of the building. The first shot hit Amber in the right shoulder and knocked her back, but the second shot hit her right in the temple and went through and through. She fell to the pavement bleeding profusely, and not moving. Stunned by what happened, it took a couple of moments before one of the young men called in to the facility—"Emergency. Prisoner down, shot. We need back up immediately, and an EMT team."

While they were attending to the aftermath, Rasheed had already gotten back in his car, and driven off in the opposite direction. He flipped open his cellphone and called Gonzo. "Mission accomplished Boss. Payback administered." Careful not to speed, he slipped onto the Brookshire Parkway and headed out of town, with no one trailing him, or knowing what he had done.

Chapter Sixty-Three

Another Hiatus

The news about the shooting of the Mayor's wife spread quickly, starting with a phone call to the Mayor himself. Amber was DOA when they got her to Mercy hospital, and no amount of modern medicine was going to change the fact. The newspapers got wind of the crime and were waiting in the hospital parking lot for the Mayor to emerge. When he did, his face tear-stained and looking haggard, he stopped for a minute and said, "I would be grateful if you would respect my privacy for the next few days while I try to arrange for the funeral, and hopefully finish up this horrible trial. Mrs. Lanceford was shot twice, once through the head, and was pronounced dead when she arrived here at the hospital. We have no leads or ideas as to who could have done this. I had visited her earlier in the evening in her cell, and things seemed to be as well as could be expected. That's all for now." And he got into his black sedan and drove off.

Judge Martin of course was notified immediately as well, and in turn notified all the participants that the trial was on hold until further notice. He was relieved that the Mayor had already testified, and might not be recalled for further testimony, though he had to be available just in case. The Judge decided the smart move was to wait and see what the funeral plans were, before resetting the schedule.

News travels fast, and sometimes it seems that it is especially bad news that travels the fastest, so it was that Benji had heard the news, and immediately called both the Garcias and Masey to tell them things were on hold.

"Son it's hard to believe how many bad things have been happening since this whole bypass project was approved. You have to wonder whether the Lanceford family's bills, spiritually speaking, have finally come due. I mean all of this cannot be a mere series of unfortunate incidents—can it?"

"I agree Mom, it seems unlikely. It's just one thing after another, and we are not even near done yet. We haven't even heard from Vernon Lanceford yet. I wonder how he is taking the news."

———————————————

How Vernon heard the news was his brother had called him, as soon as it was confirmed, from the hospital to let him know that Amber was gone.

Vernon's only response was, "I'm so sorry brother, truly sorry. I hope they find out who did this to you and your family. One thing I can assure you of, it has nothing to do with me. I'm just as shocked as you are, more like shook-up in fact. I never saw this coming."

"Nor did I, but then I never thought she'd try to have your employees kidnapped to protect me either. I feel like I must have overlooked something about Amber all these years. What could have compelled her to do such a desperate thing? I know how much she loved our life and wanted to protect our reputations, but this is way beyond the pale. I'm just speechless. I'm going to take a sedative and go to bed. I've been up all night, and we still have to finish that damn trial and I've got all these funeral arrangements to make. I did mange to call Brickman Funeral Home and they will take care of things for the next day or so. I expect the funeral will be Thursday."

Vernon listened carefully and said, "I'm so sorry bro, truly. Let me know if I can help with anything."

Sheri looked over at Vernon and he looked like a lost waif. She went over and put her arms around him, but he barely responded he was in so much shock. "Amber is gone, Sheri, Amber is gone. Tom's life is never going to be the same again." Deep down inside, there was a little voice that said, "You realize, you are partly responsible for this long litany of disasters."

Chapter Sixty-Four

The Hearse And The Mourners

Despite Amber Lanceford's association with Grace Baptist Church, Tom Lanceford decided to have a quiet funeral at the funeral home, followed by an equally quiet and private interment in a plot in the cemetery on Sharon Amity Road. He wanted things short, to the point, and not a lot of religious platitudes. A funeral for a murder victim is a different sort of thing than an ordinary funeral. One is at a loss for words, and perhaps its just as well because there are no words that can make everything instantly better for someone who has his doubts about the Almighty and everlasting life, as Tom Lanceford did. All that sounded like cold comfort to him, or heavenly compensation for earthly disaster.

The funeral was only attended by family members, and a few friends from the city council. The cortege did not have far to go from Brickman Funeral Home to the cemetery. As it happened, Thursday was Masey's day to visit Buford at the same cemetery, and so she saw the somber procession, and the taking of the casket out of the hearse, and the mourners standing around the grave, about one hundred yards away from Buford's.

She took a moment to say a prayer for the Mayor and his family. "Lord, you know I'm here for Buford, but I can't help but pity those Lancefords considering all that's happened. I'd ask you shed a little mercy on them even now. I didn't intend to ruin their lives or anything like that. I just wanted to be left alone, and still do. So I ask that you work all these events together for good, and with the least harm to the Lancefords. In Jesus name, Amen."

The breeze started to pick up in the cemetery. The cemetery had almost no trees and was on a flat piece of land. Masey grabbed her sun hat, before it blew off, and walked quietly back to her new car, which she was enjoying driving. "Life never says please, it just keeps coming," she said to herself. Friday couldn't come soon enough as she was eager to get on with, and get over this trial.

Tom Lanceford stood by the graveside for quite a while after the ceremony was over. He had spent his whole adult life with Amber, and yet in the end discovered he did not know her well enough. He thought back to his old history teacher in college who had taught "crisis often reveals the true character of a person." Perhaps so, thought Tom, and going forward he promised himself he was going to try to be a person of better character, and honor Amber's attempts to protect their reputations. He said to no one but himself, "But the catch is, you have to have good character to deserve a good reputation. A good reputation needs to be earned, not given."

Chapter Sixty-Five

Grimes, And Punishment?

Jimmy Grimes looked ill suited to be wearing a suit. Nonetheless, he was wearing one, and it was obvious to even the least observant person that he was profoundly uncomfortable and unaccustomed to such attire. Whether the collar was too tight, or the pants too loose, he looked like he had stopped at Goodwill on the way to the courthouse and had grabbed whatever he could get cheaply, and at the last minute. The results were comical. As if that were not enough, being called "James" was the icing on the cake and put him out of sorts. He had not heard anybody call him that since his third grade teacher insisted on doing so.

Jimmy (don't call me James please) Grimes was the first witness on Friday morning, and Benji was determined to deal with him with some dispatch.

"Mr. Grimes, please tell the court what your occupation is."

"I work for Salvo Sand, Gravel, and Cement."

"And how long have you been employed there?"

"Oh, I reckon for about three years."

"And during that three years time, what sort of work have you been doing?"

"Honestly, a little bit of everything, I'm a sort of jack of all trades. I lay pipe, I pour cement, I haul gravel. You name it, I do it if it's got to do with that line of work."

"And how would you characterize your relationship with Vernon Lanceford? Is he a harsh taskmaster? Do ya'll get along well? Has he ever asked you to do anything illegal?"

"We've gotten along just fine, and no he has not been mean to me at all. I come to work on time, and I am reliable. I'm no expert in the law, but I can't imagine anything he asked me to do was illegal."

"No? What about roughing up people when they didn't pay Salvo on time? What about going to the rezoning hearing and calling the question too soon? He didn't suggest you do that?"

"No, not in so many words. He had made clear to all of us how huge this bypass contract would be, it would keep us in good employment for a long time, and since all of us at Salvo get paid by the job rather than by the hour, that was very important to me. I realized that if there was lots of debate at the hearing and then a lot of protest and then a divided or even a negative vote by the council, that we would be screwed, so, I took it on myself as a citizen of Pineville to act. That's all. It was my right, and I did it, neither aided nor abetted by Vernon." You could see Jimmy was getting worked up, beginning to show his short temper.

"Uh huh. And tell me Mr. Grimes, have you ever before or since that time attended a rezoning hearing, being the good citizen you are?"

"Afraid not, what a stupid question. My job had never depended on doing something like that before last August."

"Mr. Grimes have you ever attended an anger management class or training session?"

"Another stupid question," Jimmy almost shouted. "I don't need anybody to tell me how to manage my anger. I'm just fine."

"Doubtless," said Benji. "Nothing further your Honor, in regard to this witness."

"Mr. Hightower, you may cross examine now."

"Thank you for your testimony Mr. Grimes, I just want to make sure I understood your testimony. You said that Mr. Lanceford did NOT ask you to cut short the rezoning hearing by calling the question early on—right?"

"That's correct. I did that on my own, and for my own benefit. I didn't want to lose out on that job."

"And again, to be clear, you are currently and were last month as well, a resident of Pineville, is that correct?"

"Yes sir, and therefore, I had every right to speak up!"

"Very good. Tell me why do you think it is that you had been kidnapped and taken away, in view of what you have just told the court?"

"Honestly, it's a bit of a mystery to me, because nothing I had to say would have been damaging to Mr. Vernon's side of the argument, so far as I can see. Nothing."

"Looks like someone panicked and just thought you and Mr. Colletti had some dirt to dish, doesn't it?"

"I guess, but it's a puzzle to me. I feel like I'm being punished for something I didn't do, or for something I did do which was perfectly legal."

"Nothing further your Honor."

The recess that followed was in turn followed by the news that the Mayor had taken ill and was going home for the afternoon. He was running a fever, and seemed to be coming down with the flu. Not wanting anyone contaminated, the Judge adjourned early for the day, and told everyone to show up at nine on Monday morning. It was already September 25th, and the trial had been going, off and on now, for three weeks. This of course did not bother lawyers, it just meant more billable hours for them, but it was bothering the judge and the plaintiffs, who had to abide their souls in patience, and hope next week would conclude the initial proceedings.

Chapter Sixty-Six

Take Me To Church

Masey had had enough of trials for a while, and wanted to get back to her usual routine. Even Miss Perkins seemed out of sorts when Masey was at home this weekend. She wasn't doing her usual buttering up routine when she wanted more food. Benji had agreed to accompany Masey and the Garcias to Grey's Chapel Sunday morning, and Taylor Sampson greeted them at the door, "So glad you could make it. Looks like your trial may soon wind down, hopefully in a favorable way."

"Please Reverend no more trial discussion, unless the sermon today is about Pontius Pilate or Caiaphas," said Masey.

"No worries," laughed Taylor, "and I wanted to let you know I'll be there for you next week at the trial. I've cleared my calendar so I could come see the finish of things."

Since many are called, and pews are chosen, Masey wanted to get to church soon enough to be able to sit in her regular pew. Sure enough, they arrived just in the nick of time to do so, before some unsuspecting guests took their favorite spot. The church was close to packed on this nice fall morning, but then it only held 300 at the most, counting the old back balcony. Taylor had done a good job of reviving the fortunes of Grey's Chapel.

This particular service, one of two, was a so-called "blended" service with some contemporary music and some traditional music and liturgy too. Taylor was trying hard to keep everyone engaged and at least somewhat pleased with the proceedings. In any case, everyone liked him so much, they were not of a mind to complain, especially when the church was back to growing a bit and they were going to make their budget for the second year in a row.

After the anthem "Take my Hand, Precious Lord" sung by Lealthea, a large African American woman who was one of the leaders of the choir, Taylor climbed up the stairs into the rather high pulpit, read the Scripture for the morning, which was Gal 6.7–10: "Do not be deceived: God cannot be mocked. A man reaps what he sows. Whoever sows to please their flesh, from the flesh will reap destruction; whoever sows to please the Spirit, from the Spirit will reap eternal life. Let us not become weary in doing good, for at the proper time we will reap a harvest if we do not give up. Therefore, as we have opportunity, let us do good to all people, especially to those who belong to the family of believers."

Closing his Bible, Taylor shuffled his notes and began: "For any Christian person, the notion that God has programmed a moral compass into the very nature of human reality seems obvious. By this I mean there is indeed a moral arc to human affairs. God cares about justice and injustice. And here it will be well to make some distinctions. Justice is when you get what you deserve. Sometimes people holler for justice, when really they should be begging for mercy. Mercy, by contrast, is when you *don't* get what you deserve, and what you deserved was judgment. Grace is yet a third thing altogether. It is undeserved blessing or benefit. Unmerited favor or largesse. Mostly, when people cry for justice, what they really need is mercy or grace, because all of us sin and fall short of God's high standards of rectitude. All of us. None of us have perfect knowledge of all circumstances, situations, and what would be best. None of us."

"In our text for today, St. Paul is reassuring his converts that there is indeed a just God out there in whose hands justice should be left. He reassures that you reap what you sow. If you sow evil and wickedness, it is going to come back to bite you, not because there is some sort of impersonal predetermined nature of things such that 'what goes around, comes around.' No, Paul is talking about how God runs the universe, not how the universe runs itself. If we leave those sorts of matters in God's hands, then what should we preoccupy ourselves with?"

"Paul says we should focus on doing good to all persons, especially to our fellow Christians. He calls it sowing, and the metaphor suggests that such sowing will in due course produce later benefits, later rewards. Life is not like the Publisher's Clearing House Sweepstake, where purely by a one in a million chance, somebody hits the mother load. No, Paul is saying that you actually reap what you sow, and if you sow good things, good things will bless you in some way going forward. This is not random, it's the way God has set up things, both for the good and the wicked."

The sermon continued along these lines for another twenty minutes, and Masey was lost in thought. She began to ask herself, how, perhaps, she might be a blessing even to the Lancefords when all was said and done with the trial. She made a mental note to ponder this more in the next week or so.

When the final hymn was sung, followed by the benediction, Masey said to the pastor who was standing at the door, "Fine sermon today, you sowed some good in my plot, and now I'm thinking you should reap some. Why don't you and your wife come join us for lunch down at McCormick and Schmicks at South Park? It's on us."

"I'll have to ask Jillian, but we are free, and we like the company and that food, so she's likely to say yes. We'll see you there in a bit once I close up the church." Masey was thankful for the good service, and it helped put her back on the right track mentally, as she approached the last week of this ordeal.

Chapter Sixty-Seven

Vernon's Vicissitudes

With everyone expecting to hear from Vernon Lanceford at last, Benji Moore pulled his one further ace out from his sleeve and called Grace Mc-Ghee. By this time in the trial, Grace had begun to be convinced she would not be called at all, and she had crossed her fingers that she never would be. But suddenly, she heard her name called, and slid out of her seat on the third row and came forward. She was wearing an all-white suit, with a Carolina blue blouse under it.

Grace McGhee was forty-seven years old, and while a part time employee of the city of Pineville, as a city council woman, her full time job was working at an architectural firm in Charlotte, designing bridges, overpasses, and the like. Over the years, the firm she worked with, Prime Designs, had gotten many contracts from the city of Charlotte as the city continued to grow and expand. She knew more than a little about construction projects.

Benji approached the dock, smiled, and began, "Ms. McGhee, tell us all first who your father is, and what he used to do."

"Johnson McGhee, my father, was the State Highway Commissioner for some twenty-five years. Only last year he retired, and is enjoying his retirement in Pinehurst. He loves playing golf."

"Would it be fair to say that you yourself, as a designer at an architectural firm, know quite a bit about roads and highways in North Carolina, especially here in the Charlotte area?"

"Yes indeed. I've been proud to serve our community and help it continue to grow and progress and become more prosperous."

"And so would it also be fair to say that you were very much a supporter of this bypass project off Highway 51."

"Yes, I was definitely in favor of it."

"On the day of the rezoning hearing, what was your role?"

"I was chairwoman on the day."

"So, it was you who responded to Mr. Grimes when he called the question early on in the proceedings—right?"

"Yes, I suppose you could put it that way. The normal way to read Robert's Rules is that when the Question has been called, then debate stops."

"Yes, normally, but it was within your power to allow some more discussion, was it not? You could have asked Mr. Grimes to hold his fire for a bit, couldn't you?"

"I guess, but I'd never seen that done. It's not the usual process."

"No, but it is within the bounds of the rules."

Judge Martin was getting impatient. "Mr. Moore, is this line of questioning going somewhere?"

"Yes your Honor, I'll be getting to the point jiffy quick."

"Good. Do so, as my patience is wearing thin."

"Ms. McGhee did you by any chance receive a benefit from Vernon McGhee, before you chaired the meeting on that day, a benefit, that would help pay for your child to attend Country Day School?"

And here, Ms. McGhee hesitated to respond. She fidgeted and said nothing.

"Ms. McGhee," said the Judge in his deep voice. "You must answer the question, now, not later."

"Mr. Lanceford is a kind man, and yes he provided some scholarship money for my Katie. It's so expensive to have a child in that school."

"Doubtless. I couldn't afford it. So in effect, Mr. Lanceford was giving you a bribe or an incentive to help grease the wheels of the bypass project which he had won the contract for—right?"

"I suppose you could put it that way, but I was already in favor of the project. In other words, the gift didn't really affect the way I voted on the contract."

"Perhaps not, but it certainly made you a less than impartial chair of that meeting now didn't it? If you knew you had received a gift like this, which could definitely be interpreted as a bribe, why didn't you recuse yourself, and let someone else chair that meeting?"

There was no answer. "Ms. McGhee, answer the Counselor."

"Well . . . because I wanted to make sure it got done right. I wanted to please Vernon after the nice thing he had done for my daughter."

"I see. And thus we are not talking about your pleasing your constituents, but rather pleasing the man who had given you a financial boon. Nothing further your Honor."

Josh Hightower came up and said, "I have but one question. Did, or did not Vernon McGhee ask you directly to make sure that hearing went the right way?"

"No, not in so many words. He just said, I trust all will go well at the hearing. That was it."

"Your Honor, nothing further with this witness."

The lunch recess this time was short. Everyone, including those on trial, was eager to get on with the afternoon session. Benji reviewed his notes while wolfing down a Subway sandwich with Masey. She was unusually quiet, anticipating what was to come. At precisely 1 o'clock the afternoon session was gaveled into life, and Benji stood and finally called Vernon Lanceford.

Vernon had been dressed up for the occasion by Sheri. He was wearing khaki pants and a nice tweed jacket with a tan shirt and a dark brown tie. He looked, for all the world, like an advertisement for Belk's Men's Department. Taking his time to reach the dock, he turned back and smiled at Sheri, who gave him the thumbs up.

Benji had decided on a slow wind-up to the real punch, "So Mr. Lanceford, how long have you owned Salvo Sand, Gravel, and Cement?"

"About twenty years or so."

"And has this been a profitable business?"

"For the most part, yes, but there are so many darn paving companies around here that it is a challenge."

"Indeed, a challenge. So when a contract of a lifetime falls into your lap, you feel like you've won the lottery right?"

"For sure."

"Only, it didn't quite happen just by chance now did it?"

"If you are insinuating that I bribed the council to pick my company to do the job, then you would be wrong. They just took the lowest bidder."

"Uh huh, and tell me Mr. Lanceford, since that meeting was a closed proceeding, how exactly did you or any of the other bidders know what the low bid would be?"

"Well . . . a little bird told me what the next to lowest bid was of the other bidders."

"Would that little bird be named Grace?"

"Umm . . . I'm not supposed to say."

"To the contrary, confession is good for the soul. Cough it up Mr. Lanceford, did you put in your final bid with inside help from Grace McGhee?"

"I reckon you could put it that way."

"Thank you, I don't enjoy prying things out of people with a pitch fork. And since we are on the subject of Ms. Grace, did you, or did you not, send money to the trust fund account of Country Day as a scholarship for little Katie?"

"You got me on that one. I plead guilty of being helpful to a smart child who needed a good education. Just shoot me now."

"Very funny Mr. Lanceford, but this is a serious matter because under any sort of normal way of thinking, that sir, is a bribe."

"So just call me abnormal, but not illegal."

"So let's see if we can sum up what we've learned about you: 1) you went to a widow's house and tried to brow beat her out of her lawsuit, and probably left a threatening sign in the process. We only found out about this due to the good offices of the attack cat Miss Perkins. (This produced a big laugh all around); 2) you provided money, with the aid of Vinny Colletti, your employee, after the fact, to each city councilman having won the contract, although as we heard from the testimony of Mr. Street, he absconded with the lot of it; 3) you also had your employee Jimmy Grimes conveniently present at the only rezoning hearing he had ever attended, and it was him, and no one else, who called the question prematurely; 4) we have just heard from you that Ms. McGhee told you what the next lowest bid was on the paving contract, and in addition you paid for her child's education, even before the vote was taken on the contract, never mind the rezoning hearing."

"Mr. Lanceford, tell us the truth, how much of all these shenanigans did your brother Tom know about?"

"None of it before the fact, but of course all of it after the fact, if you mean up to today. Just so you know, he's chastised me several times for my 'indiscretions', he being the white sheep of the family. And no, he did not put anyone up to giving me that paving contract. Never once."

"You seem to be doing a better job of being your brother's keeper than he was doing earlier in this trial. I have one final question, Mr. Lanceford."

"Is it true that you are dating a pole dancer from the Platinum Club and have provided her with a red Corvette Sting Ray, and are doing your best to accommodate her in the lifestyle she has grown accustomed to?"

"Frankly, that's none of your business."

"Actually it is, as it says something about your character, and your need for that contract to go through. It provides a further clear motive for all these immoral and illegal activities. Nothing further your Honor."

Josh Hightower realized he need to do some serious damage control, and so his first question was surprising, "Mr. Lanceford, would you tell the Judge and the Jury something about your relationship with your father, compared to his relationship with your brother?"

"My Dad was a tough old bird, used to run moonshine from the mountains to Charlotte. He drank a lot, and I got beaten a lot too in the process. I was the older brother and Tom always used to hide when Dad came home drunk, so I took the brunt of the abuse."

"And how long did this abuse go on?"

"All my growing up years, until I got big, and one day, when I was seventeen, the scoundrel came home drunk again, was about to deck me, and I had had enough, I beat him to the punch. Knocked him out cold. He never tried anything like that again."

"I'll bet he didn't. What happened after high school?"

"Well, Tom was the smart one in the family, so he went off to college, and I worked construction jobs around town. Eventually I saved up enough to start my own business from scratch. I did not inherit Salvo, I created it from nothing."

"There's a line from an old hymn 'we feebly struggle, they in glory shine'—would that about sum up your life as opposed to the Mayor's?"

"I reckon, but we got along fine. We never had a falling out, even when he was mad at me for some of my somewhat more marginal activities."

"Tell me Mr. Lanceford, have you ever been accused or prosecuted for illegal business dealings in the past?"

"Nope never."

"And has anyone ever complained about your not doing the paving or construction work well, to the highest standards?"

"Nope never."

"Would it be fair to say you've had a hard life, and yet you've managed to create a business and work hard, and been successful at it, despite your upbringing? Sure you've made some small mistakes along the way like all of us, but fairly evaluated, you've made a good contribution to your community?"

"Yes sir. I believe so. I ain't claiming to be no saint, but it would be unfair to say I was a criminal."

"Thank you. Nothing further your Honor."

The Judge then said, "And that completes the testimony for this case, we will now hear the summary perorations from the prosecuting and defense attorneys."

Benji had worked on this speech for a long time, honing it, editing it, adding to it, trying it out on Masey, and at home and on Miss Perkins, until she sauntered off yawning, until he finally gave up, convinced it was as good as he could manage. He arose when called, and took his lectern and set it right in front of the jury box, and began . . .

"Ladies and Gentlemen of the jury, you have now heard a large number of testimonies of various sorts, some more colorful than others, but all of it significant when it comes to seeing justice done in these matters. It has been said that justice is blind, by which is meant impartial, but justice cannot also afford to be deaf and dumb. In order to figure out what amounts to a just resolution of this court case a good deal of critical thinking is required. One must be able to separate out facts from special pleading, legality from morality, and so on. It is not an easy task, and I would urge you to take your time and get the verdict right. I'm sure we are all tired by this point of delving into all these matters, but now, above all times, is the time for concentrated and careful and clear thinking, and a just outcome to the proceedings. We all trust that you are fully capable of producing such an outcome. So let me summarize for you what I see as the salient facts of the case that should be decisive in determining the outcome of the trial."

"Firstly, in regard to the issue of whether malfeasance, collusion, tampering, and even bribery happened in order for Salvo Sand, Gravel, and Cement to get the contract for the bypass project, surely any fair person would say "yes"—there is plenty of evidence for all of that, and therefore the contract should be voided, and the perpetrators be dealt with according to the penalties of Law."

"Secondly, it seems clear that the chief perpetrators of this mess were indeed Vernon Lanceford, and his employees Jimmy Grimes and Vinny

Colletti, and that they worked in tandem with the forewoman of the city council to achieve their aim, resorting to bribery, and also to kickbacks after the fact to all the city council members. In short, it was a dirty business from start to finish. We may have some doubt that the Mayor was completely ignorant of all these proceedings going on behind his back. At the very least he appears to have practiced benign neglect, and allowed illegalities to happen on his watch, so badly did he want this project to sail quickly through the approval process. Remember it was indeed the Mayor who instigated the changing of the rules about the number of rezoning hearings for public works projects."

"In regard to the actions of Amber Lanceford, we must leave her in the hands of a high court and a greater judge, and so we say nothing about her actions except that she seems to have thought that her husband's legacy and future re-election was at stake and depended on whether or not the bypass project was approved and properly executed. As for Brad Street and his pilfering of funds from the city council mailboxes, that too must be a matter for a different court, and another time, should it be deemed a sufficiently serious crime to deserve a trial. That matter should not distract us from the main issue we are adjudicating here. Before you listen to Mr. Hightower, and his eloquent rhetoric, I would simply remind you to not to let your emotions sway your good judgment. No matter how much sympathy you may have for the Mayor, and it is right to feel badly for him and even to pray for him with the sudden tragic loss of his wife, that must not be allowed to erase in your mind the facts of the case. Furthermore, while we all may feel pity for Vernon Lanceford and his relationship with an abusive father, that cannot, and should not, prejudice our judgment about his actions many years later as an adult. I trust that none of us believes we are simply a product of our upbringing, simply automatons pre-programed to behave a certain way as adults. No, as adults we have choices about our behavior, whatever our past may have been, and precisely because we do have choices, we should be held responsible for our behavior as adults. The past does not *determine* the present or future in these matters, though it may *incline* a person in one direction or the other. Our emotions must not cloud our thinking on these matters."

"Finally, I would exhort you to do your very best to come to a fair and balanced and just decision in this matter. Over here sits a brave widow, a widow without vast resources, who mustered up her courage to object to an unjust proceeding which compromised the integrity of her property without her having a say in the matter, a proceeding without a single thought to how it might effect the lives of the Garcias either, her neighbors. All these people want is to be left in peace. They have not asked for punitive damages, nor have they sought to damage or sully the reputation of any person. They simply plead for justice. I am sure if you were in these people's shoes, you would want the same thing as well. And I believe you can and will hear their plea and respond accordingly in due time."

This speech was delivered in a good clear voice, and the pathos of it rose as Benji got to the last two paragraphs where he brought it all home. There was brief applause from some quarters in the gallery, which Judge Martin silenced with a word. "Mr. Hightower, you now have the floor."

Joshua strode to the lectern, and looked from left to right at the jurors, and could see no sympathy in their faces for his clients. Accordingly, he took a different tack than he might ordinarily have done.

"Sometimes, we all must consider the greater good of the greatest number of persons, when we make choices in regard to public works projects. Almost always, someone is inconvenienced, almost always someone cries foul, almost always someone has to move, or change their circumstances when a major road project, or mall project, or bridge project, or park project, or the like has to be undertaken. You will have noticed that despite the rhetoric of Counselors Moore and Lessing, they more or less have *not* told you that they are only representing three people, three people in a Pineville community of thousands. If there was such a groundswell of opposition to building a bypass down Buttermilk Lane, surely, surely we would have had many litigants, maybe even a class action lawsuit. Instead, we have three disadvantaged persons who are grumbling because they will lose a part of their front yard. Yes, that's all, a part of their front yard. Not all their property, not their houses, just some dirt and grass. That's it."

"Now I am going to assume that all of you are in favor of progress, of the appropriate development of a community, of increasing the number of jobs and the prosperity of Pineville, and other parts of greater Charlotte. Surely, that is a larger goal, a good goal, which should cause us to lift our eyes beyond the laments of a very few, and see the greater good of the many. And if that is our thinking, then it would be unjust to find the Lancefords guilty of what they have been accused of. This is not to deny that a few things may have been done to grease the wheels of the process, things that are often done in such circumstances to make sure of a good and proper outcome, things which strictly speaking are not above reproach."

"Call it dirty politics, call it smoke-filled room business tactics, call it what you will, but at most these sort of things usually result in fines, and nothing else, while progress is allowed to continue. In other words, I am saying that even if you think the Lancefords are guilty of some illegality, you must make sure that the punishment actually fits the crime. And as Counselor Moore so eloquently said, I am trusting that your emotions will not be allowed to outweigh your good reasoned judgments in this matter. You may not like Vernon Lanceford. You may not approve of some of his actions. You may think his private life is a mess. But this should not determine how you evaluate the matter of the legality of what went on. Let that be your sole focus, and you will not go wrong. Thank you for your time and attention." There was no applause at this juncture, only stony silence.

As Josh was walking back to his desk, the Judge arose, prompting everyone to stand. Turning and facing the jury he said the following:

"Ladies and Gentlemen of the jury, there has been lots of colorful testimony at this trial. What is germane from the point of view of the law, is whether or not this bypass project was illegally granted to Salvo Sand, Gravel, and Cement. Was there actual bribery involved? Was there malfeasance? Was there collusion between Mr. Vernon Lanceford and some member or members of the city council, and was the Mayor involved? It is your job to determine only the guilt or innocence of the Lancefords in this matter. It is my job to impose sentence. I will ask you, since the hour is late already today, to come by nine in the morning and begin your deliberations. If you have questions for me, I shall be here in the courthouse and you may send me messages. After hours you may send me text messages. Under no circumstances, and I do mean no circumstances, are you to discuss this matter with anyone other than the other members of the jury until the trial is complete. Not to the press, not to family members, not to your Facebook friends, to no one. If you cannot reach a verdict, then you will need to let me know that as well, but I would urge you to do your best to agree on a verdict. We will look forward to hearing from you when you are ready. You will be sequestered for the full time of your deliberations. You will be able to go to the bathroom adjoining the deliberations room, and a bailiff will take your meal orders as needed. We will see you in the morning."

Chapter Sixty-Eight

The Jury's Still Out

Trial by jury is an interesting phenomenon. It can produce just results, unjust results, and no results. Sometimes it's just a crapshoot, depending on the permutations and combinations of personalities and the interpersonal dynamics that exist in the little room where the jury hammers out a verdict. As for Masey, she was not holding her breath. The Judge had told the litigants that they could wait at home, and wait for the phone call from the bailiff to return to the court, because of course the deliberations could be short or long.

Whether it was the calm before the storm, or the calm after the storm, Masey felt at peace about what had happened and what would happen. She had not allowed herself to think ahead if the bypass project was allowed to go forward as was currently planned. Instead, she spent extra time in prayer on Monday morning, enjoyed watching *The Price is Right* with Miss Perkins on her lap, and in general puttered around the house, doing a little cleaning and a few housekeeping chores. She remembered to take her cell phone with her when she went to Harris Teeter at 11:00 in the morning, but still the phone never rang.

Meanwhile, in the home of the Mayor, there was much less peace of mind or heart. The Mayor felt like things had gone poorly enough that his hopes of re-election were effectively compromised, if not dashed altogether, and he worried his brother was going to end up in jail for an extended period of time. Then there was the mess with the bypass project, and the promises he had already made to some Mexican developers. He supposed that maybe he could find another route for the bypass, but that didn't bear thinking about until the verdict was in. And like the others he kept his cell phone on, and with him at all times, but when lunch rolled around, there was still no word.

Vernon Lanceford, on the other hand, was not bothering to keep his cell phone on. He figured it was likely to be bad news, and he didn't want to face it just yet. He was surprised that Sheri had not ditched him yet, indeed, they had seemed to come closer in the wake of all this bad news, like two persons together in a fox hole while the shells were being lobbed over their heads, and at them.

Jimmy Grimes and Vinny Colletti in fact went back to work on Monday morning, though with their cell phones on them at all times, and spent the morning doing some preparatory things just in case, by some miracle, that the paving project was still on. They were not entirely surprised not to hear from or see the boss, but they figured he'd surface eventually, or they would see him for sure when everyone was summoned back to the courthouse. The waiting was irritating, so these two sought to keep themselves busy, and thus distracted, by means of hard manual labor.

Josh Hightower had his own doubts as to how good a job he had done, but he was hoping he had done just enough to avoid the worst kind of verdict. Frankly Vernon's activities of various sorts had not helped matters much. There was only so much smoke you could blow in the juror's eyes when it came to some of the things he had done.

Hightower had never yet lost a high profile case before, but he had some trepidations about this one, simply because Vernon was very hard to defend. It was now Monday mid-afternoon and Hightower poured himself a large glass of Woodford Reserve bourbon, and put his feet up on his office desk, and drank slowly, sipping the bourbon which burned his throat as it went down and warmed him up internally. Suddenly his cellphone rang in his jacket pocket, startling him and causing him to spill a bit of the bourbon on his suit. Hitting the green button, he placed the phone to his ear and said,

"Yes? The jury is back in, and we should be to the courthouse by five? Will do. I'll alert my clients." As he scrambled to make the necessary phone calls, and get a washrag from his washroom, to wipe the spill on his vest, he thought, "That was pretty fast. They were only deliberating for seven hours or so."

Chapter Sixty-Nine

Judgment Day

As the fall sun was setting through the far windows in the courthouse, all the interested parties reassembled to hear the verdict of the jury. The shadows were long in the courtroom, and indeed the whole defendants side of the courtroom was cast in shadow, while Benji and his clients were still bathed in the late afternoon sun, as was the Judge. Once everyone was seated, the Judge turned to the jury and asked, "Ladies and Gentlemen of the jury, have you reached a verdict?" Masey rolled up her little legal sheet and was squeezing it tightly.

A tall African American woman, who was the forewoman of the jury, stood up and said in a deep, resonant voice: "Yes your honor we have."

The judge said, "In regard to the charge of collusion, and malfeasance, and bribery, how do you find the defendant Thomas Lanceford?"

"We find the defendant NOT guilty, your honor." With this you could see a little fist pump from Josh Hightower and several members of his team, and Masey visibly slumped down in her chair, with Benji patting her hand.

"In regard to the charge of collusion and malfeasance and bribery, how do you find the defendant Vernon Lanceford and his employees?"

"We find Mr. Lanceford and his company GUILTY in the first degree."

Then the Judge said, "Thank you for your good service. You have done well, and you are now dismissed with the thanks of the court."

Slowly the jury members filed out one by one, through the door on the left side of the courtroom. Once decorum was re-established, all eyes were on Judge Martin, who began . . .

"It is now my job to impose sentence. I have thought long and hard about this matter over the course of this month, and indeed even before this month, when I saw the item on my calendar. I personally have found the behavior of both Mr. Vernon Lanceford and some of his employees, and indeed some of the members of the Pineville city council, to be reprehensible and a violation of the public trust. The statute of limitations of what can and cannot be imposed in a bribery case in the state of North Carolina is reasonably clear, and so though I might be inclined to impose an even stiffer sentence, I have had to accept what the maximum sentence is for such a total violation of the public trust."

"Accordingly, I am therefore imposing an $100,000 fine on Salvo Sand, Gravel, and Cement, and have asked the state attorney general to void the public contract with that company. I am further imposing a three-year jail sentence on Mr. Lanceford himself, with the possibility of parole after a year. Further, I am tasking the Pineville City Council to re-evaluate the other bids and find a new construction company. Further, I am tasking them with finding an alternative route for the bypass that does not involve Buttermilk Lane" (at this juncture Masey let out an involuntary yelp and a "Thank you Jesus"). "Pineville may need a bypass, but it doesn't need to run through the front yards of the Bumgarners and the Garcias. Finally, I suspect the electorate will realize it needs a better balanced city council in the future, so perhaps wisdom will prevail at the next election."

"That concludes our proceedings in this trial. We are all free to go, except for Mr. Vernon Lanceford, who should be cuffed and taken off to jail to serve his proper sentence, beginning immediately." As this sorry spectacle played out, Sheri Lavalier could be seen to be weeping, sitting in her seat behind the row of defendants. As it turned out, she was one of the more honest and loyal persons sitting on that side of the aisle.

By the time the Judge had finished, the sun had fully gone down in the west, and Masey and Benji and the other participants in the trial emerged from the courtroom to see the city lights just winking on, lighting up the surrounding streets.

Masey was holding on tight to Benji's arm, as her vision at twilight was not good, but when she was standing on the top step of the courthouse she looked down into a sea of reporters faces and microphones. She took a deep breath and said to Benji, "Do we have to got through this hoopla?" He nodded and said, "Let's just get it over with."

"Ms. Bumgarner, how do you feel now that the trial is over?" asked a short man with a large microphone.

"Relieved more than anything else, and pleased that there was a fair and just outcome to the trial. I confess to having had some doubts along the way."

"Ms. Bumgarner, do you and the Garcias plan to further litigate against Ms. McGhee, or Brad Street, or other parties?"

"No, definitely not. We do hope someone will be tracking down Amber Lanceford's killer. But we are not after revenge, nor monetary compensation in regard to anyone. We are just Christian folk, who now want to be left alone. I have no further comments. God bless you all."

As the van that was carrying them back to Pineville rolled out of the parking lot to the flashing of various cameras, Masey finally allowed herself to relax, and unclench her fists, and think about the future.

"You know Benji," she said quietly, "I like that saying of a famous missionary whose name escapes me at the moment. He said 'the future is as bright as the promises of God.' I believe he is right, and I'm looking forward to an unclouded day ahead."

"Si," said Jesus and Maria from the back seat. "Us as well."

"Well I wonder if you bothered to check your mail early this afternoon?"

"Nope, I did not do that yet, why?"

"Because I, and I'm sure you, got a fancy invitation to a Christmas wedding for one Charlotte Tate, and Mr. Randle Radcliffe, my P.I., to be held at Grace Baptist Church, reception to follow at Quail Hollow Country Club."

"Well isn't that special. That gives us all something to look forward to as we head towards Advent. But let's not rush things. Basketball season is almost upon us, and I'm looking forward to seeing how the Tar Heels are gonna do, and razzing Taylor Sampson about his Duke team."

"Now that sounds more like my spunky Momma," laughed Benji. "Let's go have some nice dinner somewhere, and celebrate, if the Garcias have the time?"

"Si, just fine. Babysitter is hired until later. How about we go to our favorite—Me Mexico!"

" Excellent," said Benji. "We can teach Masey how to eat a hot tamale!"

"What are you talking about Benjamin, we've been handling hot tamales for weeks now, if you catch my drift." And the happy band, road off to enjoy a victory dinner.

Chapter Seventy

An Unexpected Benefaction

It had been some weeks now since the trial was over, and Tom Lanceford had settled back into his regular routines. The press, for once, had been merciful, perhaps out of respect for the shocking loss of his wife, and he had begun to think that perhaps he could indeed win re-election. No progress had been made at all in finding his wife's killer, but somehow that dark cloud seem to recede to the horizon of his mental world, and had not bothered him much.

It was a Saturday and the calendar was just turning to November, and the Mayor had allowed himself to have a day off for a change. For over a month he had buried himself in his work, keeping his head down, and hoping for the best. He had managed to find an alternate route for the bypass to Highway 51, one that only involved knocking down a derelict business or two, and did not pass through any residential neighborhoods. He thought the prospects were good that the city council would approve a new bid from another company in a week or so, and then there would need to be another hearing, this time with full debate and no premature vote! Still, he had confidence the measure would pass, and he could finally call his investors in Mexico and tell them "all's well that ends well."

Tom Lanceford had also visited his brother several times in the local "white collar" jail in Charlotte, and amazingly enough Vernon had been in good spirits, saying he was going to be on his best behavior going forward, not least because Sheri had said she would stand by him and wait for him. Vernon hinted that when he got out, there might be a surprising wedding in the Lanceford family! He was determined to be a model prisoner so he could be paroled after a year. Sheri was his motivation.

The doorbell range at about 11:00 that morning while the Mayor was sitting and writing a few emails. It was Johnny's Florist, bringing a beautiful bouquet. Flowers had stopped coming almost a month ago, after Amber's funeral. This was a beautiful arrangement of freesia and roses, and it came with a large card.

The Mayor sniffed the aromatic roses and smiled and said to himself, "Who in the world could be sending me flowers now?"

"When he opened the card a somewhat lengthy note fell out of it, which he picked up and began to scan. It read as follows . . .

> *Dear Mayor Lanceford:*
>
> *You might well think that I would be the last person writing you a note like this, but I wanted to send you something that might cheer you a little bit, bringing you a small measure of joy, as you work through your grief in losing your wife of many years. I know very well what that is like, having lost my Buford three years ago after close to forty good years of marriage. I wanted you to know that I have been very regularly praying for you, including with my Wednesday prayer group at Grey's Chapel that you might heal and go on to do some great things for the city of Pineville. I wish you nothing but blessings and good things going forward.*
>
> *I wanted you to know that I do not blame you for all of the things that did go wrong, and since I believe in a God of second chances, I've even been praying you'd have a good chance at re-election next time around. Don't be discouraged by the difficulties of the past, gain strength from those trials, and resolve to go forward in a way that makes you an even better public servant. I hope you enjoy the flowers.*
>
> *Yours very sincerely,*
> *Masey Bumgarner*

The Mayor, shaking his head, shed a tear or two, and said quietly, "That just beats all. I never saw that one coming." And he sat for a moment and was thankful that perhaps there was actually a God of second chances.

Chapter Seventy-One

Postlude Is Prelude

Three months after the trial . . .

The snow was falling lightly, and it was one of those pretty snows—big flakes and dry—not sloppy and wet. Masey had gone briefly to the graveyard to visit with Buford, before coming home and getting dressed for the wedding. She resolved to wear her dark blue suit, and the Garcias were coming over with their kids to have some playtime with Miss Perkins and to cat-sit for the afternoon so Masey could attend the wedding in peace. Miss Perkins had been making a regular habit of getting stuck in the cat door and not being able to extract herself, and Masey didn't want her stuck out in the cold or half in and half out letting all the cold air in the house.

Benji showed up wearing his best Sunday suit—the one with the Carolina blue pin stripes—and when he arrived to pick up Masey she was ready right on time, walking right out into the carport as the car drove up slowly. The snow kept coming all through the day, and was beginning to accumulate in her front yard. Benji jumped out and helped her to the passenger's side door, since she was wearing her best heels for the wedding.

"Lord have mercy, I didn't really expect all this snow today. But then again it is December 22nd, so I guess I shouldn't be surprised." She handed Benji the gift she had bought and wrapped for Randle and Charlotte, and Benji put it in the backseat of the car, alongside his own.

"Let's go for a little ride out to Grace Baptist Church, shall we?"

Masey had only been to Grace Baptist once before, for a funeral, and her memory of it was that it was a very lovely Baptist Church that had been a church plant. She enjoyed seeing so many young people in the church, and wished her own church had as many. The parking lot was packed when she and Benji arrived, and there was actually a parking attendant directing them to a spot, after Benji had made clear he had a senior citizen with him.

They arrived a good thirty minutes before the service started, but the prelude music was already going strong—a blend of traditional and contemporary Christian hymns and songs. The piano was in good tune, and filled up the worship space quite nicely with music that set the mood for the coming events. Masey looked over to her right, and saw one of the flower girls running down the side aisle, chasing her little brother, who apparently was the ring bearer. This produced a good chuckle.

Then it was time for the procession down the aisle, first the family of the groom, then the family of the bride, were escorted to the front, then came the groom's men who entered from the side aisle, and the bridesmaids came down the aisle. Then there was the flower girl strewing rose petals on the carpet from a little white basket as she walked, then the ring bearer, being shepherded down the aisle by the Maid of Honor, since he didn't seem to be able to manage on his own. Finally the Mendelsohn wedding march music signaled for all to rise in honor of the bride, who was escorted down the aisle by her obviously very nervous father. Charlotte was simply beaming and taking it all in. Various persons in the congregation were whispering about how beautiful the dress was, and there were tears being shed by both families, and their friends. The videographer was filming as best he could without being intrusive.

You could tell that this wedding had been a long time coming for both the bride and the groom. Masey noticed on her side of the aisle (she was seated with the friends of the groom) all the policemen in uniform to support their former fellow officer Randle Radcliffe. She wondered what they had in store for him at the reception, where there would be a roasting of the groom.

The minster was standing in front of the baptismal font and altar on the raised chancel floor, and once the wedding party was settled into place, he said, "You may now all be seated."

Masey was simply beaming, thinking, "Now this is the kind of public event I really appreciate being a part of," and Benji could tell how happy she was to be there for this event. She whispered to Benji, "It must have been 103 degrees in the shade when Buford and I got married in Weddington in June of 1976. This is much better."

Then the minister said, "Dearly beloved, we are gathered here today to join in holy matrimony this couple, Charlotte and Randle. Marriage is a holy estate and is not to be entered into without due prayer, reflection, and counseling, for when Christ joins a man and a woman together it is meant to be 'until death do them part.'"

Masey hardly heard the pastor, as she was lost in reverie about the day she got married, and was saying her own little thank you again to the Lord for so many good years with Buford. She whispered again to Benji, "This is so much better than that sorry ole trial, which led mostly to sadness and trouble for so many folks. But this day is about heart-joy, not heartache."

They got to the point in the service where there was a hymn to be sung, this, after all, being a Baptist wedding, and surprisingly they had picked a Reformation hymn, but then this was a Reformed Baptist Church. What struck Masey were these lines . . .

> Did we in our own strength confide, our striving would be losing;
> Were not the right Man on our side, the Man of God's own choosing:
> Dost ask who that may be? Christ Jesus, it is He;
> Lord Sabbaoth, His Name, from age to age the same,
> And He must win the battle.
> And though this world, with devils filled, should threaten to undo us,
> We will not fear, for God hath willed His truth to triumph through us

Masey elbowed Benji and whispered, "See, we are not undone, because someone was on our side in all that trial stuff."

"Amen to that. Nothing like a good wedding to wash the bad taste of the last few months out of our mouths."

And finally, finally, Masey shed the last bit of worry about her situation and got caught up in love, and wonder and praise of yet another marriage betokening life, even life everlasting. "I've still got a lot left to live for," she whispered to Benji, "and it's not just to keep Miss Perkins fed and happy either!"

A large smile creased the face of Benji as a response to this last interjection. Though the snow was coming down heavily now as he looked out the window, Benji thought it seemed more like an unclouded day in his life and that of his irrepressible Mom, rather than the beginning of a winter of discontent. Life never says please, it just keeps coming, and Benji was glad that in the twisting and turning of events, through a singular providence it had "turned round right" for him and many others celebrating on this day.

The End